In memory of my maternal grandparents, Sheila and O. Arthur Schussler, who sparked a love of Judaism and a love of life.

And to Dan, who has always believed in my voice and called me a writer.

ADVANCE PRAISE FOR WOMAN OF VALOR

"When Sally Lieberman's Orthodox family is faced with a traumatic scandal, the fallout pits husband and wife against each other. Sally, anguished and unmoored, grapples with the shocking revelation, while finding strength and comfort through running. There, she questions her Jewish identity, her marriage, and ultimately the man she believed was the love of her young life. What ensues is a moving story of family, sacrifice, and the power of mature, fulfilling love. **Golodner is a wonderful writer who tackles tough subjects with sensitivity and wit while delivering a heartfelt, satisfying read.***"*

Rochelle B. Weinstein, bestselling author of *This Is Not How It Ends*

"The literary and film worlds have devotedly explored the constraints imposed on women in contemporary religious Jewish communities, often concluding that escape from those communities is the only redress for strong, thoughtful women. Lynne Golodner's WOMAN OF VALOR *offers a different premise and alternate solutions to the tropes of misogyny, commu-*

nal insularity and subjugation that characterize many representations of ultra-orthodox communities.

Sally, the novel's main character, is the narrator, and walks the reader through her life, beginning 10 years into her choice to become an orthodox Jew, willingly leaving her secular upbringing on the heels of a humiliating, ruinous breakup with her first love. A stable, loving marriage and three children follow her entry into a large orthodox enclave in Chicago, and Golodner deftly describes the beauty and safety of belonging to a community with shared values, disciplines and connection.

Sally is happy, passionately in love with her husband, devoted to her children and accepting of the rigid religious rules surrounding her daily life. Her occasional doubts, and memories of her former life, sometimes intrude but do not disrupt — that is, until events at her son's school and a casual reconnection to her former lover change everything, calling into question all the choices Sally has made, and threatening her hard-won stability and contentment. The underbelly of a parochial community circling the wagons against the outside world pits Sally against her own ethics and maternal instincts.

Golodner's skill in developing Sally's character — flawed, authentic and dimensional — keeps the reader engaged in the real conflicts the novel presents without resorting to caricature. Sally's resolution of these dilemmas avoids the all-or-none dichotomies, and is nuanced in a believable way. **This WOMAN OF VALOR *tells an important contemporary story of faith, love, devotion and self-determination.*"**

Barbara Stark-Nemon, author of *Even in Darkness* and *Hard Cider*

"An engaging and thought-provoking exploration of identity, faith, family, and love. What if? This essential question is in some ways at the heart of

WOMAN OF VALOR. *What if my life were different?* **Lynne Golodner has written a brave heroine** *who inhabited two worlds and ultimately chooses the one readers least expect — but where there is symmetry and beauty in rules and tradition."*

Nancy Sharp, author of *Both Sides Now: A True Story of Love, Loss, and Bold Living*

"Set in a world most will never experience, Lynne Golodner's fascinating novel about an Orthodox Jewish woman's fight to protect her children from a threat within her community explores the most universal of themes. This thought-provoking story of a marriage in crisis raises tough questions about family love and loyalty, devotion to one's faith, and what it means to truly belong to a community. A deeply relatable tale in an intriguing setting."

Tammy Pasterick, author of *Beneath the Veil of Smoke and Ash*

"Overflowing with wisdom and a testament to deep, abiding love, Lynne Golodner has penned a riveting and propulsive account of a mother and wife caught between worlds, a past she ran away from that returns to haunt her and an uncertain future that threatens the sanctity of her home. Exquisitely written and profoundly human at its core. WOMAN OF VALOR is a must-read."

Ly Ky Tran, author of *House of Sticks: A Memoir*

CHAPTER ONE

A fter two hours scrubbing plates, cleansing counters and mopping the sticky kitchen floor, I was soaked through, warm soapy water drenching the waist of my shirt and the hem of my skirt. Dishes with delicate blue flowers and crystal glasses with ropey stems lined my counters, drying in the light air of evening, a stream of cool sifting through the window screen.

There was no evidence that hours earlier, fourteen people had laughed and talked and eaten five hearty courses of a long and lingering Shabbat meal around my table. The day of rest had been a full day, with guests and laughter and loud voices and warm, satisfying food. Now, the chairs were flush to the table, the cloth was whirling in the wash, the leftovers were tucked into containers and stacked in the fridge and finally, the dishes gleamed as they dried in the night. When I first came to the Orthodox Jewish community of Skokie, Illinois, I'd wondered how religious women kept their houses spit-clean while raising multiple children close in age, and now, I was doing it, without thought or complaint. It wasn't hard, even. It was the life I chose, a beautiful, structured way of going about my days according to ancient laws that had been interpreted for centuries by learned men and which I followed with the eagerness of an expatriate come to a new land and discovering its hills and valleys as if each dip and rise were a new beginning created expressly for me.

My three children were long asleep, warmth and rhythm emanating from their rooms. I crept upstairs to shed my dishwater-wet clothing and slip into leggings and a tank top. It was too late to run outside, though I would far prefer stamping the pavement and gulping in minty night air than trudging on a treadmill in my musty basement. But Barry wasn't home yet from synagogue, so I cranked the elevation to twelve and ran as if for my life. There it was: the burning in my lungs, the pounding in my chest, the searing pull of my legs going, going, going in rapid fire. One more way I knew I was alive.

My life was a series of extremes: we had no contact with the outside world from sundown Friday until three stars shone in a night sky on Saturday. We observed twenty-five-hour fast days with not even a sip of water. We came home from synagogue on a Saturday morning to the rich cloying scent of long-cooked stew bubbling in the slow cooker, nourishing my family after a brisk walk in the cold afternoon. I reveled in the exquisite pleasure of my husband's naked body entwined with mine, even though I knew it would be followed by two straight weeks of not even sleeping in the same bed according to the laws we followed. All the dictates of this life we chose. I accepted deprivation as balance for the sensual, the intensity, the intimacy of a community turned into itself, like a braid of arms wrapping me in an endless hug. It was so different from the suburban coldness of my secular youth.

The small old TV glowed with an "I Love Lucy" rerun; people in my community discouraged television watching unless you chose approved recordings or old TV shows that were less racy than current offerings. The TV in our family room was for kids' DVDs only, and we hid it in a cupboard when guests visited. Popular culture was dangerous, according to my brethren, exposing us to ideas and images and language that might mar our pure souls. I didn't quite buy into this extreme belief, but I went along with it because it was easier. I'd been Orthodox for a decade but was still considered a newbie, and the last thing I wanted was to rock the religious boat and risk falling out with my friends and neighbors.

After my run, I showered and took a book to bed. It was past one when a door slammed downstairs, announcing my husband's return. He appeared weary and tired, peeling off his jacket. Half the month, our beds were separated so we didn't touch during my cycle or for seven days after, but the rest of the time, we pushed the beds together and covered them with a king-sized sheet. I missed him desperately when I was *niddah*, and I saw the longing in his eyes as he watched me across the table or from his lonely bed in the shadows of the night.

"You look comfortable," he said, disappearing into the closet. Hangers clanged. He rustled for a few minutes before emerging in flannel pants and no shirt, the soft fuzz of tight curls on his chest lurching my stomach. I loved laying my head against him, his heart beating into my temple. The beds were apart now, so he climbed into his, lay on his side, mumbled, "Love you," and settled into sleep. I didn't know how he could sleep so easily when he enjoyed a long Shabbat nap after our guests left and before he was expected back at synagogue. But I knew how hard he worked during the week, so I left him to his Sabbath rest.

Still buzzing from my run, I reread the same paragraph three times before turning off the lamp and laying my head against the pillow. Barry's soft breath whistled in the dark. Moonlight shimmered through the window. After a half hour with no sleep, I kicked off the covers and went downstairs.

Shadows painted the floor from the bright light of the moon through the window. The trees seemed to dance in the darkness. Leaves were finger puppets in a wordless story. In the den, I flicked on a desk lamp, pouring yellow light over papers and books and softening the bright glare of the computer screen.

Over the past year, I'd reconnected with high school and college friends online, people I'd known before I sealed myself off in the religious Jewish world. I hadn't realized how much I'd missed Ann Copeland, my childhood best friend, until we started corresponding. Those late-night conversations felt like a tether to an old version of me, a woman in a world I'd once called home. And while I didn't want to go back to the cold distance of my wealthy, austere childhood, sometimes I missed its simplicity, its lack of rules and abundance of quiet. While I was immersed in my chosen world of rules and hemlines, Ann became a journalist in Oregon, and her emails offered a taste of a life I might have lived if I hadn't come to Skokie as a twenty-four-year-old with a broken heart. Ann had a daughter but had never married, and she was happy, confident in her ability to pave her own path, not looking over her shoulder for the approving nod of older mentors or supposed friends watching every move.

I scrolled through my email, clicking open missives from old friends, childhood playmates, former colleagues. Reconnecting with old friends was innocent enough, and I'd told my husband about every single one of them. Barry loved hearing about my former life and the people who populated that cast of characters. But when John Hogan popped up in my inbox, I didn't tell Barry. I don't know why I hesitated, because my husband knew everything about my past: that John's sudden breakup after three years of dating propelled me into Orthodoxy, that I'd loved John and hoped I'd marry him, and that I had been devastated when he left me with no explanation. I'd never kept secrets from my husband before. I'd yearned for this all-in, heady love before I met Barry, and I loved him too much to hide any part of me. I also didn't keep secrets from Batya, my best friend, next-door neighbor and compatriot in the turned-religious road. Barry trusted me wholeheartedly, though Batya could read a lie on me as if it were written in capital letters and permanent marker across my face. But I'd told neither of them when John's name appeared on my screen, with his beseeching words, *I've missed you; where have you been for the past ten years?.*

My stomach knotted at the sight of his words, and suddenly, his voice was in my ears as if he sat beside me. Instantly, I remembered the way we curled into each other after a long day of buzzing office work, the synergy of us sprinting over grassy hills as we ran, racing to see who could go faster, falling in on each other at the end as if the real destination were the two of us.

While it was harmless to scroll through photos of a guy who grew up three houses down from my childhood home and was now a father of five and entrepreneur living on the same flower-lined boulevard as my parents, peering into John's life was different. The rabbis would say I was tempting fate. My husband would question why I was so curious, why I had any interest in a man who broke my heart and never looked back. Batya would give me an earful about all the reasons why I should not step in his direction, and I didn't disagree with any of it. What could I possibly want from this connection? Since I didn't know, I let his email linger unanswered for weeks until I forgot the message was there.

And then one day, he messaged again, asking why I hadn't accepted his friend request, saying he just wanted to hear about my life and reconnect. I was curious, I'll admit. Had he been thinking about me all these years? Did he regret his abrupt departure? Did he know how badly he broke my heart? Had he hurt, too, even though he initiated the breakup? And, I wondered, had he ever loved me in the all-in, full-body way I'd loved him, thinking we'd spend our lives together, wanting to make me his forever home?

But even as I wondered these things, I knew I should thank John. If he hadn't dumped me, I would not have found my true love and the life I was destined to live. I might instead have suffered through an empty marriage in an echoing suburb, leaving my kids to walk to school alone as I had, their lunches made by kitchen staff like mine had been when I was young, with no one to kiss my cheek on cold mornings before sending me off.

When I answered him, finally, I expected a quick hello, a few emails fluttering back and forth, and then a fizzling out. We inhabited different worlds. We would have nothing in common. So I accepted his friend request. And went about my ordinary life.

But if I were honest, I think I knew it would not be just one email. We corresponded for weeks, without frequency or urgency, easy notes that were no different from the ones I sent to other long-lost friends I'd reconnected with. Until one day, this message came:

Sal,

Sorry it took me so long to reply. I was away on business and thought I'd have time to write, but I didn't. Meetings all day and dinners that lasted way too long. I am a true workaholic. I guess if I had more going on in my personal life, I might not be, but after we broke up, I was so concentrated on building my career that I didn't let myself get distracted by anything but work. It was really hard for me to get over you, to stop missing you. You were the best thing that ever happened to me, and I can't believe I threw it all away. There, I said it. I guess it's safe to say in an email, and besides, you're married now, with kids.

But what I really want to know is, how did you become religious? That's the part I just can't understand. You? Religious? Orthodox Judaism? Seriously? Am I emailing with the same girl I was in love with for three years, the same girl who never stepped foot in a synagogue the entire time we were together? You were barely Jewish back then. I can't imagine what your parents think about such a change. The senator can't be happy. Explain that to me, dear Sally, because I'm not sure I'll ever get it.

Yours, John

It was a question I got all the time from old friends or people my family knew. They couldn't believe the hippie with long hair had turned into a wig-wearing wife. I still hadn't found the right words to quickly and efficiently explain how the beauty of this world captivated me or why I hid myself in so much clothing to be faithful to the modesty mandates. It took hours to describe the solace I found in the routine of ritual and the safety of gender roles. But most people didn't want a long, detailed answer. They were momentarily curious, and the curiosity passed as quickly as it came, their eyes glazing as I stumbled through my answer.

Become religious? Why?

I was raised in a wealthy suburb of Detroit with a beautiful view of Lake St. Clair and long expansive lawns lilting toward stately manor homes. There, life was about choice and independence and earning more money than you could ever spend. My father was the conservative senator from Michigan, and my mother the proper, manicured, elegant politician's wife who wouldn't admit that she came from warm Jewish ancestry.

We did things then to impress the neighbors, to win votes, to put forth a face of what America could be. But there were echoes beneath the surface of that life. And loneliness. I was raised mostly by nannies and butlers and cooks and drivers. I saw my maternal grandparents once or twice a year. My life felt like a show on a stage, the audience seated far away, their applause fading as they left for their warm, welcoming homes.

I came to Orthodoxy by mistake, but I was so glad I found it. Nursing a broken heart, I didn't realize that what I needed, what I desperately wanted, was a family to pull me in and tell me that I mattered. And that's what I found when a magazine assignment sent me to interview Orthodox Jews in Chicago, and I stumbled upon Shiri Schwartz, a rabbi's wife and community leader who loved cooking and raising her brood and pulling people like me into the bosom of the community. My new way of living offered reasons for everything. I didn't have to make choices; they were made for me. Which freed me to go through my days with ease and confidence.

But John wasn't asking about my life now; he was making a statement of regret. It was hard to get over me? I cringed at the words, *when we broke up*, and wanted to write back, "*We* didn't break up. *You* broke my heart, you fool."

I should write him a heartfelt *Thank you* for leaving me. That heartbreak primed me for the life I was meant to live. But how could I say, *It's your fault I'm a religious married woman who covers her hair*? He did not deserve credit for my beautiful life. His departure brought me back to my grandparents, who became my anchor. He brought me to the true love of my life. Because John left me, I was the mother of the three best children in the world.

So why was I scrolling on a computer late at night while the people who formed the backbone of this life I loved slept soundly in their beds?

I glanced at the desk calendar, flipping through the days to see when I'd last visited the *mikvah*, the ritual bath I visited to end my time of physical separation from my husband. I needed to touch Barry's skin, to nestle in his arms and feel the motion of our bodies braided together until the two of us ceased to be and we became one. I needed to fill my nights with something other than desperate emails in the dark to an old love.

CHAPTER TWO

On Tuesdays, after I dropped the kids at school, I made my way to my *tehillim* group, a motley crew of women reciting psalms and sipping coffee. Leah had hosted our group for three years. We recited the lyrical Hebrew as a meditative mantra wisping up to heaven on behalf of those we prayed for. The sick. The infirm. Those who lost their way. Those hungry for a *shidduch*, a match with their one true love. Women desperate for another baby who crumbled when a red stain appeared on their underwear. I sometimes found myself swaying to the beat as we palmed prayerbooks, our voices in rhythmic synergy.

I pushed the handle on the front door of Leah's brick colonial and called, "Hello?"

"Come in," she sang from the kitchen. The smoky aroma of fresh coffee melded with the sweet cinnamon of something in the oven. Leah was known for her crumb cake and rugelach, which she made every week for us. *Thank God I ran yesterday.* Hopefully the calories burned were not less than the calories I was about to consume.

In the kitchen, Leah bustled between oven and counter, pouring coffee into porcelain mugs on a matching tray, arranging warm pastries on a platter. A shiny snood covered her hair. She wore a long-sleeved white T-shirt under a denim jumper, her feet nestled into Crocs.

"Hi!" She dusted her hands on a towel and came around the counter for a hug.

"Have you heard yet?"

Leah shook her head. Her oldest son, Yoni, was hoping for acceptances from several *yeshivot* in Israel and Lakewood, New Jersey. April was late but not impossible for locking in a post-high school learning destination. Yoni was a late bloomer whose grades weren't great. Only in the past two years had he turned things around academically, and his *Yiddishkeit*, his Jewish knowledge, was exemplary. He had glowing recommendations from rabbis, so we all felt optimistic, reassuring Leah that he would find his place before long. Because my children were still young, I had no idea how the Orthodox post-high school education system worked, but I nodded along with the women who'd grown up in this world, hoping one day I'd figure it all out.

"The rabbis will see that he's had a transformation," Leah said. "He's so bright. Sometimes the brightest ones take the longest to find their way. God willing, we'll hear soon."

"You will," I said, patting her shoulder. "The best kids always find a placement."

Yoni was the oldest of nine children, spanning from 17 to 4. I didn't know how Leah baked like a professional chef with school schedules to juggle and a house she kept quiet and spotless.

"If I do my part, God will do His," she always said when I asked how she juggled everything so beautifully.

"You'll hear soon, *im yirtzeh Hashem*," I muttered. "He's done so well for two years. That stands for something."

She smiled.

The door slammed, followed by a chorus of hellos. Chavi, Rivka, Debbie, Shiri. Hebrew names and English, straight-and-narrow paths through girls' schools to seminary to wedding alongside women who attended co-ed high schools and had party- and sex-filled college escapades before finding their winding path to religion, marriage, and motherhood. Batya trailed in, her year-old daughter Talya in her arms amid a bundle of blankets. Talya reached for me, and I gathered my best friend's baby into my arms, closing my eyes and inhaling the powdery scent of a little one as she lay her head on my shoulder.

My friends hugged and air kissed. Leah lifted the tray of pastries and pointed to the insulated coffee carafe, which Batya grabbed as we followed her into the living room.

"Rivka, grab the tray of mugs, will you?" Leah called over her shoulder.

"I've got napkins and milk," Shiri sang out.

Although we called the group for 9:30, we never got started until 10. We recited psalms for a half hour then schmoozed and ate and sipped until 11:30, when many of us raced out to pick up children from nursery school. Together, we had a collective thirty-eight children.

Leah pulled a well-fingered paper from her pocket and began reading names.

"Let's *daven* for these people, recovering from surgery or who recently had babies: Rochel bas Leah, Minna bas Mushka, Leah bas Gitel, Shira bas Leah, Menucha bas Batsheva..." Her voice droned, the names blurred.

Leah named people needing emotional support, who had fallen "off the *derech*," a subtle way to say they weren't observant enough or had stopped following our rules. Each week when she read that list, the silence grew thick, as we listened for familiar names and tried to match them with scandalous stories. As pious as these women were, several were mother birds with fluffy feather breasts insisting they did not gossip. I was sure my tehillim buddies were as curious as I was about what prompted someone to leave this peaceful path. I was so new to it, I couldn't imagine going the other way.

The lists read, we picked up our dog-eared booklets of psalms and began to mumble. Leah called out page numbers, and we obediently flipped. Lips moved, emitting a stream of Hebrew, a lyrical sing-song of old poetry intended to save souls. Our very existence rode on these prayers. Or maybe that was just what we told ourselves.

CHAPTER THREE

I'd come to this world in the most unexpected way, as a journalist at *Chicago Magazine*. Recently graduated from the University of Michigan, I was eager to start my adult life as a writer employed by the Windy City's gorgeous glossy and living in tandem with the man I thought was the love of my life. But when John surprised me with an abrupt breakup carrying no explanation and seemingly no remorse, my world broke into pieces. I shifted like a shadow between my quiet apartment and my cubicle-filled office that buzzed with journalistic energy, waiting for the cloud of sadness to lift. So when my editor waved me into her office for a special assignment, I shuffled in, hoping for a story that could distract me.

"I want you to write about the Orthodox community of Skokie for the first of a series of features on Chicago's ethnic enclaves," she said. "You're Jewish, right?"

I shuffled uncomfortably, crossing my arms in front of my chest. My father was the austere senator from Michigan, who raised me and my sisters in the pristine Protestant suburb of Grosse Pointe. My mother came from a Jewish family, though we rarely saw my maternal grandparents, who were my only connection to my Jewish heritage. Strolling through the echoing rooms of the sprawling estate on Lake St. Clair where I grew up, you would never guess it was a partially Jewish home.

"I mean, yes, technically I am Jewish," I stuttered, "but not really. I know nothing about it."

"Good, you'll be objective!"

A low hum of newsroom bustle buzzed under fluorescent lights. I stood in my editor's doorway. A single potted plant drooped limp on her windowsill, and there were two photos on her desk—one of her husband and another of her dog.

"Why would they talk to me?" I asked. "I don't even know where to start."

"Focus on fashion or food," she said, sipping from a giant Diet Coke. "Or say you're interested in learning about your heritage."

"I'm half Jewish," I said, falling onto the couch. "Barely. I don't know anything about it, and that would be a lie—I am not interested in learning more about *my people*. If you could even call them that. Besides, isn't that disingenuous? Don't I want to have some journalistic integrity?"

She threw up her hands and leaned back in her swivel chair. "I don't care how you do it," she said. "Just do it. This is the series I want to run over the next six months. After this one, you'll move on to Little India in Oakbrook Terrace and then the Muslim Community Center, which has something like 3,000 people every Friday for prayers."

"Sounds like you know more than I do," I joked. "Maybe you should write it." I tried for a snarky smile but got only an eyebrow raise in response.

"Funny. You're the writer. And I'm your boss. So go to Skokie. Check out the shops selling modest dresses, gorgeous hats, beautiful artwork and ritual items. Use your expense account to eat at kosher restaurants. I hear there's this lava cake dessert that looks like the black hats Hasidic men wear—the brim is a circle of chocolate that slides down as the cake melts. Dress up and go to a synagogue. Meet people. Ask questions. Dig in, do your research, and give me an update in two weeks."

Two weeks?! "Yes, ma'am." I saluted before retreating to my gray cubicle, where I had tacked up a *New Yorker* cartoon and a flier for a pub crawl I'd covered the prior spring. Other than that, there were no personal effects. How had I worked there for nearly a year and managed not to personalize

my surroundings? An elderly co-worker who managed the monthly calendar and took classified ads over the phone had a red wool sweater slung
over her chair, a vase that she filled with fresh flowers on a weekly basis
and six pictures in frames on her desk. Another reporter had a collection
of pencils sticking out of the foam ceiling; he tossed them up when he was
bored or pondering a story. Sometimes they loosened and fell, smacking
him on the head; he left them littered on the floor. Every desk but mine
had some semblance of personality, some lived-in feel.

I started a Google search and found synagogues, schools, restaurants
and stores. For the better part of an hour, I copied information into a
document then dialed the number for the Women's Orthodox League,
which sounded like a good place to start. There was a phone number next
to the name of the president, Shiri Schwartz.

She answered on the third ring, high-pitched voices chittering in the
background. "Hello?"

"Hi. Is this Shiri?"

"This is Mrs. Schwartz. Who is this?"

"Sally Sterling, from *Chicago Magazine*. I'm writing about the Orthodox Jewish community, and I wondered if I might meet you for coffee so
we could do an interview."

"Why would *Chicago Magazine* write about us?"

"We're doing a series of stories to show the many cultural and ethnic
sides of Chicagoland." I spoke quickly, hoping she wouldn't slam down
the phone. "I'm Jewish but I grew up secular, so this assignment will help
me learn more about my own background." I winced as I said it, but it
worked.

Her voice softened. "Oh, that's interesting. Sure. I'll meet you at the
Starbucks on Dempster. But not today. Tuesday? 10 a.m.?"

It was Thursday, and I didn't want to wait to get started, especially since
my update was due in two weeks.

"You can't meet sooner?"

"The first thing you need to know, honey, is that in the Jewish world, Thursday is the busiest day of the week. We are shopping and cooking and cleaning and getting ready for Shabbat. You know what Shabbat is, right? Every Jew knows Shabbat, even if they don't celebrate it."

"Yes, I know," I said, swallowing defensiveness. Why did her words trigger me? Who cared what this lady thought of my lack of Jewish knowledge? "Any chance you could make Monday work? I'd love to get started on my research, and you are my first stop."

I could almost hear her smiling. "Really? I'm your first? Well then. Okay, I can make Monday work, but it'll have to be at one. I have a WOL board meeting in the morning."

"Great. Starbucks at one on Monday."

"You know what? Come to my house. That way we can really talk," she said, whipping off her address, which I scribbled down. "Or better yet—do you want to come for Shabbat lunch? You can't take notes, but you can get to know how we live. Say you'll come."

I had nothing better to do that weekend than mope over John's absence and replay the breakup in my mind. But I'd be so out of place, unfamiliar with the prayers and rituals. They'd think me a total fool. My stomach knotted.

"Please, I'd love to have you join us for Shabbat," she pleaded.

"Okay, I guess," I stuttered.

"Park down the street, in the school lot," she said. "And walk to our house, please. We don't drive on Shabbat."

"Right. Thank you. I look forward to meeting you. Oh, and Shabbat Shalom!" *Take those Hebrew words, lady!*

I sat back on my wheeled chair, hands cradling the back of my head. All around me, people buzzed, shuffling papers, clicking through Internet searches, pouring cold coffee from the carafe in the communal kitchen into mugs stained with overuse. It was the first time that I was excited about a project since the breakup, and I hadn't thought of John all day.

I popped into my editor's office. "Hey! I landed an interview with the head of the Women's Orthodox League. She invited me to her house for Shabbat lunch and then an interview on Monday."

"Women's Orthodox League? What is that? Like the Junior League but Jewish?"

"Pretty much."

"Cool. You'll be moving in impressive circles." A smirk underscored her sarcasm.

"Judge all you want. This is going to be a great story."

"Better be," she said. "I'm thrilled with your enthusiasm."

"Okay, so I'm wondering if I can do some on-the-ground research tomorrow. I'll need an outfit that is modest enough to wear on Saturday, and I'm sure I don't have anything."

"I can't pay overtime for weekend work or expense your clothes, but sure. Have fun! Be in the field tomorrow—no need to come in." She waved me out as her phone buzzed.

At my desk, I tossed an extra reporter's notebook and a handheld tape recorder into my bag. Out the window, the sun sank into the horizon.

CHAPTER FOUR

"**S**al?"

Wednesday morning, Batya's voice echoed across the linoleum. The door banged shut as my next-door neighbor and best friend walked into my kitchen.

"Hey." I kissed her cheek.

She smiled, setting Talya in the family room to play with plush toys, plastic cars and thick-paged board books. Batya perched on a stool by the counter as I washed breakfast dishes.

After Shiri, Batya had been my first friend and the main reason Barry and I bought this house after we married. She, too, had not grown up religious, and like me, she loved our way of life. She wore wigs as her preferred method of hair covering, while I opted for scarves and hats, reserving my wig for Shabbat, holidays and weddings. I felt funny putting glossy hair, shorn from another woman's head, over my own lustrous locks, even though my friend looked gorgeous in her sleek, chestnut, straight-hair wig.

The hair framed her face above a black knit vest and long-sleeved T-shirt, topping a denim skirt a whisper above the floor. Younger girls wore skirts just long enough to cover their knees when they sat—four inches was the rule at Bais Yitzchok, the local girls school, and the principal was known to pop into high school classrooms with a ruler, sending girls home if their skirts fell short of expectations. The young moms of my community opted for super-long, floor-sweeping skirts, and sometimes, I felt like a princess in my generous, full skirts.

Batya's dark-brown eyes were like pools of melted chocolate. She swiped thin lines of brown kohl along her bottom lids, which made her eyes shine. She was one of the few women I'd met who looked radiant no matter what she wore, with or without makeup.

Barry didn't care how I covered my hair, only that I did so to fit in with our community and follow the modesty mandates. Plus, no woman could serve on the women's council if they didn't fully cover, and it was preferred to do so in public with a wig.

Early on, when we were dating, Barry had laid out his expectations.

"I want to marry someone who will cover her hair," he said. "Hopefully, she's a good cook, and likes to do it, and I want a woman who will wear only skirts, no pants." He looked at me expectantly, waiting for my energetic nod. While I had already committed to this way of life, it was strange to hear his demands, as if I had to fulfill a checklist to be admitted access. I had never dated men who were so direct in their demands for a partner—but I also liked how transparent and no-games this way of dating was.

I was already all in—but what would happen if one day, I grew tired of all the rules and restrictions? Would he stop loving me? Would he leave me? Would I be alone again?

But I nodded and smiled. "Of course," I said.

"And the mikvah," he mentioned.

I pursed my lips. It was something I'd heard about but didn't know much, other than that it was a deal-breaker for most religious men.

Later, I'd asked Shiri for details. She'd become my mentor in all things religious.

"When you get engaged, we'll go over the specifics, but basically, you separate from your husband when you have your period, count 'clean days' after it ends, and don't touch until you dunk in a ritual bath," she explained. "It's the unmarked building behind the community center.

And you'll sleep in separate beds—but you can push them together when you're allowed to touch."

I must have looked stunned, because she reached out a hand and said, "Don't worry. It's not that bad. You'll appreciate the time apart, and when you come back together, it's wonderful. This practice enhances the connection between husband and wife. Take my word for it."

When Barry and I married, I followed all the rules, checking to make sure there was no spotting on my "clean days," a term that made me cringe. I mean, was I not clean because I bled each month? It felt like sexism on steroids, considering that my cycle allowed me and all my friends to bring more Jewish souls into the world, which was a major focus of this community! And yet menstruation was the reason many rabbis said women could never touch the Torah, never carry the holy scrolls in our section of the synagogue—which expanded to mean we couldn't sit near it or study certain tracts. It wasn't Barry's fault. He'd grown up with all of this, so it didn't seem odd or misogynistic to him. He was a product of his environment. And I was a product of mine, as much as I'd tried to leave it behind.

Most days, I twisted colorful scarves into intricate wrappings that I'd learned from Israeli women, covering my hair and feeling like an exotic treat. When I ran outside, I pulled my long curls into a bun at the nape of my neck and pulled on a baseball hat or bandana. People could see my hair—though not all of it and not long and flowing as I loved it. Barry pursed his lips when I did this.

"You need to cover all your hair," he said. "It's not modest to go out like that. It's like you're giving other men a taste of what they shouldn't be seeing."

To placate him, I pulled a small scarf over the bun and tied it into a tight knot so it wouldn't come loose. I didn't understand why he cared so much. No one knew me like he did, in my full splendor. Nor would they. I was as committed as he was, sometimes more so because I chose this world. And when I ran, it wasn't like I was doing a strip tease for neighborhood men. I blazed past on sidewalks and streets or ran in the woods up and over grassy knolls. My heart thumped, my face shone with sweat, and I moved faster than any gaze could focus on wisps of my soft, shiny mane.

John had loved my curls. "Your hair," he'd said almost every night we were together, stroking his long, sturdy fingers through my tangled locks. "I love this mess so much," he'd say, burying his nose in the thick of it, breathing in the smell of my coconut-y shampoo.

I startled back to the moment at the sound of Batya's voice.

"What are you thinking about?" she asked, shaking my Venti Starbucks cup to see if there was anything left in it to sip. Finding it empty, she raised her eyebrows, walked over to the garbage and tossed it in. "Mind if I make a pot of coffee?"

I shook my head and turned back to the sink to finish the breakfast dishes. I stared out on our little backyard, with its playscape and barbecue. There were a few toys scattered on the grass that I had forgotten to put away in the garage. I hated when the yard looked messy.

"Nothing."

"Come on. I know you! Your mind is racing. It's like I can see little wheels turning behind your eyes. What are you worried about?"

She opened the fridge and pulled out a can of ground coffee. At the coffeemaker, she scrunched her nose at the used grounds and damp, stained filter I'd left in the device. She lifted it out with two fingers, shoving me aside with her hip and opening the garbage under the sink to dump it. She knew where I kept filters—in a cupboard next to the coffeemaker, where I also kept my favorite cookbooks and bills waiting to be paid. She knew pretty much everything about me, so it was hard to hide from my best friend. But I did not want to tell her I was back in touch with my first love. I could already hear the litany of reprimand that would pour forth. She scooped generously from the can, dumping new grounds into the basket. The alluring scent of fresh coffee filled the kitchen.

Batya was one of the best parts of my life. I'd had good friends over the years, best friends even, but none like our soul-sister connection. It had nothing to do with religious observance, though that gave us more time together in quiet and contemplative ways—at our tehillim group, swaying beside one another in synagogue, talking in the kitchen on a random weekday as we cooked for Shabbat, taking our kids to the park and chatting on a bench while they ran and climbed, and so many meals where we lingered around a finely laid table for hours. Nearly every week, either my family trundled over to her house or her brood invaded ours; it didn't feel like Shabbat without Batya and Tzvi and their chittering children filling our house. It was a friendship built on sharing life, and I was grateful to have her at my side.

I desperately wanted to tell Batya about John's emails, but I didn't want to face her reaction—a mix of horror and finger-wagging: *How could you? You're married. And he's not even Jewish. You're tempting fate. Stop now. Nothing good can come from this. Why would you even want to be in touch with him? The man broke your heart. And Barry should know, regardless.*

I hadn't hidden my former life from anyone. I was an open book with everyone in the community, wanting to be an example of someone who embraces observance fully and completely, without shame or regret. *If I hadn't lived that way, I would not have chosen this one*, I said when someone asked about my transformation. Early in our friendship, Batya and I swapped stories of childhood and our journeys toward religion. She knew John as a character from another story, a past life, dead and gone. If I mentioned late-night emails and rekindled friendships, she'd say temptation leads to bad acts, even by good people. That you couldn't straddle worlds. So I couldn't say anything. Now I had secrets from the two people I loved most. It didn't occur to me to just stop emailing John and all the people from my past. Not for the first time, I wondered if picking up my journalistic mantle with a few freelance assignments might fill the hours I would otherwise spend emailing old friends. And lovers.

"It's seriously nothing," I said, wiping my hands on a towel.

Her gaze told me she expected more than a shrug-off. What could I say that was convincing? What could I say that she would believe? She looked at me expectantly, waiting for me to speak.

"Okay, well, Barry wants another baby."

I assumed this was true, but it had not been a conversation between us. I hoped this little half-truth was good enough to satisfy her curiosity.

Her eyes popped. "Really?"

Batya had five kids: Ahuva and Bracha, then Shmueli—Donny's best friend since birth—Ephraim, who was Shira's age, and Talya. She had told me time and time again that she was happy to have babies until her body wouldn't produce anymore. Her husband, Tzvi, was a successful banker with family money who was the love of her life. I'd often thought of Batya's story as a Lifetime movie—popular suburban girl spends a college semester in Israel at Hebrew University and embraces the best of the Orthodox world, coming home in long skirts and long sleeves with the kind of deep and lasting love that most women yearn for. She was happy, in love with her husband, in love with her life, in love with her role as a full-time mom and religious woman, and her secular parents embraced her observant lifestyle, sharing Shabbat meals and holidays as if nothing were different.

"Yeah, he really wants more kids—and Simi is three, so we should think about it, but I'm just not there." The words kept coming. Wow. Was this how I felt? If not, I couldn't believe how easily I could lie to my best friend.

"And you don't?" Batya's voice tried to sound judgment free, but I knew she believed we should have as many babies as we could to fill the world with Jewish souls. Yes, my sweet, beautiful, happy friend was a zealot.

"At the risk of withering to dust under that judgmental glare of yours..." She blushed.

"I don't know. Not now. I have my hands full with these three. Having another child doesn't just add one more to your load—it multiplies everything. I want to be a great mother to all my kids. I don't want my focus to be distracted." I swatted her shoulder. "Now can you back off, please?"

I pulled two mugs from the dairy cabinet, grabbed the carton of *cholov Yisroel*—extra-kosher cream—from the fridge and trooped to the coffeemaker.

"Really, I wasn't judging," Batya said. "You have to do what's best for your family."

"Yeah, right," I laughed.

From the next room, Talya squealed and flung toys, which landed with a muffled thud on the carpet. We smiled, loving the innocence of babyhood. That much was not a lie. I did love the sweet happiness of my children at every stage, and I loved watching them discover all the details and textures and scents of life.

Batya stayed for another hour before Talya stumbled into the kitchen, rubbing her eyes. My friend scooped up her daughter, nuzzled her nose into her dimpled neck, and the little girl giggled. Batya kissed me on the cheek and breezed out the door, leaving my house quiet for a little while before it was time to get Simi from school.

I hadn't responded to John's last email, the most probing one, though all the possible replies fluttered through my head like a butterfly seeking a place to land. I could ignore the email, delete it, forget it ever came. Any contact with the man I once believed was the love of my life would be bad news for the life I was currently living. I could so easily walk away... Why didn't I?

I pulled on leggings and a long-sleeved running shirt with a flowy cotton skirt over top and slipped my feet into ankle socks and lace-up sneakers. I threw my hair into a tight bun under a baseball hat, carefully tying a scarf to cover it, my husband's face bright in my mind. If I doubled down on observing the rules of my life, maybe it would distract me from online temptations. Now I knew why the rabbis admonished the community to stay away from the digital sphere. It could only lead us down a dangerous path. I folded the jogger stroller into the trunk of my minivan. In the preschool parking lot, I jumped out of the car. Teachers waited with the children by the front door. Simi stood with clasped hands, his little backpack slung over both shoulders.

"Mommy!" he called, running toward me and leaping into my arms.

"Hey, bud," I said, nuzzling. "I brought snacks. Mommy's ready for a run."

I drove to Dawes Park in Evanston, parked and clicked open the stroller. Simi climbed in, holding his blankie in one arm and a plastic bag of goldfish crackers in another. I tucked an apple juice box into the cupholder, locked the car and popped my key fob in the fanny pack clipped around my waist. "Ready?"

"Ready!" he chirped, leaning back. I could see his eyes glazing and knew he'd sleep well as I pounded the path.

The day was bright and warm. So many Orthodox women suffered from Vitamin D deficiencies because they covered every inch of skin, never letting the sun seep into their pores. I turned my cap backwards, gazing up at the glaring sunshine, which warmed my face. I rolled up my sleeves to just before my elbows, a permissible leniency. God, I missed wearing tank tops in the light air of spring. I got so hot when I ran!

My feet hit the pavement with the *tap tap* rhythm I'd always loved about running. Meditative, hypnotic. Birds called. Trees rustled. Sunshine glimmered off the green water of the lagoon, rainbows refracted in the spray of the fountains. In the distance, the deep blue of Lake Michigan sparkled like diamonds in the light. Clouds feathered against an open sky.

Pushing the stroller, I picked up speed as wind buzzed in my ears. My chest burned, but that would pass. For the first mile, every inhale was fire searing into my lungs and spreading through my limbs. And then, the sweet freedom of pushing past my wall like a gazelle leaping in the grasses. Pigeons strutted under benches, pecking at crumbs on the ground. An old man stared at the lagoon, flicking popcorn into his mouth, never breaking his gaze. I passed nannies and young mothers pushing strollers, older couples holding hands as they walked. And then I hit the moment where I saw nothing, thought nothing, felt nothing, just went. My body moved on its own. I did not have to guide, steer, acknowledge. My heart thumped a drumbeat, husky and constant, a soundtrack for my body, in tandem with the syncopated rhythm of my movements.

My Fitbit buzzed at four miles, and I turned around to head back to the car. Simi would have a good long nap in the open air and bright sun, and I'd be calm, better able to manage my thoughts, and the bustle of my after-school household, with tired cranky children and dinner to make. Rivers of sweat streamed down my face, soaking the little hairs at the back of my neck and seeping into my shirt. The backs of my knees, creases of my thighs, between my legs and under my arms were damp.

I wasn't far from Skokie, just far enough to run free. I loved my neighborhood, especially its long Jewish history. Though the town's name originated from a Potawatomi word for "marsh," it was anything but a natural setting. Concrete sidewalks and asphalt streets created a grid of commerce, including kosher restaurants, synagogues and *shteibels*, bakeries and shops filled with religious books, ritual items and modest clothing. The town began as a German-Luxembourger farming community, drawing Jewish immigrants in droves after World War II. The last census showed we still comprised more than half its population. Which was why I often drove outside its borders to run, escaping the judging eyes of friends and neighbors.

Back at the car, I slipped Simi out of the stroller and into his car seat. He whimpered in a half sleep. I tucked his blankie into his lap, and he leaned his head back, closing his eyes once more. I folded the stroller and packed it into the trunk.

The sweat had cooled, and now my shirt clung to my skin, as if I had jumped in the lake fully clothed. I glanced at my face in the rearview—blotchy and red. I flipped the hat around so the bill stuck out front, tucking in stray curls as I drove to Shira's school, gulping at my insulated water bottle I'd tucked into the cup holder.

I passed familiar houses, post-war bungalows that populated the neighborhood. The Klempmans' yard littered with tricycles, wagons and push-toys. The Rothschild abode, sullen and clean swept, as if no one lived there. I looked for familiar faces in passing cars and on the sidewalk. At my daughter's school, I pushed the button to slide the side door open. She clambered in, weary and quiet.

"Long day?" I asked as I drove away. She nodded. I reached back to hand her a plastic bag of trail mix and another of apple slices that had started to brown in the hours since I'd cut them. "Here's a quick snack for the ride home."

She dug in, chewing vigorously while staring out the window.

At Donny's school, a half mile from Shira's, I repeated the ritual—sliding door open, child jumping in, close the door, hand snacks over, drive away. Simi rubbed his eyes, awakening with quiet whimpers. I reached behind my seat and patted his leg. "We'll be home soon, kiddos," I said, steering toward our house.

"How was your day, Donny?"

"Humph."

I glanced at my son in the rearview mirror.

"Something wrong?"

He shook his dark curly head.

"Tell me about your Hebrew classes; what parsha are you studying?"

"I forget."

"Did you read Rashi?"

He shook his head again. While Donny was the quietest of my children, he usually chattered nonstop when I picked him up, eager to recount the details of his day.

"What about your English subjects—anything interesting today in science? Math?"

Again, a headshake. And then quiet. He chewed his snack slowly, as if he wasn't really tasting it.

After I parked the car in the garage, the kids clambered out, pulling their bags into the house and dumping them at the door. "Donny, hang back, honey, for a moment, will you?" I called, locking the car and shutting the garage.

He kicked at the floor, staring down.

"What's going on, sweetheart?" I knelt to his eye level. The other kids had run into the family room, where I could hear the jingly music of Uncle Moishy from the TV. "One tape," I called to them. "Then the TV goes off."

Donny's tongue darted out to lick his lips. He wouldn't make eye contact. I grazed the side of his soft face with my hand, trying to turn his gaze in my direction. He hunched into his shoulders, shrinking back.

"Look at me, sweetheart," I said. "What is going on?"

Tears pooled in his eyes, and he pursed his lips. "I can't tell you," he said.

I pulled him to me. "You can tell me anything," I whispered into his hair as tears spilled out, dampening my shirt. He shook with sobs. I patted his back and whispered, "*Shhhhh*," over and over, until his crying subsided.

"It's okay," I said. "Whatever it is, I can help you. I can make it better."

"No, you can't!" he wailed, wresting himself free and running from the room. His feet pounded up the stairs, and the door to his room slammed.

My heart pounded. What could have happened? What could my boy not tell me?

I dialed Barry's cell phone.

He answered after one ring. "Sal? Everything okay? I'll be home in an hour," he said.

"I know. I'm sorry to bother you at work," I said.

"What's wrong?"

"I don't actually know. It's Donny. He's in a state, and I can't get him to talk to me. Something happened at school that he says he can't tell me about. I feel sick."

"Okay, I'll leave now. Be home in a half hour. Love you."

I picked up the kids' bags and set them on the bench in the mud room where they were supposed to deposit them after school but never did. I neatened their shoes into pairs on the mat by the door. I knew I should start on dinner, but my mind was racing, inventing horrible stories to explain my son's behavior. A classmate had hit him. But no, I would have gotten a call from the school if he'd been in a fight, and there was no bruise on his face or arms. A teacher had yelled at him. But no, he would have told me about that, even if it upset him.

What could he not tell me?

I chewed on a finger. Could a teacher have hit him? Or something worse? I loved my community, but I'd heard rumors of scandals kept quiet so as not to leak dirty secrets to the non-religious world. I'd heard of unlicensed day cares in religious homes where babies were burned by boiling water left unsupervised on a kitchen stove. I'd heard of pious husbands seeking prostitutes secretly and families who refused to pay taxes, not recognizing the federal government as an authority they must obey. We were far from perfect.

I tried to banish all the ugly thoughts, but they kept poking at me. Teachers crossing unfathomable lines. My little boy being touched or hurt in unthinkable ways that I was supposed to protect him from. Secrets sailing through the school, the headmaster oblivious or worse, wanting to keep everything quiet so as not to disrupt the perfect pious profile of our world. These things happened in insular communities. The news media salivated to report on them, creating painful exposés revealing how far the righteous could fall. The secular world loved to uncover dirty, dark secrets about communities built on faith. And unfortunately, sometimes the more rigid the rules, the more people needed to act out to shed the shackles. It could happen here. I just hoped it hadn't.

CHAPTER FIVE

"So what do we know?"

Barry and I sat in the study, door closed, kids mesmerized by the second Uncle Moishy video I allowed them to watch, despite my earlier admonition to only watch one. Donny was still squirreled away in his room. I hadn't followed him, though I'd wanted to, and when Barry walked in, I'd flung myself at my husband, despite the fact that I hadn't gone to the mikvah yet. I had an appointment for that night.

At first, he jumped back, so used to the mandated physical distance between us. "I thought..." he said as his arms closed around my back. He pulled me close, pressed me against his body. His heartbeat calmed me. I nestled into his chest, stifling my sobs and trying to breathe evenly.

"What if it's the worst?" I whispered.

He rubbed circles on my back. "Shhhh. We don't know anything until we know something." He stepped back to look into my eyes. "So what do we know?"

I dried my eyes on my sleeve.

"I'm going to the mikvah tonight," I said. "I normally wouldn't cross the line, you know that. But you also know that the law is that we can't have sex during my niddah time, not that we can't touch—all the rest is a fence around the law, so we don't screw up. We haven't done anything wrong by hugging or touching. Loosen up. Eye on the ball. The bigger issue here is our son."

He nodded. "It felt so good to touch you," he whispered, sweeping a stray hair that had escaped from my hat and grazed my forehead.

I smiled weakly. "We don't know anything," I said, straightening my shirt and sliding my hands along my skirt to smooth it. "All I know is that he is sullen and isn't saying much, and then he cried and clung to me and said he couldn't tell me what had happened."

Barry hefted a sigh and exhaled audibly. "Certainly uncharacteristic."

I nodded. "And since I called you, my mind has been flipping through all the horrible things that it could be. All the stories I've read of religious people gone terribly astray, stories of abuse..." My voice trailed off.

Barry grabbed my arms and squeezed the flesh. "It won't be that," he said.

I wriggled free, rubbing my arms where he had held too tightly. "How can you know that? It's happened in religious communities before—a lot."

His brow wrinkled. "Sorry. Didn't mean to grab you so hard."

I shook my head to shrug it off. "We're both upset," I said.

"Well, honey, we don't know anything has happened. We just know that our seven-year-old is upset. That's all. So don't let your mind go to the worst possible place."

The family room had gone quiet. "Uncle Moishy's over," I said. "I have to get dinner started."

"I'll talk to Donny," he said.

"You can try." I shrugged.

"Who wants to help with dinner?" I called to Shira and Simi.

Little feet clattered into the kitchen as both of them sang out, "Meeeeee!" They pushed chairs from the table to the counter and climbed up.

Good. A distraction. Now, what would I make? It was Thursday, with a mountain of Shabbat prep ahead of me, so I'd make it an easy meal. Tuna noodle casserole and a salad. Not much for them to help with. I'd make cookies, too, for an impromptu dessert, out of the ordinary for midweek but a distracting indulgence.

Cooking was one way I'd learned to build connections since I became religious. It started with my burgeoning friendship with Shiri, who, after the first Shabbat lunch invitation, kept inviting me back for meals and, later, to stay at her house for the entire Shabbat. But when I did, she'd tell me to come over early and help her cook Friday afternoon. I had loved the way her children hovered around to help and how the connection bonded them in sweet ways. Growing up, my family meals—when we had them—were made by a cook and served by hired help. There was no bonding over cookie dough, no easy jobs for young children to feel close to the fabric of the household. I vowed that when I married and had a family, making home-cooked meals would be one important way I would establish love and nurturing in my house.

I set the mixer near Shira and took two sticks of margarine from the refrigerator, along with baking soda and two eggs. I pulled flour, brown sugar, and refined sugar from the cupboard, grabbed a bottle of vanilla, kosher salt, and chocolate chips.

"Let me get the noodles going, and then we'll make cookies for dessert, okay?"

Shira and Simi broke out into big smiles.

I pulled cut carrots and cucumber slices from the fridge and set them on a plate between them, with a little glass bowl of ranch dressing for dipping. "This will hold you over until we finish."

They fisted the veggies and started dunking.

I set a pot to boil and pulled a package of egg noodles from the pantry, along with three cans of tuna and a can of condensed mushroom soup. This time I'd have to forgo the sauteed onion and celery—I just didn't have time to do it all perfectly, and the kids wouldn't miss it. From the fridge I pulled shredded cheese, sour cream, and mayonnaise, along with vegetables for an easy salad—a cucumber, three tomatoes, three green onions, and a head of romaine. I washed the leaves and put the wooden salad bowl in front of Simi.

"Can you tear the lettuce for Mommy?"

He nodded solemnly as I set a colander of damp leaves in front of him. I knew I'd have to tear his torn leaves even smaller, but it gave him something easy to do.

Once the noodles were in the boiling water, I turned to Shira. "Okay, unpeel the margarine and dump the sticks into the mixer bowl, honey."

Her little fingers pulled the foil wrapping back, and the margarine slid into the metal bowl.

"Do you want to measure the sugar, or shall I, and then you can pour it in?"

"I can!"

I showed her where on the cup to fill it to, and she dug it into the sugar jar and scooped up enough white sugar, carefully eyeing the line I'd indicated.

"Remember to pack the brown sugar tightly. Here's a spoon to help."

She scooped brown sugar from its jar and patted it down into the cup until it reached the three-fourths line. "Great. Now dump it in."

"Can I turn it on?" she asked.

"Let's do the eggs, and then yes."

"You do the eggs, Mommy," she said. "I don't want my fingers to get gooey."

I smiled, cracking the eggs into a glass bowl and checking for blood or irregular marks. Seeing none, I slid them into the mixer.

"Okay, now turn it on to the first level," I said.

The mixer whirred into motion, combining the sugars, margarine and eggs into a smooth batter.

"I'm done!" Simi called.

"Nice work," I said, pulling the salad bowl and glancing at the giant green sheaths. Turning my back, I tore them smaller and left the bowl by the sink, where I'd peel and cut other veggies to add in. The noodles were soft, so I drained the pot into a colander in the sink and set the oven to 350 degrees. Then I mixed all the casserole ingredients into the pot, where

I would dump the cooled noodles and blend everything together with a wooden spoon before sliding it all into a greased 9x13 baking dish.

"Can I do the chips?" Simi called, jumping down off his chair and pushing it over to the spot between sink and stove. He knew not to get too close to the burners, trained well in the times we'd made matzoh balls together, nearly every week for Shabbat. I loved involving my children in food prep—not only was it fun and good time spent together, but they were learning lessons in math and science and getting to know family recipes at the same time. Which weren't necessarily my family recipes, but recipes culled together from Barry's family and my chosen one, the friends who'd mentored and welcomed me into this community. I hadn't expected to love cooking so much, but it made me feel independent, like I could sustain my family from the work of my hands. Growing up, my mother was too busy supporting my father's political career and traveling with him to meet constituents to cook. The first time I made challah, under Shiri's watchful gaze, I felt like I had climbed a mountain.

"Sure," I laughed, grabbing a bag of potato chips from the pantry. The baking dish filled with the noodle mixture and set on the counter, Simi reached into the foil bag, grabbed a greasy handful, and mushed his hands together to crumple them into small pieces, which he rained down over the top of the casserole.

"One more handful," I said, surveying the thin, salty layer. He finished, and I held on to him with one hand as I dragged his chair to the sink. "Wash your hands," I said, turning the faucet to warm and moving the soap dispenser closer to his reach.

The casserole went into the oven, and I turned back to Shira and the cookies.

"It's time for the dry ingredients," I said. "Measure out two and a quarter cups of flour." I pointed to the two-cup mark on the big glass measuring cup. "We'll do the last quarter in this." I handed her a small metal quarter cup.

She measured the flour and dumped it into the bowl. I added in a teaspoon each of vanilla, salt and baking soda and then told her to whir it again. The batter became thick, clinging to the mixer blade. I scraped it down with a spatula.

"Now the chips," I said, measuring a full cup of chocolate chips and handing it to Shira, who dumped it in and turned the mixer on one last time to blend it all together.

"Can you do the scooping?" I asked.

She nodded with serious eyes. I grabbed two prepared cookie sheets and handed her a small metal scoop. As she filled the cookie sheets with rounds of dough, I returned to the sink, where Simi was splashing in the water and laughing. His shirt was doused, but he was happy, so I let him continue as I peeled a cucumber and sliced it, the tomatoes and the onions and added everything to the salad bowl. The rest of the house was quiet. Was Barry making any progress with Donny?

When dinner was ready, I called upstairs. "Barry, Donny, dinner!"

They solemnly descended the steps, my son's hand clasped tightly to his father's, their faces drawn and pale. They took their places at the table, and Barry offered a half smile, eyebrows raised, compassion in his eyes.

"Don't forget the *bracha*," I said, wagging a finger at the kids. "*Mizonot*, for noodles," I reminded them.

After moving their lips in a hasty blessing, they scooped food into their mouths at an alarming pace. I stared at the faces of each of my family members. Shira and Simi had my lightness—golden hair and fair skin—and they were oblivious to the heaviness in Donny's eyes. They kept up an endless stream of chatter about their day, about books they were reading and friends they wanted play dates with. I grabbed a napkin to swipe at Simi's cheese-encrusted lips. He recoiled as I rubbed.

"Do you want me to wash your face instead?" I asked, and he shook his head, closing his eyes as I removed the cheese from his soft skin.

"Can I please be excused?" Shira chirped, pushing her chair back from the table.

I nodded. "Clear your places," I said, watching Simi follow his sister.

"Me too," Donny said sullenly, not looking up as he left the table, plate in hand still half-filled with food.

"Go get ready for bed, you guys," I said. "No baths tonight."

They scampered up the stairs. I heaved an exhale, releasing the tension I'd held in Donny's silence. "So? What did he say?"

"Not much." Barry lifted his shoulders. "Only that Mr. Fineman is mean to him."

"His math teacher?"

Barry nodded.

"Okay, well, should we call the school? Set a meeting?"

Barry shook his head. "Let's give it time. We need to hear more before we take action. Tomorrow is just Judaic subjects anyway, and Sunday too. He won't have him again until Monday. Maybe over the weekend we can tease out some details?"

Something gnawed at my stomach as he said this, but I bit back my hesitation. "If you think it's best," I said. "But I feel, I don't know, like it's something big and we have to nip it in the bud before it gets worse."

"That's your imagination running away with you," Barry chided. "I know you're worried about our son. I am, too. It's not like him to be so quiet and sullen. But we will get to the bottom of it. I'm confident he'll come to us with it over the weekend. After all, the peace of Shabbat does wonders."

"Okay, I trust you," I said, not believing my words. My mother's instinct told me to roll right in, trundle over everything and everyone to rescue my son from what I knew was an awful and damaging situation.

"I'll clear up," Barry said, grabbing his plate and the casserole dish from the table. "You get ready for the mikvah." He winked, his mouth lifting in a sly smile.

"Thank you," I said, returning the grin. Then I groaned. "I have so much cooking to do for Shabbat! How did I let it go so late?"

After all these years, just a look from my husband could send tingles through every nerve ending. All I wanted was to climb into bed next to him and stay there for hours. And here was the downside of my chosen life: so many obligations and so little time. I had no choice but to cook for the Sabbath, and if I didn't get to it tonight, Friday would be a bear of a day.

But maybe I should let it be. How lucky was I? So many women complained of distance in their marriages. I wanted my husband more than I could have imagined eight years into our marriage, and the feeling was more than mutual. I wished I didn't have to separate from him for half of every month. I would gladly lie naked beside my beautiful man every single day if I had the option. Shiri always said the separation would enliven the times we could come together, and she was right, but I wished we never had to be apart. I feared the silences and the separations might reveal all was not perfect in my storybook life.

Chapter Six

I never expected that a magazine assignment would turn me religious. But the women were so embracing, so welcoming, and I loved the way their husbands gazed at them over flickering candlelight, singing full-throated and loud the poetic Hebrew of "Aishet Chayil (Woman of Valor)" before Friday night dinner. I wanted that connection, that safety, that enduring love.

I took longer than the two weeks my editor wanted to develop a far-reaching, flowing story about this world I came to love. I spent three months there before my story published, shining a bright light on a community few people knew. I was rarely at the office, spending my days observing prayer groups where pious women recited psalms for the welfare of neighbors and friends. I scribbled notes over lunches in pizzerias, cafes and bakeries. Under Shiri's embrace, women vied to invite me for Shabbat meals or to stay in their homes from Friday afternoon until the stars sparkled in the Saturday night sky. I began to recognize faces and remember names. Walking down Skokie streets, I waved to women toting toddlers and pushing strollers as they called to me by name.

I bought long-sleeved shirts that covered my collarbone, pulled on opaque tights in black and brown and navy blue and alternated on weekdays between two denim skirts, one which hung to my ankles and one that fell to mid-calf. I sometimes looked in the mirror and wondered who stared back—that woman covered in so much cloth couldn't be the coquettish co-ed who preferred tank tops and short-shorts to hike Sleeping Bear Dunes in northern Michigan with my college friends.

But I didn't hate my reflection. I was merely curious about why I found comfort in the approval and embrace of these chatty women.

And then, when I married Barry, I saw something different when I looked in the mirror. I saw how he saw me, how I epitomized his dream of a life partner, a lover, a best friend and companion. Our wedding took place on a late-autumn day when the first wintry chill blew through the Windy City. We had taken over the first floor of the Congress Plaza Hotel. Although they weren't happy about my becoming religious, my parents made sure the press covered my wedding so constituents could see the elegance and mystery of the senator's happy family, even this newly Orthodox part of it, which they might cringe over privately, but when facing the public, they beamed as proud, loving parents. I got ready in a suite on the twenty-third floor with my mother, Barry's mother, and all our sisters.

My sisters were stiff in their matching dresses, made from the same pink fabric with a gentle brocade pattern in patches of velvet. Each woman wore a different style—Barry's sisters were suitably covered with sleeves and long skirts, while my sisters hadn't followed my request to cover elbows and knees. But I didn't mind. They could wear what they wanted on this day. I was not focused on them, only on the future I would walk toward down the carpeted aisle in the hotel ballroom. My sisters could sit back from the festivities and watch, or they could join in the full-throttle dancing. I was excited to exchange the world of my childhood for a vibrant new one. Barry's sisters were glamorous in their long, full skirts and sleek wigs, bouncing babies on their hips.

Before the makeup artist came to me, Barry's mother grabbed my face between her fleshy hands and hovered close. "Welcome to our family," she whispered, fluttering moist kisses on my forehead and nose.

I closed my eyes and let them come, like a rainfall after a drought. When I opened my eyes, I darted a glance in my mother's direction. She stood tall and somber in purple-gray silk, watching the whole scene, her eyes glistening, her red lips pursed in a question. When I caught her eye, she looked away. *I'm sorry, Mom*, I thought but didn't have the courage to voice the words. If only she had come to me, sat with me, laid her hand over mine. I would still have marched forward into this loud, dynamic religious community, but I might have invited her to come with, if only as an occasional visitor. One small gesture was all it would take, I thought, but nothing came.

In contrast, my nana sat by my side for all the preparations, a wide smile on her face, her eyes crinkled with excitement. As I ventured into Jewish observance, I renewed my connection to my maternal grandparents, who were eager for the relationship. My mother was their only child, my sisters and I their only grandchildren, and my parents had limited our access to them throughout my childhood, not wanting to immerse too deeply in their very Jewish, albeit secular, world. But now, we spoke by phone several times a week, and my grandparents came to Chicago many weekends, often staying at Shiri's house with me and immersing as fully in Shabbat as I did.

I invited them to the Shabbat festivities the weekend before my wedding, which my parents did not attend. They would not have enjoyed it, I rationalized, though I didn't give them a chance to decline. My grandparents reveled in being my most important family at this auspicious time.

After the wedding planner set my veil atop my head and secured it with a sequined tiara and a dozen bobby pins, I was swept downstairs by a swell of women—sisters, mothers, aunts and grandmothers, the wedding planner, and well-meaning female friends, hovering around me like bees around their queen. Into the elevator, down all the many floors to the long, carpeted hallway, where I walked somberly toward a riser and perched in a tall wicker chair wrapped in white tulle. Guests wished me *mazel tov*, kissing, waving, the little girls—cousins, nieces, the children of friends—oohing and ahhing as they stroked my dress, pointed to my tiara, touched my manicured nails painted in the palest pink shade.

And then, trumpets sounded and men were clapping and deep throaty voices belted out sounds that weren't quite words, music carried on the swell of a sea of men in black levitating along the carpet, arms linked, their feet barely touching the ground as they danced my groom to me. Barry was wrapped in a white cotton robe, a *kittel*, the garment that a man wears on his wedding day, and which at the end of his life, he is buried in.

His face glistened with sweat. His eyes clenched closed, his father and uncle held him up, their arms linked at elbows. He seemed to falter, to sway, like he would fall if they let go. I forgot everything that I was feeling and focused on him, his black curls hard with gel under his kippah, his closed eyes sunk into his face.

Ai-ai-ai, chatan v'kallah... The men sang about a groom and a bride. At the edge of the dais, Barry's eyes opened and a loopy smile spilled across his face. His lips seemed to quiver, though I'm not sure they moved at all. He lifted his arms out of the clasp from the men on his sides and reached for my veil, lifting it over my head and tucking it back against my hair. He bowed his sweaty forehead to mine.

"You are absolutely the right bride," he whispered, evoking Jacob, Rachel and Leah, when one bride was switched for the other. His breath smelled sour from fasting all day. I wrinkled my nose and clamped my lips shut, fearing I would emit the same acrid scent. As the room started to spin, he turned away, and the crowd of guests roared with approval. He clasped arms with his father and uncle and danced back the way he had come.

The rest of the wedding was as energetic and overwhelming as the *bedeken*. While I had carefully crafted a menu featuring my favorite wedding fare—including little hot dogs in flaky puff pastry and light-as-air Hungarian layer cake—I barely ate a thing except for a small plate of hors d'oeuvres that the wedding planner brought to us after the ceremony, when we were sequestered to consummate the marriage—an ancient tradition which had turned into an opportunity for the bridal couple to hide from the chaos and eat after fasting all day. We devoured carrots and celery with ranch, three mini hot dogs apiece, and six mini egg rolls.

"Water, I need water," I gasped.

Barry poured a second glass after I gulped down the first.

The wedding band bounced klezmer tunes in the hallway outside the ballroom, and a wordless hum drifted from the hundreds of people talking and milling about as they ate from the buffet. Barry and I settled into momentary quiet.

"My wife," Barry said.

"My husband." I reached a hand to him.

His hands were moist.

"From all the dancing?" I said, tapping my forefinger against the pad of his palm.

"Nerves," he said.

"Really?"

He nodded. "This is the most important decision either of us will ever make."

He stood and came over to me. "Don't ask me to get up," I laughed. "I could fall asleep right here, right now, in this dress."

"It's been a day. Our wedding day," he whispered.

His breath tickled my earlobe and sent shivers along my neck.

"My wife," he whispered again, stroking the back of my neck with two fingers.

I closed my eyes and leaned toward him. His tongue darted along the bottom of my ear, and his teeth tugged at the lobe.

"I told you I would know what to do," he said, his hand grazing my shoulder and trailing down my back.

"Do we have to go to the reception?" I croaked.

"I think we might be missed," he laughed, lifting the hair off my neck and fluttering little kisses along my spine.

"Do we care?" I mumbled.

"A little."

He peered into my eyes, smiling coyly, playing with me. "Let's save something for later," he said. "Ready?"

I breathed in deeply and shook my head. "No. But I might never be. Let's do this."

I reached for his hand and let him pull me up and lead me out of the room and into our shared life.

We danced for hours. And after all the speeches were finished, after the frenetic spinning and bouncing ended, after the men stopped singing and stomping and the women stopped clapping and cheering, after everybody left, kissing us and pressing into our hands gifts and cards stuffed with money, after the very last people waved their goodbyes and fell into their cars and drove away into the dark night, it was the two of us in a quiet hotel room with no sound but our beating hearts. I was so tired that I worried I would not be able to sleep or have energy to consummate my marriage, even though I had waited for this moment pretty much since our first pizza date, when his dark eyes peered deep into my soul and I wanted to touch his thick curly hair. The wedding band had been so loud that my ears continued to ring long after we left the ballroom and rode the elevator silently, warily, upstairs. I sat on the edge of the king-sized bed and peeled off my sequined wedding sneakers, massaging my sore, swollen feet.

"Let me," Barry said, kneeling on the carpet.

I lay back on the bed, the tulle of my skirt flouncing around me.

His hands pressed into each toe, rubbing in circles and moving down the ball of my foot toward the heel. My heart pounded. His hands moved up the back of my ankle, pressing on either side of the bone then moving up my calf, his thumbs digging into the flesh, working out the knots that had formed from all the dancing.

"Feel good?"

"Hmmm mmmm."

The throbbing in my chest moved down my body. My breath came quicker as his hands moved higher.

"Why don't I help you out of that dress?"

He grabbed my hand, pulling me to standing. "Turn around." His fingers lifted my hair and peeled back each pearl button from its little hole in the fabric, all the way down my back to the bottom of my spine. His hands slipped inside the dress, his palms hot against my shoulders. He pulled the fabric down off my arms.

"I'll hold it while you step out."

"I have to hang it up," I said. "It's so delicate."

When the dress was off, Barry carried it to a chaise in the corner and laid it flat. I stood before my new husband, my stomach fluttering as if I had never stood naked before a man. This would be the first time he would see my body, and he would be the last man to do so, to cherish it, to touch, to know my contours and scents. There was something beautiful, exciting about committing to one man for the rest of my life. This person held all my hopes for a bright future in his trusting hands.

"Look at you," he said.

His shirt was wrinkled and untucked. He was still in his shoes.

"It's not fair to be the only one naked," I said.

I reached for his shirt, flicking each button open until it dangled off his torso. I pushed it off his shoulders, and it fell to the floor. He pulled his undershirt over his head and dropped it beside the crumpled button-down. His chest was smooth and covered in a light moss of tight dark curls. His arms were sculpted, muscular. How had I not known? He lifted the buckle on his belt and pulled it free of his pants.

"Keep going," I said.

Thick, dark curls. Piercing eyes. A soft smile on lips that were as pink as a summer rose. His eyes held mine as he shed the rest of his clothing, and a man stood before me that I had never known, a man I would come to know better than any other, whose strong, muscular thighs and throbbing body were more than ready for me. Every nerve-ending pulsed, every tender touchpoint. I bit my bottom lip and closed my eyes.

Our wedding night was intense and passionate, yet tender and sweet. We were beyond exhausted when we began, and by the time we finished, tangled up in each other, we had surpassed exhaustion and bordered on the edge of surreal awakening. I lay against my husband's chest, eyes closed, daring sleep to take me, not wanting to let go of this fantastic ending to a dream day.

"Did I surprise you?" he whispered into my hair.

"Definitely," I said.

"You didn't think I'd know what to do," he said.

"I hoped you would."

"And were you satisfied?"

"Absolutely."

I closed my eyes and settled into the briefest sleep. Morning came quickly, and the tumble of relatives and guests clamored for the new couple at the wedding brunch in a smaller ballroom. I pulled on a neat navy skirt with a peplum polka dot blouse and, for the first time, tucked my hair into a full-brimmed hat, a message to all that I was now a married woman, off-limits to the wandering eyes of any man other than the one whose name linked with mine. I peered at my reflection in the mirror, not sure I recognized myself, uncertain if I liked what I saw, afraid I was a little girl playing dress-up, playing with fire.

Barry walked into the bathroom and stared into the mirror. "You look so beautiful," he said, coming up close.

"Really?"

He nodded. "You look like a wife."

CHAPTER SEVEN

From the wedding night onwards, Barry and I had been in sync. Our life settled into a flow, and each day began and ended with us sharing close words, a lingering glance. Some days, he could anticipate my words before I spoke them.

Thursday night would be agonizingly long as I prepared for Shabbat and went to the mikvah and had an intimate reunion with my husband. I wanted Barry intensely and knew that we might come together quickly the first time but then settle in for a second course, staying up into the wee hours of the morning. I could not immerse in the mikvah or even arrive to the unmarked building to prepare until after night fell and stars twinkled in the sky.

Before we married, I studied with Shiri to learn all the laws of married Orthodox sex. Which was the only sanctioned sex in our world, anyway. Mostly, it revolved around my monthly cycle. From the minute I started bleeding until it ended, plus seven "clean" days, I was off-limits to my husband, and we had to observe that time carefully. No handing anything to each other, no sitting on a couch with one cushion, no holding hands, no pouring wine for each other. We must sleep in separate beds. We mustn't see each other naked, not even a shoulder or a knee. I had to put down the platter of chicken at dinner rather than hand it directly to him. It was a time to work on our emotional relationship, all the books said, and it certainly helped the desire to build, but I also felt a little like my body was dirty, untouchable, because of the very thing that made me a woman. Barry reassured me how much he wanted me and how if we didn't have these rules, he'd devour me regardless of what time of the month it was. It was nice to hear but hard to believe because he'd never had period sex, so the point was moot. Of course, I didn't really want sex during my cycle, but as soon as it petered out, I was raring to go, and I had to wait another seven "clean days" until I was within his reach. That part grated on me most and seemed to drag slowly until my inevitable immersion in the pure waters of the mikvah.

At the ritual bath, which mixed rainwater with city water, I dunked three times while a bewigged and modestly dressed woman watched and declared me "Kosher!" after each dunk. I'd sat in a full tub for a half hour then showered and washed every inch of me clean. The mikvah lady checked my fingers and toes, scanned my back and front, looked everywhere for anything out of place that would prevent me from immersing—she collected stray hairs from my back, removed fuzz from between my toes, examined my nails to make sure there was no dirt lurking beneath the nailbeds. After, I quickly pulled on my clothes and slipped my wet hair into a snood then drove home, my headlights illuminating the house where my husband stood with a big goofy grin. I was barely inside before he engulfed me, sprinkling kisses along my face, my neck, and pulling me up the stairs to our room, where he couldn't close the door fast enough. It was kind of exciting to have this wedding night–level eagerness month after month, and I laughed as he nuzzled me and pulled me onto the bed, which he had already moved together as if it were one large king-size, waiting for us to tumble onto it.

"Is it me you want, or the sex?" I often joked.

"Does it matter?" he joked back.

I slapped him lightly. "Barry! Always say it's me, never just the sex. Always me."

He laughed and pulled me on top of him. "Of course it is, Sally," he said, sucking my tongue into his mouth. "Sex with you. My one and only."

After, I lay on my back, staring at the ceiling as Barry snored beside me. It had been wonderful to reconnect with him and lose myself in his touch after the heaviness of the day. Focused on the mikvah and then on reuniting with my husband, I let go of the ruminations over Donny's situation. But now they returned, shadowy lurking on the periphery of my vision. I'd forgotten to close the curtains. The moon painted streaks on the wall, the waving tree branches like evil fingers reaching for me with an uncomfortable truth.

I tried to fall asleep for what felt like hours, but when I looked at the clock, it was only 1:30. I swung my legs over the side of the bed and pulled on a sweatshirt. I had intended to head to the kitchen, to at least make the challah dough so it could rise until morning. To get all the cooking done, I planned to call Nana to come help me, since she and Papa joined us every Friday night for Shabbat anyway. We could talk while we chopped, diced and sauteed, two pairs of hands to make the work lighter and faster.

Downstairs, the blue light of the computer beckoned. Just a quick peek at emails, and then I'd head for the kitchen. In the desk chair, I looked for the same moon that had followed me through the house, a watching eye, a bright awareness. Among the emails was John's incipient question about my religious life. I should have deleted it. I tilted my head toward the ceiling, picturing my sleeping husband, his taut thighs under my gripping hands. I should never have connected with John in the first place. I highlighted the message and was about to delete it, but something about the waiting questions bothered me.

It was that he lurked on the periphery of my life, my happy life, wanting to press inward. And that I let him, keeping it secret from the man I loved more than I ever knew I could love, the man who had become part of my soul. I was betraying him with my silence. I deposited the email in the trash, set the computer to sleep and headed for the kitchen.

CHAPTER EIGHT

There were times I wished my grandparents could move right into our house, become a true part of my family. But they were far too independent for such an arrangement, and besides, we didn't have room. Still, I inserted them in our lives at every turn, inviting them to school performances, birthday parties, playdates in the park, Friday night dinner, and holiday meals, of course. They reveled in my observance, deepening their own, so gladdened were they that one of their offspring had finally embraced the faith and heritage they held so dear. Nana accompanied me to Torah partners; as Batya and I pored over a text, Nana leaned in with the elderly study buddy Shiri had matched her with. A similar age and life experience, they became fast friends, opening the community to my grandmother faster than she could have done on her own.

That Friday morning, Nana came over with a ready smile and her favorite apron covered in bright yellow lemons tucked into her purse.

"Thank you so much for helping," I said, kissing her soft cheek. "I had the mikvah last night and only did a little bit of cooking. How will I ever get it all done?"

She smiled knowingly and winked. "The mikvah, eh? Papa and I never did that, but I imagine it might make things very special." She stroked my cheek, pulling the apron from her purse and tying it around her waist.

"Yeah, well," I said, my face burning. "I don't know about special. Anyway, we have two meals to make, plus the challah to braid and bake, and cakes for dessert."

She patted my shoulder. "Two sets of hands make fast work," she said, reaching into the pareve drawer for a knife.

Nana hummed as she cooked, and I relaxed into the reassuring lilt of her voice.

In the years since we'd reconnected, I'd tried to suss out where the break had formed, where and why my mother had so drastically departed from her parents' warm embrace. Or if what I knew as a warm embrace had not been quite so warm when my mother was a child. Nana was tight-lipped, and Papa discouraging. They refused to discuss it whenever I broached the subject. So I'd let it go, even as I continued to wonder. Every so often, I'd slip in a subtle question, but they were keen and would not give any details. It was their business and my mother's and none of mine.

We made up for lost time, me eagerly drinking in the stories they had long wanted to tell, of their backgrounds, their families, their upbringing, their identities. I came to feel that my becoming religious was not so much a departure from what I knew but rather a return to what I did not realize lived in me already.

Nana's grandfather had been a revered Lithuanian rabbi who died in the Holocaust. His son made it out and emigrated to America, giving life to a whole new generation but abandoning his father's religious path in the wake of such tragic loss. Nana and her five siblings represented an array of Jewish observance, adopting every denomination and way of observing that 20th century American Jewry had to offer. And while Nana had joined Papa's fervently Reform family when they married, the traditions of her grandfather's past lived in her, a dormant flame ignited by my new life.

"This challah is delicious, honey," Papa gushed at dinner.

At the end of the table, Barry smiled. "My Sally is the best baker and cook," he said.

I blinked away the compliment, knowing full well that his praise was motivated in part by our spine-tingling reunion from the night before. My grandparents couldn't know the details of what went on in our bedroom, nor would they want to, but I felt like it played across my face like a silent film, revealing our most intimate moments to everyone.

"Barry," I hissed, smiling in spite of myself.

"Can't a husband compliment his wife?" He tore a bite of challah with his teeth, not a sensuous act, but it seemed sex tinted the way I viewed everything today.

I looked away. "Who wants soup?"

The kids' hands shot up, and they sang out a chorus of, "*Meeee!*"

I laughed. "Nana? Papa? One matzoh ball or two? Barry, I know what you want," I said, winking.

He chuckled, and I blushed again. Eight years in, and he could still transform me to a puddle of wanting! Nana followed me into the kitchen to help carry in bowls of steaming soup.

While we were playful and light, Donny sat silent in his seat, staring down at his hands. He had refused to accompany Barry to *shul* to start the Sabbath as he usually did, instead clinging to my side as I finished the salad and set the table. He'd been unusually quiet during pre-dinner singing, reaching under the table for my hand and holding on tight far beyond the reassuring squeeze I gave him. I hoped this Shabbat would make him feel safe enough to reveal what was bothering him. I hadn't invited any guests for dinner, and we were only going to Batya's for lunch, which was like family. She always invited her parents and my grandparents, too. A supportive cast of characters. But we would go to synagogue in the morning, as usual. Would Donny refuse to go? If we hung back, our absence would undoubtedly inspire the curiosity of the neighbors, and that was all I needed, prying eyes and probing questions from a community too consumed with the details of its members' lives.

The next morning, Barry planted a long, probing kiss on my lips before he breezed out the door to shul. He wanted to make the early *minyan* because I was concerned we would not make it at all, given Donny's current state.

"I'll go and come back so we can be together as a family before going next-door for lunch," he said.

I patted his shoulder in thanks then lay back on the pillow, staring at the sunlight peering through the window.

I peeled back the covers and pulled the blankets tight as I got out of bed. Easier to make it right away than have the sheets skewed all day. I fluffed the pillows and stood them on their edges against the headboard then smoothed the covers with my hands. Neat as a pin.

I washed up and pulled on my Shabbos robe. The kids would clamber downstairs in pajamas, slowly waking on this one easy day of the week. I stood cereal boxes on the kitchen table along with colorful plastic bowls, child-sized spoons, and 2% milk. Simi bounded in first, bright-eyed and huggy. He threw his arms around my legs and bounced, his motion to tell me he wanted to be picked up. I hefted him to my shoulder and planted kisses along the perimeter of his face.

"Stop, Mommy," he giggled, turning his face to prod me on.

"You love it," I said, blowing a raspberry into the folds of his neck. He was gradually losing his baby chubbiness, but I loved the layers that remained. Each of my kids morphed from pudgy baby to wiry children, and I wanted to hold on to this one as long as I could.

Shira came down a few minutes later. Donny did not descend for another half hour, as sullen as he'd been the night before. I leaned close to plant a kiss on his cheek, but he recoiled.

"A mother can't kiss her son anymore?" I said, ruffling his hair but growing concerned.

They ate quietly then put their bowls on the counter and disappeared into the family room. Since Donny came down last, he was last to leave, and

I sidelined him, hoping for a few moments of more revealing conversation than we'd had over the last forty-eight hours.

"It's not too cold outside," I said. "Why don't we bundle into some fleeces and sit on the deck?"

"For what?"

"To look at the morning," I said, tweaking his elbow. "To listen to all the sounds of a quiet Shabbat. Since we're not going to shul, we might as well enjoy the slow morning."

His eyes blazed at mention of avoiding the synagogue. "We're not going to shul?"

I shook my head. "I thought we could use a quiet morning at home together," I said. "What do you think?"

His face brightened, and he bobbed in agreement.

"Grab your fleece. And put on thick socks."

I bundled a coat over my Shabbos robe, tapped the snood that held my hair to make sure no wisps had escaped. My feet already warm in slippers, I shuffled to the deck, a kitchen towel in hand to wipe dew off the chairs.

CHAPTER NINE

Tea steamed in the mug in my hands. I'd swirled hot water from the Sabbath urn into a packet of hot cocoa for Donny, and he stirred the spoon round and round as the warmth puffed into the morning above his cup. In the trees, birds cheeped and clicked, sounding like a swarm, but when I gazed up to see their feathered bodies, I spotted only a pair of orange-chested American robins, squawking in energetic conversation. I admired their boldness, speaking as if they were the only creatures around.

Donny blew on the cocoa, pushing away steam. A chipmunk chittered at the edge of the deck then scurried underneath, its tiny feet scratching against the concrete. A light breeze swept the yard, pimpling my skin. I shuddered into my coat. "It takes so long for spring to arrive, doesn't it?"

Donny smirked. I could see the sinews of his body relax, elongating as he stretched his feet over the wood planks and cupped the mug close, the steam warming his face. It was good to see a glimpse of his lighter self.

"The other day at school, Mr. Fineman..." Donny's voice trailed off.

"Your math teacher. Yes. What did he do, honey?"

I sipped my tea and avoided looking in his direction, praying my nonchalance would open the door for details to spill forth. He set down the mug, twisting his hands in his lap. His teeth worked his bottom lip. I wanted so badly to reach out, to hold his hand in mine, to smooth his hair and murmur reassurances, to make it all go away. I wanted to pull my boy to me and stroke his back and tell him I could protect him from a dangerous world. But I stayed in my chair, watching sunlight filter through tree branches and fall in neat lines on the deck.

"He..."

My stomach clenched. What had this man done to my son? I could not rush the telling of this story. I knew my child. If I pushed, he would retreat further into himself, drawing a solid wall tight around him that no one could penetrate. I had waited several days to get this far. I'd wait as long as it took until I knew, and then I'd fly into fierce mama bear action.

"He...he said I must be dumb," Donny said.

That could not be all. Such a comment would wound him, yes, but it would not crush him to the point of needing to stick by my side, avoid his friends at shul, avoid the school he loved attending. It was like all the fun had drained out of him.

"And...he hit me," Donny said.

I closed one lip over the other, biting back words. I wanted to rage, to stomp, to storm across town to the Finemans' house and break into their Shabbat, screaming and ranting. I crossed my ankles and sat deeper in my chair.

"He hit you?"

Donny nodded and reached out his hands. His knuckles were red and swollen, as if he'd been struck across the knobby bone. Both hands. Raised and angry with welts.

I grasped his hands and lifted them to my lips to kiss them. "He struck you across your knuckles? With what?"

"A ruler." His eyes were filling. He bit his bottom lip to keep from crying.

"He did it again and again, and it really hurt," he said, his voice shaking. "Just once?"

He shook his head, and the tears silently slipped from his eyes, wetting his cheeks. He made no move to wipe them away, just sat on the deck chair, weeping without convulsing, without word, without movement.

"Was this the first time?" I asked.

He shook his head.

"How long has this been going on?"

Inside, I seethed, but I didn't want Donny to pick up on my anger, my rage. I had never hit anyone in my life, but I wanted to pummel this man until he was purple and couldn't crawl out of range of my fists. I wanted to pin him to the ground.

Donny sipped the cocoa then put the mug down on the deck railing. "It's been going on all year," he whispered.

All year? *All fucking year?* I gripped the armrests of my chair to steady myself.

"Mama..." He put a hand on my arm. He couldn't see my emotions. I had to shield him from carrying the burdens of yet another wayward adult. He was the innocent here. It was not his job to comfort me.

I reached for his mug and set both cups on the ledge then pulled Donny onto my lap. He lay his head on my chest and curled his knees up until he was a ball in my arms. I held him tight.

"Oh honey...why didn't you tell me? It is never okay for anyone to strike you—not a teacher, nor a parent, not anyone."

He sniffled, crying silent tears, shaking in my arms. His shoulders hunched into me. And then, when the tears slowed, he looked up and said, "He sometimes asks me to stay after class and I don't want to, but he tells me I have to and that I can't tell anyone, and then he tells me to turn around and he hits me on my tush, too."

Oh my God. My poor boy. If steam could puff out of my ears, now would be the time. I felt like one of those cartoons where the character's head comes apart with clouds of smoke floating to the sky. If that man had appeared at my door at that moment, or even out on the street beyond, I would have pushed him to the ground and slit his throat. Or run him over with the car. How could a teacher entrusted with the care of young children inflict violence on these precious innocents? How could anyone do such a thing?

I had to know the exact details. How could I ask if he'd touched him beneath his clothes? If he'd pulled down his pants to spank him? If he'd fondled or groped or looked?

As if he could read my mind, Donny shook his head. "He never undressed me, Mommy," he said. He hadn't called me Mommy in at least two years.

I rocked him in my arms, waves of regret and guilt and rage coursing through me. My heart thumped. My head pounded. My mouth was like felt.

"It's over," I said. "You will never see that man again. I promise you are safe. And you can always tell me anything, no matter how scary or horrible it is. I will never be mad at you, honey. You can tell Mommy anything, and Tati, too, even if another adult tells you not to. Especially if another adult tells you not to."

His arms wrapped through mine and he clung to me, his fingers clawing at my coat.

CHAPTER TEN

Barry was back from shul by 11, by which time I'd dressed and roused the boys to don dress pants and sweaters and Shira to pick a dress and tights and a matching hair ribbon. Simi and Shira played quietly in the family room, but Donny shadowed me wherever I went. I begged him to sit on my bed while I changed in the closet, though I could see from his face that to be out of my sight inspired fear. His eyes darted like a cat in the dark. I handed him a favorite stuffed giraffe from his bed, one he hadn't clung to in years.

"Hold this," I said. "Let Grimmy keep you company while I get dressed."

After, I convinced him to settle in the family room with his siblings so I could talk to his father. I pulled Barry onto the deck, where the day had warmed enough to go without a coat.

"Now I know," I said.

"What? What do you know?" He leaned toward me, his knuckles whitening.

"Donny's teacher has been beating him," I said.

"What?"

"Mr. Fineman."

"Beating him?"

I nodded. "With a ruler. Across his knuckles and on his bottom."

"God!" Barry spat out the word. His eyes blazed.

I hadn't realized until that moment that I had been holding my breath, wondering how he would react, if he would defend the man because he was religious and insist this could not possibly happen in our world. I knew my husband, knew what a good and sturdy man he was. I knew we were a unit, connected, tight, in this together.

But I'd heard of *frum* people sweeping under the rug unforgivable transgressions like molestation and abuse and unsafe conditions to protect the sanctity of the community. To prevent the government from intruding. To keep a perfect profile so the outside world would not look down on our curious ways. Because I came from the outside world, I could not understand how anyone could ignore illegal, immoral or dangerous behavior just to protect public opinion of their community.

He threaded his fingers through his dark curls. "Obviously we need to do something," he said. "But before we go crazy, let me have a private conversation with the headmaster. I mean, what if it's an exaggeration?"

A chill rippled through me. "Are you kidding? I believe our son. I saw his knuckles—they are red and swollen. All of them. That doesn't happen from falling on the playground. And he has no reason to lie."

I stepped back from my husband, glaring at him.

"Sally, I hear you. And of course, I believe Donny, too. Why would he make this up? All I'm saying is, let's handle this quietly. We need to investigate. We need to find out the truth."

"I know the truth," I said, pushing away from him as he stepped closer. "My son is being abused. And it sounds like my husband—his father—is trying to pretend it's not happening. Are you honestly choosing the school over your family? Don't you see how he clings to me? That is not normal behavior. He is not exaggerating, and you are horrible to even suggest it."

"Let's not take this to an extreme," he said, reaching for me.

I crossed my arms in front of my chest and backed away.

"This *is* extreme, Barry," I said. "You're a fool if you think this will stay quiet. And if you can't side with me on this, I will seriously wonder if you are the man I thought you were."

"Just wait until I can find things out, Sally," Barry pleaded, reaching for my hands. "Please. Let's keep this within the community. And how do you know it was on his bottom, too? Did you look?"

I shook my head, realizing that for the past several months, Donny had insisted on taking showers, rather than baths, and didn't want me in the bathroom after I'd turned on the water and checked to make sure it wasn't too hot. I had assumed this was part of growing up, wanting privacy and feeling embarrassed in front of your mother. But he was only seven. It was too soon for such a high degree of modesty, unprompted. Now I realized he was hiding his shame and blaming himself. Poor kid. And what an ignorant mother I had been. Right under my nose, and I hadn't even suspected.

"I trust my son," I said. "He's not going back to that school. That teacher needs to be fired. And if you think I'll keep this quiet, you do not know me at all."

"Woah, hold on," Barry said, stepping in front of me and gripping my arms. I tried to wriggle free, but he tightened his fingers. "Baby, please. We are one in this. You know that you, our family, are everything to me. I would never forgive a person who abused my child. Please know that. I just need to find out the whole story. Let me speak to the headmaster. Let me take care of this."

"I will stand by our son no matter what," I said. "No matter what it does to *our community*." I said the word as if it left a sour taste in my mouth. "Our children need our support and protection, unequivocally and without question. Not the community. And if you push me on this, you will see me walking away."

"Are you threatening to leave me?"

I gulped back tears. That was the last thing I wanted. What *was* I saying? Barry was the love of my life, my best friend, my partner, the father of my children. I wanted nothing more than him and our precious children.

But if he wanted to hide his head in the sand, then yes, I realized I *would* leave. I would scoop up my children and run for the hills. For if my role of mother was put up against my role as wife, my children would win every time.

"I love you more than I ever thought possible, Barry," I said slowly, quietly. "But to be a mother, well, that is an entirely different kind of love that consumes every fiber of my being. And if one of my babies is threatened...you do not want me to say who I would choose."

He moved closer, his eyes boring into mine. "We are a family," he said. "We've had it easy, Sal. We hardly ever fight. We are almost always on the same page. This is a big deal. Bigger than we can even contemplate at this moment. And if you can even consider leaving me over it so quickly, well, I will have to call into question everything I thought about us, too."

The nerve! Why didn't he see that my perspective was the only way to look at this?

We stared at each other, eyes like laser beams penetrating past skin, into the heart, carving a hole through which all the trust and certainty and connection seeped out. Everything we had, until now, taken for granted. The tree in the yard rustled in a slight wind, leaves fluttering. The midday sun gleamed overhead, painting the planks of the deck in broad bright strokes of light. On the sidewalk in front of the house, stroller wheels creaked and the crisp clop of dress shoes padded along the pavement, the *click click* of women's low chunky heels and the scuff of little boys kicking their toes into the concrete. Our town was alive with motion as people left synagogue, heading for festive lunch tables. There was a hint of warmth to the air, but a chill still bit at its edges, and the air between Barry and me pulsed with rage and questions and sadness.

I wanted to close the gap between us, to step three short strides and lean into his arms, nudge my head against his shoulder and breathe in the musk of his aftershave and the deep scent of his skin that I knew so well. I wanted to say, *We can work out anything. We are both committed in love to our children and each other.* If I did, this would be over, and we would find the tether that tied us to each other, find a way to face our son's abuser together. *It won't be that easy,* chanted a little voice in my head. *This is different, bigger, and he is going to protect the community even as he seeks to protect our son. You alone can save your son. You alone can see clearly beyond the confines of the damn community.*

And so I stayed where I stood, arms crossed in front of me, jaw set, lips pressed tight.

"Yoo-hoo!" Batya called from her kitchen window next door. I pressed fingers to the puffs of skin beneath my eyes, swiping at any threatening tears. *If they look red and puffy, she'll know something's up.* I pasted a smile to my mouth and turned toward her window, waving.

"Hey!"

"We missed you in shul today," she said. "Ready for Shabbos lunch?"

Shoot. We're going next door. My grandparents would see instantly that something was amiss. I had reveled in the intimacy of just family and best friends for Shabbat lunch, but now I wished another family were coming as a buffer to distract my best friend from prying about the obvious tension between my husband and me. I had to paste a smile on my face and make it convincing.

"Can't wait!" I called. "Let me get everyone ready. We'll be over in 15."

I wanted to strap on sneakers and race through the neighborhood, running off worry and fear and anger and easing the knots in my stomach by burning in the afternoon air. But running on Shabbat was forbidden. Among the many prohibitions on the Sabbath, we weren't supposed to exert ourselves, and we couldn't take a hot shower if we did. And anyway, I could not run from this.

CHAPTER ELEVEN

While Barry and I had the usual disagreements of most married couples, he was right when he said we rarely fought. For eight years, we had had it pretty easy. It was strange at lunch, as if the distance between us were palpable, pressing the air down. He wouldn't look at me, which gnawed at my resolve. How could he turn his back on me at a time like this? And what if he did leave me? I was just spewing words in anger, but if he pulled away, the community would rally against me and leave me out in the cold, abandoning all love of the newly religious to cling to someone who had never veered from our ways.

Did he love me so little that he could just turn his back? It was like a wall had gone up between us, and try as I might to soften his glance or get him to look at me tenderly, I could not reach him. Donny insisted on sitting next to me instead of playing with Shmueli. In fact, when the kids finished eating and fled from the table to play outside or in Batya's toy-filled basement, Donny told his lifelong friend that he was going to stay at the table a while longer. Shmueli stared at Batya, who shrugged and waved him off, but she peered at me with a question in her eyes that I was not ready to answer. I would tell her about Mr. Fineman in time, but not in front of my son. I didn't want his trauma to play out again and again as adults looked his way with shame or accusation. Batya would be as horrified as I was, but I couldn't promise others in the community would be equally sympathetic.

Nana, too, sent questioning glances in my direction, but I pasted on a smile to beam back at her. I kept close to Donny to avoid any real conversation with the adults at the table.

With the kids gone, except for Donny, I moved us both closer to Barry's side of the table, settling into a chair beside him, with Donny on my lap. Heat emanated from my husband, and the tension in my shoulders eased for a moment. Here was my sweet man, my partner in life. I slid my hand under the table to rest on his thigh, a peace offering. He jumped, startled, turned to me and glared. I sank into the chair, pulling my hand back to my side. My face flushed with heat. I looked around, hoping no one had noticed our interaction, but Batya was staring straight at us, aware of everything. *Damn her. She was too good a friend, too perceptive.* The flush crept down my neck and up to my ears. Shamed, I glanced at Nana, who sat across from Donny. Her age-spotted hands rested on the table. She had come to our house before lunch, and I had told her about the abuse. After listening intently, she'd pulled me to her, rising on her toes to peck my cheek.

"Oh honey," she murmured, patting my back. "I am so sorry. But children are resilient, and Donny will be okay. We will route out this wretched teacher and make sure he never hurts another child again."

I was heartened by my grandmother's support. It couldn't erase the rift with my husband, but it was reassuring to know that I was not alone in my agony.

"Barry wants to keep it quiet until he can talk to the headmaster," I said. "I'm furious. But also scared. Now he won't talk to me, and I feel so alone."

She knitted her lips together in a tight line. "Marriage is not easy," she said. "Your grandfather and I have had rifts in our many years together. But we got through them, and you will too. Barry loves you, and you love him. Give it time."

I shrugged, leaning toward her. "I guess I have no choice."

She stroked my shoulder and offered a plaintive smile.

What was she thinking as she sat across from us at Batya's table? She hadn't had time to tell Papa, and he buzzed in conversation with Tzvi and Barry.

"Sal, help me with the dishes," Batya said, lifting the platter of cold salmon in one hand and grabbing the big metal salad bowl with the other. Scrapes of soggy lettuce saturated the bottom of the bowl. I stacked empty kugel plates—Batya's peppery-sweet yerushalmi kugel was legendary.

I glanced at my son, who looked calm, finally.

"Donny, honey, why don't you and Nana go read on the couch," I said. I patted his shoulder and pecked a kiss onto his hair. Tzvi had opened a tome of Talmud, and he leaned over it with Barry and Papa, chittering about its contents. Papa moved his chair closer to join in the learning as Nana ushered Donny toward the family room.

"What is going on," hissed Batya when we got to the kitchen.

I pointed to the door that led to the yard, dumping the plates on the counter and heading outside. Checking to make sure the windows were closed, I pulled the door behind us softly.

"You cannot even begin to imagine," I said. My breath left me in a much-needed exhale. I bent over. "Ohmigod, this is not happening." I pressed a hand to my forehead and closed my eyes. "I think I might be sick."

"Are you pregnant?"

I slapped her arm. "Is that all you think about?" I chuckled, feeling lighter already. I leaned against the deck railing. "No, I am not pregnant. It's much worse."

She cocked an eyebrow.

"Don't look at me all judgmental," I chided. "Listen. This is serious, Bat."

"Okay, sorry. What's going on?" Her hand on my sleeve was reassuring. I hadn't realized how much I needed someone's touch to tell me I would not have to face this alone. I wished Barry could tell me it would all be okay, that *we* would be okay.

"So, you know how Donny has been really clingy lately?"

She nodded.

"Well, I found out why."

This was harder than I had anticipated. I felt embarrassed, ashamed, as if I had done something wrong. What would the community think of me? Of my family? Geez, why did I care? My son! A swarm of emotions choked my throat, lodging the words I wanted to offer to my best friend. Would she judge me? Would she blame my son, distance herself from our family? No—Batya would never do that! But the community might. I gulped.

"Sal, what is it?" Batya looked worried, her face straight and serious, her warm brown eyes begging me to speak.

"Donny's been abused at school," I said.

Her eyes widened. The hand still on my arm tightened its grip, her fingers clenching, pinching my skin.

I winced and pulled back.

"Sorry," she said, patting my arm. "What do you mean?"

"Well, apparently it's been going on all year, and I can't believe I didn't notice or suspect anything," I said. "What kind of mother doesn't see that her child is being beaten?" I stifled a sob, my hand clamped to my mouth.

"It's not your fault," she said. "Why would you even think to consider such a thing? You couldn't know."

"But I should have, Batya! He's my son, my baby."

"Tell me what you know, Sally." She rubbed my arm in even, soothing strokes. There were no trees in her yard, but I watched the leaves on the tree in mine wave as if they, too, were trying to soothe my discontent. I stared at the dark green, like fingers fluttering in the breeze.

I told her everything, about Donny retreating into himself, his admission and his shame, and then the détente with my husband over our different reactions. By the end, I was weeping into her shoulder while she rubbed circles on my back. I had not felt this much emotion in so short a span of time since…well, since John Hogan broke my heart ten years earlier.

"You have to reconcile with Barry," she said. "You're both reacting in normal ways to such a shock. But you need each other to get through this."

I sniffled and nodded. "I know you're right," I said. "But if he goes to protect the community before our son..." I shook my head. "I can't accept that. I just can't. It's reprehensible."

"Men and women approach things differently," she said. "That's why Hashem made us two halves of one whole."

"Oh, cut the religious crap about gender roles," I said. "Now is not the time."

She looked stricken.

"Batya, come on, this is not the time to preach to me," I said. "You know I am normally fine with the way our life lays out in different expectations for men and women, but right now, with what I am facing, I refuse to chalk our reactions up to a gender difference. That's a cop-out. Don't argue this with me."

She remained silent, watching me. Batya was usually the force of strength in our relationship, and I was normally content to let her lead. But not today. Today, I was mama bear, and no one could talk me down from standing on my hind legs and growling. When something gets between a mother bear and her cub, the life of the interfering creature might literally be on the line.

"The guys are going to be wondering what we're up to," she said. "Let's go back in and finish cleaning up. I have dessert to bring out."

I nodded, patting my eyes with the futile hope that no one would notice I had been crying.

The rest of lunch passed without much fanfare. Barry didn't look up when I returned to the dining room, and Donny hovered to my side, staying there until we were home, full and content and quiet in the late afternoon.

"Let's all take a little Shabbos rest," I said. "Kids, you don't have to sleep, but let's just have some quiet time in our rooms, okay? Mommy's tired."

We shuffled off to our respective rooms, and I peeled off my dress and tights and *sheitel*, climbing into sweatpants and an oversized sweatshirt and letting my hair breathe. I leaned against the pillows, willing my eyes to close but unable to sleep. Barry clicked the door closed and sat next to me on the bed.

"We need to work through this," he said, reaching for me.

I stayed on my side of the bed, arms folded. "How could you turn your back on me so quickly, so easily? You wouldn't even look in my direction at lunch."

Tears welled in my eyes again. I bit my tongue to hold them back.

"Never in all our time together have you done that, Barry," I seethed. "Not once. There's never been any question about how connected we are. Until now."

Barry sighed. From the window, a slight wind sailed in, little fingers of coolness caressing my face and cooling the heat of anger.

"Barry, I want to reconcile with you more than anything, but I am afraid," I pleaded. "Afraid that you'll abandon me and choose the community over our marriage. Afraid that I will be all alone in trying to defend my son and protect my children against a community that you have always known but which is still new to me."

I gulped, unable to keep the tears from streaking my cheeks.

"You are the love of my life, and I do not want to lose you," I said. "But my children must be protected at all costs. Even if it means turning against the community."

"It's not good for children to see their parents at odds," he whispered. "Sally, come to me. Please. We must face this together."

But I was on a roll, my anger swelling like an ocean wave. I stood, hands on my hips. While all I had wanted earlier in the day was Barry's tender touch reminding me that we were a unit in everything together, I could not bring myself to soften, to go to him.

"Listen to me," I insisted. "When Donny needs help dealing with this, I will find a therapist for him. And I won't care if the therapist is Orthodox or not. I don't care about protecting the reputation of Orthodox Jews. I will do what my son needs, with or without your support. And I think he needs to be at home for a while. He'll finish the school year here with me and maybe even start next year homeschooling if I can't find a school where he feels safe and where I can be assured that he will be protected."

"It's not good for children to be at home all the time," he said. "They need socialization, and they need to become independent, the sooner the better, or they'll always cling to us."

Barry slumped on the bed, exhaling like the wind. He said nothing, his eyes engulfed in sadness, staring in my direction but not quite looking at me. I knew that look. He was done fighting for now. Whenever we had a disagreement, there came a time when his eyes glazed and he would no longer respond. At that point, I had no choice but to stew away from him. The coming night would be a long one, with no sleep to escape into, no salve for my sadness, no reassuring embrace from a loving husband.

I hunched into myself, fingering the blanket. If I looked at him, my resolve would crumble, but all I wanted to do was fling my arms around my husband and hold on for dear life.

Earlier, I had planned to ask him to stay home after *Havdalah*, to talk things through, but I no longer wanted that. I needed to be fierce, to show my son that he would always be safe in his home, with the support of his parents. I knew deep down Barry felt the same way, so why was I pushing him away, making him out to be an Orthodox ogre?

I left our room and headed for the kitchen, to mix tuna with mayo, slice hard-boiled eggs, scoop marinated herring into little bowls and cut vegetables for *seudat shlishit*, the third meal. I wasn't hungry, but I arranged crackers in a pinwheel on a plate and stacked challah rolls in a basket. I called the kids and Barry to the table, where we ate in relative silence before retreating to books in the family room, together but separate. Simi was the

only one who seemed oblivious to the change of atmosphere, *vrooming* his
cars along the carpet and talking to his stuffed animals.

When it was full dark, I pulled out the Havdalah candle, cup and spice
box. The children were quiet and tired. Barry had gone upstairs to pull on
proper clothes, and when he came down, he went into the family room
and hugged Donny tight to his side. Then he came to the kitchen, struck a
match and lit the Havdalah candle as we gathered around it. Normally, we
would sing, but his eyes were blank as he mumbled the prayers separating
the holy from the mundane, ending our weekly day of rest. At the end of
it all, he put out the multi-wick flame by dipping it in grape juice, glanced
at me with a look I could not interpret, as if a question hovered in his eyes.
He placed the candle on the table, turned on his heel and left.

Chapter Twelve

The next week was a blur. Nearly every day, I felt backed against a wall—my children crowding me with needs and a desire to be close; my husband avoiding me but inhabiting the same spaces, barely speaking; my best friend hovering like a fly I needed to swat away but who persisted in staying near; and my community, like low-lying cloud cover making the air thick and heavy. I wanted to call Shiri to talk to her about the situation, but I was afraid she'd respond as Barry did, and I didn't want my surrogate mother in this community, the woman who had nurtured my entire transformation, to cast me out in the cold. Nana called daily, coming with Papa for dinner on Sunday, bringing muffins and coffee on Tuesday and offering to help cook Thursday night. Her presence was a comfort because I could not let Barry get close until I knew we were aligned in defense of our son.

He called the headmaster on Sunday, but the conversation yielded little concrete information. Apparently, this was not the first such complaint against Mr. Fineman. When I pressed him on what we would do next, what actions we could take to chase the man out of employment and work with the school to change its protocols to make it safer for the children, he shut me out. "I'll handle it, Sally" was all he said.

I could not call the headmaster myself without looking like I didn't trust my husband. Besides, I didn't know if the man would even take my call. Everyone would see me as the pushy woman who wasn't always religious and who could not let her husband handle difficult situations. The head-master might insist that it was inappropriate for him to speak one-on-one with a woman, even a mother of one of his now former students. I felt helpless, which made me angry.

The only good that came out of those days was that Donny's little body relaxed, his limbs sighing in relief when I said he would never return to that school and would instead stay home with me for the remainder of the school year. The bruises on his knuckles healed. He seemed calmer, less afraid.

Leah asked no questions when I called to say I would not make it to the tehillim group on Tuesday. Batya slipped into my house most days with Talya on her hip, eager to make coffee and talk. I was surrounded with support and love, but I ached for the one person I wanted most to make everything better, my husband. I missed him more than I ever imagined I would, needing his touch, his caress, his gaze to tell me I was not alone, nor would I be, ever again. The familiar sadness of my lonely childhood came rushing back, a gaping emptiness I had not felt since I stepped into this world a decade earlier.

Even though I was to blame for our distance, the longer we stayed apart, the harder it became to imagine reconciling. I didn't know what to say or what action to take, and just when I contemplated approaching him, I remembered that the situation with Mr. Fineman was unresolved. He was not punished for abusing my child. He was still employed at the school, endangering the lives and emotional well-being of countless children. And I was muzzled, unable to warn the community that there was a fox in our midst, creeping into the henhouse.

So I boiled over with anger and contempt, researching attorneys to prosecute this transgression but never calling any of them. I didn't want to be cast out of my community. I didn't want my husband to leave me. I didn't want to lose the careful castle I'd built on top of the clouds.

Sometimes, late at night, I looked for divorce attorneys but then erased my search history from the computer. I would not leave Barry over this. I didn't want to leave him at all, ever. And then I'd see my husband's face pleading to let him handle it, to walk away, to shield the community while also protecting our child, to not cause a scandal, thinking he could achieve both without hurting anyone. And I'd shrink into myself, recoiling from his embrace, which was only imagined, never real.

Chapter Thirteen

I t was not easy to homeschool. I had never considered teaching my children all that they needed to know. And now, thrown into the role of primary educator for my bright, eager seven-year-old, I was failing.

I searched online for resources, curricula, sample schedules from other parents to teach me how to structure our time. When would I run? Where would Donny be while I sprinted down the sidewalk? How would I manage grocery shopping and cooking and cleaning while Donny sat at the kitchen table with textbooks?

As a result, I was late to everything and bad at managing my house. Many days, I turned into the circular driveway of Simi's school at 12:15, the last in a long line of cars. My little boy waited with his backpack on, eagerly searching the faces for his mommy, often the last to leave. I hated the thought of my children waiting for me, feeling forgotten. I remembered the pit in my stomach when I'd waited at my elementary school for a nanny or the maid to collect me. Other kids ran into the open arms of a loving parent, and I stood in the dust of the playground, clinging to my school bag as I watched all my friends leave for warm, happy homes. The teacher tasked with waiting for all the kids to depart always seemed to sigh impatiently, tapping her sturdy black shoes, chastising me with her glare.

Simi waited under the blue-and-white awning over the front door, where teachers in black skirts, black tights and short wigs talked and waved as parents whisked away their children. He held his lunch box in two hands and sucked on his lower lip, his backpack strung over his shoulders. A baseball cap hid his face from the sun. When he saw me, his eyes widened into a smile. He looked up at his teacher, who nodded, freeing him to run to me. I scooped him up, inhaling his little boy scent of just-washed hair, sweat and dried paint.

"Sweet boy," I murmured. His arms locked around my neck.

I carried him to the car, nuzzling his cheeks as he giggled. Donny waited in the car with the windows open. Did people wonder why he was no longer in school? Or did they already know? At least Simi didn't hold a grudge against me for my tardiness.

"Mommy, stop that." He rubbed his face against mine so that I really couldn't.

"How was your day?"

"Good. Dovi took the ball from me at recess for no reason."

He didn't pout as he said it.

"Hmmm...why would he do that?"

"I don't know. We had brownie bites for snack. Morah Chani made them. They were so yum."

He scrambled into his car seat and waited for me to fasten the harness buckle. At home, I put Simi in his bed for "a rest," not caring if he flipped through books or sang to his stuffed animals, as long as he had some quiet time in his room, where he inevitably fell asleep for at least a short nap. I sat Donny at the kitchen table with schoolwork and ducked into the den, scanning my emails, deleting department store eblasts and calls from community organizations looking for volunteers and donations.

It had been weeks since I deleted John's probing email. He must have accepted that I would not respond. But since the explosive news from Donny and my persistent distance from my husband, I wanted to talk with someone who wanted to talk with me. I combed through the trash bin in my email, grateful that I hadn't cleared it out recently. And there it was, John's last letter, asking me to tell him about my life, wanting to hear from me. I should let him go, finally and forever. Keep the past in the past. But I ached with loneliness. Who knew when Barry and I would reconcile? And if he didn't succeed in getting Fineman fired, I doubted I could come close to him again. It would underline how far apart we really were. If I let John slip away, who would I have left? He had called me the love of his life. He'd said it was a mistake to let me go. I took care of everyone around me—who would take care of me? Who cared about my happiness? Certainly not my husband! I moved John's email back to my inbox and clicked *Reply*.

Dear John,

I'm so happy to hear from you. I've been thinking about how to respond, what to say, since your email arrived, so don't think I'm blowing you off.

Too desperate. I erased the last sentence.

You ask a question I ask myself every day. I'm not sure how I got here. But this is where I've landed. Yes, I live in a religious world. I have loved the past ten years. I feel like I finally found my home. But something happened in the last week that is causing me to question everything.

Truth be told, I'm not sure you would like me like this. I look nothing like you remember. I am covered and quieted. My hair that you loved so much is hidden from public view. I don't mind it, really. Actually, it's pretty special to reserve myself just for my husband. And we have the three most amazing children in the world. I love being a mother.

Fifteen minutes had disappeared since I sat down. The clock ticked. In the kitchen, Donny scratched a pencil against a notebook and shuffled pages. Upstairs was quiet. Simi must have fallen asleep. I had time before I had to pick up Shira. I bit on my thumbnail, unsure what to write next. I'd already said too much. It still wasn't too late to delete the whole thing and wipe him from my mind.

Not sure what else to say. Let's keep talking. Love, Sally

I hit *Send* before I could regret it.

Chapter Fourteen

Nearing two o'clock, Simi shuffled down the stairs, blankie hanging from his arm. Shira's school let out at 3:30, and Donny had closed his books and escaped outside, thunking a basketball against the concrete. The sun angled through the window, striping the kitchen table. The bright spring air would do us all good.

"Wanna go to the park, sweetie?"

"Yay!"

"Let's get your brother."

Never crowded and partly shaded, the park had a little kids' structure to one side opposite a taller structure for bigger kids. Both were set into a foundation of woodchips to cushion inevitable tumbles. There were two banks of swings—one for little ones, and another for kids who could pump their legs on their own. There was a spinny thing that made me nauseous when the kids insisted I sit with them on it, but they loved riding it fast. And there were three go-nowhere metal horses that Simi loved to rock back and forth madly. When all three kids were here, they each ran off to the playscape they felt most comfortable with, and I loved that all of them could find pleasure in one place, all within my sight.

Simi ran to the shortest slide and started to climb up it from the bottom. "Let's do it the right way," I called, reaching for his hand to guide him down and over to a ladder. When he was mostly up, I scampered to the other end to catch him.

At the top of the slide, Simi looked to the right and, seeing other children running along the playscape, decided to follow suit. "*Ahhhhhhhhh*," he yelled, taking off down the length of the structure. A little boy smiled at Simi and ran alongside, screaming into the air in unison.

Simi climbed up and down on an arched ladder, never looking down between the rungs, as I'd taught him. *We only become afraid of falling if we look at how high we are*, I'd said.

Donny had gravitated to the bigger playscape and was climbing and sliding at his own pace. There were no other seven-year-olds here in the middle of a school day, and I wondered if he noticed or thought about his friends at school or even cared that he was playing alone. I waved when I could catch his gaze, and he smiled and waved back. The wind was light, old oak trees and evergreens standing sentry around the park's perimeter. The squirrels were out in full force, darting along the grass.

A pair of chatting mothers pushed two little girls in pigtails and pinafores on swings. An elderly nanny dozed on a bench while her charge zipped between structures. A puppy on a leash was tethered to a tree, behind which rested a bike with a baby seat.

A hawk circled overhead, cawing. Simi ran to me, grabbing my leg. "Safe!" he yelled, panting. Drops of sweat beaded the sides of his soft face. "My mom is safe!"

I cradled my sweaty son to me before he ran off again. Who would provide safety for me? I missed Barry terribly. This rift hadn't been going on for long, but each night, the silence in our bedroom was stifling. I lay in bed in the dark with my eyes open and my heart pounding, wanting to reach out to my husband. And he never reached for me.

Finally, the boys gravitated to the swings. Simi tucked into the little black bucket seat, his legs dangling, while I pushed him from behind. Donny pumped higher and higher, the speed threading wind through his hair.

"Higher, Mommy," Simi called, and I sent my son soaring toward the sky.

As his striped polo swung closer, I flattened my fingertips against his back and gave another hefty push. His body pulsed with warmth. I wanted to hold him to me, to be comforted by my son's unbridled ease. The back and forth of the swings lulled us both.

Evergreens encircled the playground, a fragrant border that offered privacy and quiet, set back from the busy street. Birds soared overhead, hawks wheeling under a cloudless sky. In the peace of the moment, I wondered if I would hear back from John.

CHAPTER FIFTEEN

It's an odd thing, finding a person from your past after many years have slipped away. Since John had last seen me, I'd fallen in real love with a good man and been pregnant three times, birthed three children. My body had morphed, and while I was lucky to lose baby weight quickly by running, my shape had shifted each time. My hair was flatter and duller from covering it. Would he still find me attractive? Did I want him to?

My mind danced with shocking fantasies, of uncovering my hair and letting my curls cascade to my shoulders as I sat across from him in a low-lit restaurant in the heart of Chicago. I knew Barry couldn't read my thoughts, but I shrank into the shadows of our house anyway, embarrassed, guilty, wanting to erase all the damage done and start over.

John responded to my email within a day, asking about my transformation, my children, my life, and why I wasn't writing more than in my journals. I considered his questions and gave careful answers, pondering what mattered to me now, what I wanted to show this man from my past. I'd been on the fast lane into the frum world and had dropped pretty much everything that I thought mattered to me before I came to Skokie. When I quit my magazine job to study Judaism and immerse in this community, it wasn't because I wanted to stop writing. But stop I had, and in the last decade, I had dropped my dreams of writing award-winning magazine stories or, someday, a book. While Barry was an attentive and caring husband most of the time, he never asked about that part of my life, mostly because he hadn't been part of it. How could he know that I'd once dreamed of becoming a well-read writer with lots of work in the world for readers to consume? As I covered my hair and my elbows and my knees, as I followed the modesty mandates and spoke in the clipped tones of religious women, I shed the eager, reaching college graduate who had big dreams and big talent.

I asked about John's life and learned that he had been alone since we broke up, never married, never fallen in love, though he'd had a few dalliances with promising women in the years since he left me. He lived alone in a sleek high-rise on the Gold Coast, he was excelling in his career as a renowned architect, but he went home to an echoing abode with expansive windows that looked out on the seething city. He was as lonely now as I had been for the first 20 years of my life.

We emailed for a few weeks before deciding to meet. I kept waiting to see if Barry would reach out and end this rift. But he showed no interest in reconnecting. I knew it should have been me ending the stand-off, but I just couldn't bring myself to do it, especially since he said nothing about pursuing legal action against Fineman. We remained in silence, skulking in our corners, sharing the same house but not the same life. I told myself that any move, any slight show of desire, and I would end the email exchange with John. It never occurred to me to do it anyway and double-down on my marriage. I was afraid of being rejected by the man I loved the most, afraid that we had sunk to a place we could not come back from.

The more I missed my husband and the lonelier I felt at home, the more intense became my emails with John. There were nights I sat in the study, heart thumping, my body yearning for a man's touch. I would have been satisfied—thrilled, even relieved—with the touch coming from the man who shared my room. I couldn't really imagine John replacing Barry, but I needed someone's searching voice to quiet my concerns, to distract me from the unfinished business of my life.

John sent pictures of his home: slick, angular furniture, all leather and glass with hard edges and dust-free coffee table books. I looked around me at the piles of pillows in my family room, the old couch where the children jumped, the old TV set where they watched *Sesame Street* and *Caillou*. My house was filled—with people, with stuff. And with love. His was beautiful, like something out of *Architectural Digest*, but empty, silent, sleek. My floors were well-trod, the wood planks fading with use. Though I dusted, mopped, and swept constantly, my home was worn and, most of the time, happy. I argued with myself as I clacked at the keyboard. *Stop writing to him. You love your husband. Don't damage your entire life. Go back to Barry.*

But we were ships passing, never going to bed together, Barry staying longer at the office than he needed to and leaving most nights after dinner to learn with his *chavruta*, study partner.

John and I decided to meet on a Wednesday, for lunch. I arranged for Simi to go home from school with a friend, whose mother was part of my tehillim group, and I asked Nana if Donny could spend the day with her and Papa. She had no idea about John since she and Papa had not been part of my life back then, and I hadn't said a word about our emails. Truthfully, I was ashamed and didn't want to see the look in her eyes when I admitted I was distracting myself with another man. Batya would have taken both kids, but she would have also asked questions that I did not want to answer. I'd have a few hours before I had to pick up Shira. John suggested Ricki Lee's in the Loop, a new restaurant that had been lauded in the *Tribune* for its homey feel and farm-to-table menu. It wasn't kosher, but I preferred a place outside of my watchful community so I wouldn't risk running into anyone who would recognize me and ask questions about the strange man at my table. I'd order a salad, skip the dressing, and drink water.

To avoid the dilemma of parking and for ease of time, I took an Uber. Accounting for the inevitable traffic, I left an hour before we were to meet. The drive was slow, taking a full forty-five minutes before arriving at the restaurant. The long drive had done little to calm my nerves. The minute I pulled the door open and saw that he was already seated at a table, my stomach lurched. His warm chocolate eyes beckoned, his hands hidden under the table. Was he nervous, too?

I pushed through the throng of people at the front of the restaurant. A din of chatter blanketed the place. He'd chosen a booth, thank God, the better to hide in, the better to muffle our conversation.

"Hey," he said, standing up and wrapping me in a tight hug.

He still wore Polo cologne, which mixed with sweat, musk and the curious scent of campfire that always trailed after him. How could he be so much the same after all these years? I breathed him in, closing my eyes, letting him hold me. It felt good to be touched.

Finally, I pulled back to look at him. He wore a green polo, chinos and boat shoes. "Day off?"

"I couldn't go to work knowing I was going to meet up with you," he said. "I called in sick."

"Really? That's so not you."

He bit his lower lip. "It's been ten years, Sal. I've changed."

"We both have." I slid into the booth.

"Yeah. But look at you. Look at you!"

I smiled. What did he see?

"You're just the same."

I snorted, picking up the menu to have something to do. "No, I'm not."

I'd run that morning then washed and dried my hair, hoping to fluff some life back into my curls. While I normally wrapped all of my hair when I covered it with a scarf, today I had loosely tied a silk triangle over the top of my head, letting my curls spill out beneath it. Leaving the house, I'd ducked into the taxi, holding my sweater over my head so Batya's prying eyes couldn't see my mostly uncovered hair. I hoped no other neighbor caught a glimpse.

I had tried several outfits before deciding on a knee-length, curve-hugging denim skirt and pale-pink, long-sleeved T-shirt with a chunky necklace and white-striped sneakers with white ankle socks. It was the least religious outfit I could pull from my closet. Did John see me, Sally, the outgoing writer he had dumped, or did he see a religious woman, frumpy and frocked, hidden away from the male gaze?

"Your eyes still sparkle, and your full lips I honestly want to bite—sorry!— and you're buzzing with energy. You always were." The words on the menu blurred.

"Okay, wow," I mumbled. "Sorry, I'm nervous. But it's good to see you."

"Yeah. I can't believe it's been ten years, Sally," he said. "You were the love of my life."

What? I looked at him, eyes narrowed, brows hunched. Nothing like jumping right in. I steeled myself for the what-happened-to-us conversation that I had played out on the ride downtown.

"So we're doing this?"

"Well, it's like a big egg on the table, isn't it?"

"Not an elephant in the room?"

"I hate to be cliché," John laughed.

"You try too hard to be original." The knots in my stomach tightened. I sipped water. "Okay, then. Why did you dump me? And why didn't you call? And why are you back now?"

"Coming out swinging," he said. "I know you won't believe me, but I wasn't dumping you."

I snorted. "John, don't even."

"No really, Sal. I needed to think, to figure out what I wanted in my life. I was too attached to my love for you."

"What does that even mean? That's crap," I said. "*It's not you, it's me.* Right. Ultimately, whatever we had wasn't strong enough to hold on to while you *figured it all out*."

"Fair enough. I can see that now. I was stupid. Immature. I didn't know what I wanted. Maybe I was afraid of being happy."

"Oh my God, that is such a cliché. I feel like it's a bad movie playing out at this table. Come on, John! You're better than that. That is such a cop-out."

A woman approached the table in a pink smock and white apron, with an order pad and pen. Saved by the server.

"Welcome to Ricki Lee's! Have you eaten with us before?"

I smiled at her. "No."

"Great! Welcome. Let me tell you about our specials."

As she described a deconstructed lasagna, a roasted chicken butternut squash salad and the vegan special—a mushroom and bean burger with shredded carrots, alfalfa sprouts and avocado—I watched John. He stared back, seeming not to notice the server. Oh, the poor woman trying to take our orders. We couldn't care less about food.

"I'll have a house salad, no dressing," I said, handing her my menu. "And a side of fruit."

John raised his eyebrows. "I'll try the vegan special. With fries. Thanks."

She collected his menu and walked away.

"Vegan special?" I asked.

"Like I said, I've changed."

"Okay. Introduce me to this new John. Who looks an awful lot like the old one."

"That's not fair. I mean, look at you. You're totally different than when we were together. Why couldn't I be?"

"Fair enough. But let's get past the muck, okay? Why reach out now? What are we doing here?"

"Do you really have to ask? You never stopped loving me. And I never stopped loving you."

"You're awfully confident, aren't you? Why would you assume that? I am married, with children."

I tried to conjure my husband's face, his strong hands, his dark curls. I tried to picture us entangled in our bed. I missed Barry so much, like there was a literal hole in the middle of my body. Why did I think reconnecting with an old flame from a life I had deliberately left behind would be easier than returning to my husband?

But even as I summoned images of the man I'd pledged my life to, my breath caught in my throat and my stomach was back to clenching. Had John really never stopped loving me? I would finally be vindicated if that were the truth. But did it honestly take ten years to realize the strength of his feelings? And was he arrogant enough to believe I would abandon my family, my marriage, my entire life, for him, just because he sent a friend request?

"Say I'm right. Say you never stopped loving me. Say you want me even now."

"John, I'm married! I am a mother. I am religious—religious! I have a whole life that does not include you. And I love my husband."

"Then why are you here with me now?"

Game, set, match to Hogan.

I dug into my purse, searching for my phone to show him pictures of the kids. I thumbed through hundreds of images from the park, the backyard, dressed for Shabbat. I picked one particularly cute one. Shira had tied a ribbon in her hair and was helping Simi adjust a little newsboy cap on his head. "Look at them," I said. "This is my life now."

John's eyes softened. His eyes shimmered with unshed tears. "She's a little version of you," he said.

"Yes," I said. "And the boys are the sweetest little things you'll ever meet. Adoring and trusting and so full of joy and energy. I would never leave them. My oldest is the spitting image of his father. Whom I love very much."

Even though I kept saying it, I knew being here challenged that sentiment. *The lady doth protest too much...* I felt a pang of sadness poke at my stomach. *Barry, where are you? Why can't we bridge this divide? Save me from temptation! Save me from my own stupidity.* Except it wasn't up to my husband to save me from anything or prevent my transgression.

John handed back my phone as the server approached with plates. "Salad and fruit," she said as she plunked down the food. "And the vegan special! With fries. Can I get you anything else?"

"We're good, thanks," I said.

"I always imagined we'd have a little girl who looked like you," John said quietly. "I thought there would be time to make up for my mistakes. I figured we would find our way back to each other."

"You left me," I said between my teeth. "I wasn't going to chase after you. And it took you ten years to get in touch. On Facebook."

I poked at the salad with my fork. I had no appetite, though the plate was beautiful—resplendent greens with wisps of strawberries, thin cucumber slices, slivers of purple onion. *Damn.* I'd forgotten to ask for no onions. The sharpness of onion made everything non-kosher. I sighed. I felt like someone was kneeling on my shoulders, making it hard to breathe.

"Is something wrong?"

"The damn onions."

"What about them?"

"It's nothing." I laid my fork beside the plate and sipped water to loosen the clog in my throat. I bit my tongue to hold back tears. I would not cry in front of John Hogan. I would not lose it here, the first time I'd worn mascara in weeks and in a public place!

"Sally..." He reached for my hand. I could feel his pulse in his palm. His fingers stroked mine. I could feel the wanting in the soft skin of his fingers, and I looked up at his beautiful face, his warm eyes, his soft lips. I wanted to taste him, to tug at his bottom lip with my teeth, to feel him close, to not have to let go. To erase the way he'd hurt me. To pretend like the last ten years hadn't really happened, that we'd been together the whole time, uninterrupted. That nothing bad had happened to my son, that my husband wasn't a shadow against the fabric of my life.

"We don't have to do anything," he said. "There's no harm in staying in touch, right? I know how much is at stake for you. I don't want to hurt you. I never did."

Suddenly, I was angry. So angry that I thought I might breathe fire.

"Are you kidding? You broke my heart and never looked back. Not a call or a text or an email. Nothing. How arrogant are you to prance right back into my life as if you have a right to!"

"I can't apologize again," he said. "I meant it when I said I fucked up. I can't take it back. I can't erase it."

My eyes were hot with tears. I blinked, breathing through my nose to stop the emotions from surging, but it was too late.

"Oh Sally." John stroked my hand as I crumbled.

Was I crying for him? Or for the mess of my current life? Or for release from all the pent-up feelings of the past weeks?

After the tears slowed, I slid over to his side of the booth, lay my head on his shoulder and closed my eyes. "You were everything to me," I whispered.

His hand lifted my chin, forcing me to look at him. My face was splotchy, my nose clogged. And then he was kissing me, and I was leaning into him. My lips to his, breathing in his breath, his hands lifting the hair at the back of my neck, my hands pulling him to me. We pressed into each other, as the din of the restaurant continued on around us, the clanging of plates, the clicking of cutlery, the ring of a register and a bell dinging as the door opened and closed and opened again.

CHAPTER SIXTEEN

I got home with just enough time to shower and change before picking up the kids. I needed to wash John's scent, and the memory of him, off me. I had been so distracted by his emails and the anticipation of seeing him that I had barely made a dent in Shabbat planning, which meant I would be up late, long after the children fell asleep, running to the grocery so I could cook Thursday night and Friday morning.

Outside, the sky was white. I peered out the window. I missed the tall, leafy cover that I had grown up gazing out at and running under. I hung my towel on a hook and walked into the closet in search of a ground-sweeping denim skirt and long-sleeved T-shirt, grabbed a snood from a basket and tucked my wet hair inside it.

I collected Shira from her school then picked up an incredibly tired Simi, thanking Rivka for keeping him all afternoon. At my grandparents' house, I hugged Donny. Nana looked at me over his head, eyebrows raised in a question. I didn't want to tell her about John, especially not now. What if I disappointed her so much that she and Papa regretted moving here to be close to me? What if their image of me soured? I couldn't deal with another person I loved looking at me with a face of disappointment.

"Want help for Shabbat?" she asked as I stacked Donny's books in a tote bag.

I chewed my lip. I did want help, but I didn't want to risk spilling my secrets. I shook my head. "That's very sweet of you, but I think I've got it," I said. She narrowed her eyes at me in a question but pressed her lips together.

"Okay, love you, honey," she said, kissing my forehead.

A wave of shame washed over me. "I love you, too," I said, biting back tears as I pressed into her shoulder then darted out.

Shira and Simi waited in the humming car. Nana stood on the porch, waving, a question in her eyes. She clearly wanted to talk, but I couldn't look at her. I'd told her about Donny's abuse and the rift with Barry. She would never understand why I met up with John, and to speak it aloud would make my transgression more real. I didn't want my closest confidantes knowing how much I ached for my husband, how lonely I was that I was so easily tempted to step outside my marriage. I hoped Barry and I would come back together before I had to announce anything and I could sweep this mistake away into memory. The car was quiet as we pulled into the garage. Simi had fallen asleep in his car seat. I unbuckled him and lifted him out, his body warm and heavy.

"Mommy," his little voice trickled in my ear.

I rubbed his back as I stepped inside and laid him on the couch.

In the kitchen, Shira and Donny pulled open cupboards, looking for snacks. I kissed Shira's head and stroked Donny's cheek as I pulled crackers from the cupboard and a block of cheese from the fridge. "Tell me about your day," I said as I sliced the cheese onto plates.

"Nothing much happened," Donny said. "Gigi and Pop Pop were fun. We made popcorn and watched a movie."

"What movie?"

"*Cheaper by the Dozen*."

I chuckled. "A classic."

He stuffed cheese into his mouth. "Can I have some more, please?"

"Absolutely. How about some carrots, too?"

They nodded.

I peeled and sliced carrots then cut celery stalks into thin sticks. I rinsed grapes and dumped them in a bowl, which I set on the table.

"Esther's having a Shabbos party this week," Shira said.

"Oh, that's nice. Do you want to go?"

She nodded as she chewed.

"Great. I can walk you over. Do you know what time?"

"Four. She invited the whole class. Morah said she had to."

I could see Shira's teacher declaring this on behalf of Esther's family so as not to hurt anyone's feelings. "It's nice to include everyone, honey," I said. "You don't want to leave anyone out."

"I know." A dribble of cheese spilled from her mouth.

"Napkin." I pointed to the pile.

She swiped at her face and crumpled the napkin, dropping it on the table.

After they finished eating, I washed their dishes, put away what they had not touched, and started on dinner. On Wednesdays, I made pasta, easy and quick, so I could pour energy into Shabbat prep. This week, I had been so consumed with John that I had forgotten to invite guests. Most of our friends would be otherwise committed by now. And no one had called to invite us. Strange.

I dialed Batya, who answered on the second ring.

"Good time?" I asked over the clang of dishes and pots and children's voices.

"Oh Sally! You know this is the witching hour," she laughed. "What's up?"

"Okay, I won't keep you. I'm so behind this week for Shabbat. I've invited no one and haven't even mapped out my menus. I'm panicking."

"Wow, you left it late!"

"Don't rub it in."

"What's going on? You're usually so on top of things."

"I've been...distracted."

"By what?"

"Tell ya later. I'm calling because I wondered if you would be so gracious as to join us for a meal? The late invitation is no commentary on how much I adore you, of course."

Batya was the consummate host, inviting big families to her house for Shabbat meals. Her ample brood was rarely invited due to their size. And she only had five children. I could not imagine how families with nine or eleven fared in the way of invitations.

"Thank you. You know I'd love to have Shabbat with you! But we've already invited guests for lunch, and I like it to be just us for dinner. Everyone is so tired Friday night."

"Aw, well. I thought I'd try."

"Come here!"

"What? Oh, a pity invite. No thanks!"

"It's not a pity invite. I would love to have you. And we have room. I invited one family, the Rosens. They only have six kids, and two are near yours in age. It'll be fun. Say yes."

"Well, okay, if it's not too much of an imposition. I'll make a salad or a dessert—or both!" She was such a gracious and generous host and never seemed to buckle under the pressure of all that she took on.

"Of course, you will. Salad and dessert, both. Done! Thanks, babe. We can walk home from shul together."

"You're the best. Love you."

"Love you too!"

Less cooking and no Shabbos day mess. Plus spending the afternoon with my best friend's family was as calming as crawling into my most comfortable sweatpants and curling up under a blanket with a book. It would be a good Shabbos, and the company would distract me from thoughts of John and worries about Barry.

I filled a pot to boil and grabbed my notepad from beside the phone. What to make for Friday night, and which salad, which dessert for Batya? I was too distracted to get into my usual flow.

Simi padded into the kitchen, hair spiky from sleep, his left cheek red from where he had laid his head. He threw his arms around my legs. "Up!"

I lifted my little boy. He leaned against my chest. I rubbed his back and breathed in his sweet-sour scent. Soon, he would go from baby to musty boy. If Barry and I were in another place, if John didn't hover on the periphery, I would have another baby. I longed for my husband's touch, for his lingering gaze, for all the rightness to return to our marriage.

I pulled a juice box from the fridge and popped the straw into the top. Placing it on the table, I sat Simi on a chair and returned to planning. I dumped a box of pasta into the boiling water. I pulled a cucumber, a head of romaine, three tomatoes, a red onion and a green pepper from the fridge and grabbed the salad bowl from a cupboard. Now, what to make for Shabbat dinner?

"Hello!" Barry's voice boomed from the back door.

"Tati!" The kids ran toward the door like a herd of cattle.

I wiped my hands on a towel and followed them. They loved their father so much. And why shouldn't they? He was a kind, fun, loving daddy. And for all the time I'd known him, he was a kind, fun, loving husband.

I waited for the sea of children to part and leaned in to brush his cheek in an air kiss. "Hey," I said. "Good day?"

He nodded, not meeting my eyes. He hung his coat in the closet and dropped his leather satchel in the study. "Let me wash up." He headed upstairs, where he would change into more casual clothing, wash his hands, splash water on his face. The pasta was nearly finished. I was halfway through making the salad. "Donny, Shira—please set the table!"

"Me too!" Simi stomped.

"You can do the napkins. Remember how to fold them?"

He nodded.

I looked at the notepad where I usually carefully scrawled the dishes for each Shabbat meal, beside a column of guests. The page was still empty.

CHAPTER SEVENTEEN

L ater that night, after the children were tucked into bed and the dinner dishes were cleaned and put away, I found Barry in the living room. The lights were off. He sat in silence, shadows from the streetlights casting long angles of light along the floor. In his hand, a crystal highball held two fingers of whiskey.

"Rough day?" I said, sinking onto the couch. *Please, shift this silence. Please, distract me from thoughts of John.*

"Not particularly."

"Oh." I ran my fingers over his hand.

He bristled, withdrawing into the corner of the couch.

"What's going on?"

"I've been so tired lately," he said in a quiet voice.

"I know. There's so much going on. It's hard to keep up with it all."

"It's more than that, Sally."

The house was stunningly quiet. The children had stayed in their beds after I finished reading and turned out the lights. They burrowed into their pillows, closed their eyes. Fell into an easy sleep. In fact, dinner, baths and bedtime had been too easy.

"What is it?" I asked, suddenly scared.

"The headmaster isn't going to fire Fineman," he said.

A searing pain stabbed my chest. I could not grab air. I clawed at the couch to steady myself.

"I know," he said, eerily calm.

"What are you going to do?"

He looked at me with wide eyes. My heart throbbed in my throat.

"Me? Isn't it we?"

"Okay, what are *we* going to do?"

He threaded his fingers through his curls, snagging on the tightest ones and wresting them free of knots.

"I honestly don't know," he said. "I want to ask the rabbi for guidance."

I snorted. "He's not going to do anything. No one is." Sadness consumed me, like a brick on the chest. We were an island in this Orthodox world, adrift at sea, no one coming to rescue us.

Silence pulsed between us.

"This is a criminal act, Barry," I said.

"I wouldn't call it that," he cautioned.

"Oh, wouldn't you?" My heartbeat seethed through every inch of my body. My skin vibrated. I thought I might lift off the couch, hovering above my husband like a menacing genie.

"Let me tell you something, Barry," I said carefully. "This is a criminal act. A grown man beat our son. Repeatedly, for months, in the sanctity of his school, where he is supposed to be safe, protected. And there is no recourse apparently for this type of abuse. At least not in our community." I spat the last word.

His eyes were hooded. He stared at the floor, and I didn't blame him. If he had looked at me at that moment, my fiery gaze might have decimated his entire being to a thin trail of smoke—gone, erased with just a glance.

"In any other community, lawyers would be called, charges filed, and he would lose his job as he fought for his freedom," I said. "Immediately. His firing would have been step one. But not here. Not here! Here, it's all about *the community*, not letting the public see the Jews faltering. Not creating a *hillul* Hashem, a desecration of God's name.

"Well, let me tell you something. It *is* a desecration of God's name for an adult to abuse a child. Show me in the Torah where it says to sweep under the rug anything that gets uncomfortable or calls our communal reputation into question. Show me where it says that a husband and father should kowtow to the school headmaster instead of protecting his son!"

I was yelling, and I hoped I didn't wake the kids. My body shook with rage. I was entirely alone in this fight for my family.

I lowered my voice and turned to my husband, whose downcast eyes and hunched shoulders I ignored. I didn't want to see his empathy or his pain. It was easier to blame him than it was to blame the community I'd chosen as my new family, my whole world.

"I had hoped we would find our way back to each other, to fight for our son together, as we've always been close and connected." I spat the words at him. "But I can see now that was a foolish hope. What has happened to you? What has happened to us?"

Say something, Barry. Please. Turn us back from this cliff.

But he said nothing. He sat on the edge of the couch, leaning his elbows onto his thighs, his hands stroking his hair over and over.

CHAPTER EIGHTEEN

That night, I separated our beds, even though I had not gotten my period. I wanted no chance of touching, no reminder that my husband could be tender and sensual and someone I wanted. But I couldn't sleep. I stole to the den after two, padding in bare feet, my cotton nightgown grazing the wood floor.

There were two unread messages from John. Had it been that same day that I'd met up with him?

Dear Sally,

Ohmigod how good it was to see you!! Like a dream come true. I am so glad I reached out and so glad you responded. I feel like a little boy on Christmas about to tear open all my gifts under the tree. It's like no time has passed. And now I just want more of you. More of us. When can I see you again? I'll meet you any time, any place. Just say when.

Always and forever yours, John

Like Christmas. As if I needed a reminder of how different we were. Visions of my parents' ceiling-scraping tree shimmered in my memory, wrapped boxes scattered beneath the fir boughs. Embroidered stockings dangled from the white hearth above our marble fireplace. Christmas mornings, we raced in matching pajamas to sit on the Turkish rug and wait for our parents to call each name, hand over one gift then another, from smallest to largest. A tiny metal menorah, no taller than six inches in height, hid on a shelf by the picture window, a relic from Mom's childhood that she had promised her parents she would hold on to. We never lit it, never pulled it into our holiday display, but it remained in full view, even when Dad held political fundraisers in the house. As a child, I hadn't really noticed it, but now I wondered what it meant to my mother, if perhaps there was a tiny part of her that didn't hate her background.

Funny that when I thought of John's reference to Christmas, I went back to the single symbol of Judaism in my childhood home.

In the second email, he suggested a meeting place for Thursday, which of course I could not do. Not with all the Shabbat cooking to do, though now all I wanted was to steal away and escape the silence of my home.

A deep sadness seeped into my chest, like a weight dragging me down into deep, dark waters. The man I had yearned for wanted me more than he ever had a decade earlier. Our chemistry was alive, though a voice in my head nagged that it was only because I was mad at Barry and feeling alone in my marriage. I could have married John—would have!—if he hadn't cowardly bowed out.

But Barry—oh, Barry!—my love, my passion. My life. I thought back to our wedding night, to the eagerness with which I anticipated mikvah appointments so I could return to his embrace. Why couldn't he see what our family needed? Why was the community more important than our vulnerable children? Than our marriage? What had changed my husband into this cowardly automaton chirping the party line?

If Barry would return to me, all yearning for John would disappear, I just knew it. Married couples fight. They grow distant. They don't pack it in and have affairs. Was I that weak? At the first sight of trouble, I'd cut ties and run to another man? I was worse than both of them.

The cursor pulsed. I should tell him to leave me alone. I should insist it was a mistake to reconnect. I needed to honor my vows.

On the bookshelf beside the desk sat a little crystal clock that Barry had bought during a trip to Israel. Instead of numbers, Hebrew letters indicated the time. It had been a few months after our wedding, when we were giddy with new love and I was pregnant with Donny. We were excited to build a family. In Jerusalem, we'd peered into glass-fronted shops. When we'd come to one with clocks in the window, Barry had said, "It's our time. Let's buy something to commemorate the way we feel right now."

We'd pressed inside, a little bell dinging our arrival as we'd pushed in the door. A fast-talking salesman had fluttered to our side, pointing to elegant crystal clocks in varying sizes.

"Something special, from *Yerushalayim*," he'd said, invoking the Hebrew word for Jerusalem as he'd sized up Barry's dangling prayer fringes and black hat, my scarf-wrapped head, long sleeves and floor-length skirt. "Keep a part of *Eretz Yisroel*, the land of Israel, with you always."

Barry had palmed the small, square clock, which glimmered with rays of sun angling in from the window, piercing out in rainbows of light through cuts in the crystal. "This one," he'd said, beaming at me and asking the man to wrap it carefully for the flight home.

"Better for you to ship it to America than pack it on the plane," the man had said, and we'd agreed, sparing no expense to guarantee our beautiful future.

Its *tick-tick-tick* from a shelf in our den was a reminder that time marched on, regardless of momentary indulgences. It was 2:45 a.m., and I had a long day ahead. Cooking for Shabbat. Homeschooling Donny. Carting Simi and Shira to and from school. Not to mention the wash and the cleaning and, if I could squeeze it in, a run to release all my pent-up emotion. I would spend the afternoon chopping and dicing and baking and simmering, while Simi napped on the family room floor, thumb in his mouth, his soft blankie wound around his arms as a comfort, Donny at the kitchen table studiously staring at workbooks. And then I'd pick up Shira, make dinner, go through the bedtime routine, and after they were asleep in their beds, return to the kitchen and continue cooking until everything was complete and covered tightly in foil and plastic.

I did not respond to John that night. I put the computer into sleep mode and padded into the family room. I lay down on the couch, huddling under a throw blanket. The cushions were soft and lumpy. I sank in, wishing it would swallow me up, wishing it would cradle me in its embrace and tell me that everything would be alright. But I didn't think anyone could say that.

Chapter Nineteen

"Mommy!" Simi was at eye level to my head on the couch, his little hands shaking me awake.

I blinked my eyes open. "What? Are you okay?"

He nodded. His hair was tousled from sleep. He wore blue footy pajamas. His cheeks were red.

I reached out to stroke one. "Are you hot?"

He nodded.

The sun was rising through the family room window, but the sky still held the last wisps of night.

"Well, let's get you out of those pajamas and see if it helps." I sat up and stretched.

"Why are you sleeping here?" Simi laid his head on my lap, his hands reaching behind my back and holding on.

I patted his curls. "Come on."

He followed me upstairs and into my bathroom, where I relieved myself, brushed my teeth, and washed my face. I ducked into the closet, slipping off my nightgown and pulling on a blue cotton skirt and flowered blouse. I grabbed a pair of ankle socks from a drawer and a baseball cap to stuff my hair into.

"Okay, now you."

I directed him to his bedroom—a small space made cozy by bright paint and sticker decals of smiling animals. I lifted the blinds on both windows, letting in the day, and cracked a window to air out the room. Early mellow sunlight washed over the walls. There was always another day, a fresh start.

"Did you use the toilet?"

Simi nodded.

"Okay, what do you want to wear?"

He pulled open a drawer and grabbed royal blue sweatpants and a shirt with colorful cars.

"Perfect. Underpants? Socks?"

He pushed the drawer closed and reached on his toes for a top drawer. I lifted my boy onto the bed and pulled the clothes with him. He unzipped the pajamas and shrugged out of them. I pulled the legs free of his feet and deposited the pajamas on the floor then pulled the shirt over his head and held the underpants for him to step into. He slid the sweatpants on, one leg at a time.

"Well done, sweetheart!" I slipped a sock over each foot, dumped the sweat-damp pajamas in his hamper and straightened the sheet and blanket on his bed.

Simi followed me into his sister's room, where I ran a hand over Shira's silky hair and planted a kiss on her cheek.

"Morning, honey," I whispered.

She breathed in and reached up.

"Time to get ready for school." I pulled up the shades, bringing in the light. "It looks to be a beautiful day."

Next, we traipsed into Donny's cave of a room. As I lifted the shades, light poured across the carpet and up the far wall. When Donny turned seven, he begged us to repaint his room in more of a "big boy color"—trading soft pastels for blues and browns. It was a darker space now, which I didn't love, but it suited his new tastes. I'd repainted the furniture, scraping off pale-blue paint and sanding it before repainting it a deep navy. Two windows brightened the room.

"Hey bud." I shook his shoulder and kissed his cheek. "Morning. Time to get up."

He shimmied down into the blanket and pulled the pillow over his head.

I laughed. "Already a teenager, eh?"

He groaned.

"Breakfast in five!"

I loved seeing how much lighter he acted, how he relaxed into being safely at home. I hated that it took practically an entire school year of abuse for him to come back to himself, and I wondered if deep down, there might be some stubborn scarring that may never heal. I looked for signs of it but didn't even know what to look for.

I clasped Simi's hand and led him to the bathroom, where I squeezed toothpaste onto his Snoopy toothbrush and handed it to him. He grimaced as he shoved the toothbrush along his teeth.

"Remember the tops and the backs," I said.

He scrunched his nose.

"Good job."

He squeezed a paper cup, gulping down the water instead of spitting it back into the sink.

I pulled the thermometer from the medicine cabinet and stuck it into his ear. "Keep your mouth closed until it beeps," I said. He clamped his lips tight.

His temperature came in at 101. I poured children's Tylenol into a plastic measuring cup. "Drink this," I said.

He winced but downed it, and I filled a paper cup with water to hand over once the medicine was gone.

By the time Shira and Donny appeared in the kitchen, dressed but rubbing their eyes, I had whisked eggs in a bowl and poured them across my largest skillet, sprinkling salt and pepper over top. I moved the eggs around to shift the liquid to warmer parts of the pan, watching the eggs take shape. From clear deep yellow to firm light yellow to puffy, airy and ready to eat.

The toaster pinged, and I pulled out crisp slices, depositing them on three plates then scraping a mound of eggs onto each one. Butter and jelly were on the table. I gave each child a plate, poured orange juice in small plastic cups.

"Wash and say the bracha," I reminded them, and they trooped to the sink, dumping water from the two-handled ritual cup over their hands and mouthing the blessing for hand washing before eating bread. They shuffled silently to the table, mumbled another blessing for bread and snapped bites of toast to break the silence.

"Let me check on Tati."

Upstairs, my room was dark and musty. My bed was neat and tucked, his a mess of sheets and blankets. The shades were tight against the windows, pinpricks of light peeking through at the corners. I trilled the shades up with a snap, which woke Barry, and then cracked open a window to air out the room.

"Nice that you feel you have the luxury of sleeping in," I snorted.

"Don't be rude, Sally," he said.

"Simi's fever is at 101," I said. "And I haven't even started on Shabbat cooking. Can you help today? Clearly, someone has to stay home with him, and I need a run to the grocery."

I'd never been so cold and businesslike to him. I knew I was making things worse, but I couldn't help myself.

"Let me get dressed," he said, stretching. "And yes, of course I'll help."

I huffed out of the room. Downstairs, chairs scraped against the floor. Dishes clattered in the sink. *I'll do them later.* We shimmied into coats, and Shira grabbed her school bag.

"It's not fair that I'm the only one going to school today," Shira whined.

"So stay home," I retorted.

Her eyes glimmered. "Really?"

"Sure. Why not?"

I lifted Simi in my arms and marched upstairs, depositing him on Barry's bed. "I'll go to the grocery; you stay home with this one," I said and marched out of the room.

Herding Shira and Donny into the minivan, I slid the door closed, making sure they were buckled, and reversed out of the driveway. Maybe my anger would dissipate at the grocery store. Or maybe I'd need to run it off later.

Chapter Twenty

"Cake!" Shira chimed as we passed the bakery section heaped with plastic-wrapped sheet cakes, bags of rugelach and sprinkle-coated cookies. My grocery cart was full with deli meats, frozen puff pastry, carrots and potatoes and onions, a melon and two containers of strawberries, a round of beef that I would roast for hours until it was so tender it would fall apart and ooze with juices. There was a five-pound bag of bread flour and two cartons of eggs. A bottle of vegetable oil. Two bunches of broccoli for kugel. A pullet of chicken cut into eighths for soup. Fresh dill, parsley and parsnip, plus a can of matzo meal. I would make challah dough that afternoon and leave it to rise until Friday morning, when I would braid and shape the loaves and bake them in time for candle lighting so they would come to the table warm, soft and steaming. I would make chicken soup and let it boil for three hours then skim the surface on Friday. I'd make the matzo ball dough and let it chill before shaping the balls and bobbing them into a pot of boiling broth. All of that I could do Thursday afternoon and evening. I'd leave the broccoli kugel and the roast for Friday. And now that all the kids were home, I'd pull them into the preparations—more hands would make it go faster.

Oh no. I had promised Batya a salad and dessert. I steered the cart back to the bakery, where I plucked a chocolate babka and a cinnamon babka. Store-bought would have to do. I loved baking, but there was only so much time.

Shira thrust a hand toward the table, pointing at the rugelach. "Can we?"

I sighed and snatched two bags. "Sure."

My kids trailing along beside the cart, we took up a wide berth as we traversed the aisles, which were clogged with bewigged women busily grabbing ingredients for Sabbath dishes. I steered back to the produce aisle, where I collected lettuce, cucumbers, tomatoes and red onion for a salad. Was that enough? I could make one of my fancier salads, with mandarin orange slices and a sesame vinaigrette. I wheeled back to the dried goods and cans, finding sesame oil, sesame seeds and canned fruit.

It took twenty minutes to check out, the lines extending from every register back into the aisles—a Thursday in the Orthodox community. Housewives in headscarves with their youngest children stacked in the cart or shuffling alongside it, waiting to purchase all the ingredients they'd need for a day of rest. Who exactly was Shabbat restful for? Likely not many of the women in my community. Come Sunday, I'd need a rest from the day of rest, but we'd be full into a new week, with too many things to do.

Several of the women shot inquiring glances my way when they spotted Shira and Donny toting alongside my cart. *Let them wonder*, I seethed. *It's none of their business.* Except everything was everyone's business. And I wanted everyone to know about that menace, Fineman. I just couldn't be the one to tell them.

After piling all the plastic bags in the trunk of the minivan and returning the cart to the corral near the store door, I cracked the window and turned the radio to a contemporary station.

When I parked in the garage, I quipped, "Help with the bags, please."

The kids hefted a bag each from the trunk and lugged them into the kitchen.

"Put everything on the table," I chirped.

Simi was on the couch watching Elmo. Barry sat in the kitchen, poring over a book of Talmud. Shira joined her brother in front of the TV, but Donny looked at me with questioning eyes.

"You can watch, too," I said.

"Mom, I'm too old for Elmo," he said.

"Then read a book," I said. "Or play outside where I can see you."

Donny huffed into the family room and dropped to the floor, pulling a book onto his lap.

I was ready to explode with anger and disappointment, longing and regret. It took a few trips to get everything inside. Barry didn't even look up as I went back and forth with bags looped onto my arms and hands. I wished he would help me, but knew I'd just bark at him if he did. Oh how I longed for the time not so long ago when he'd grin at me and take the bags from my hands to make my life easier. How I loved that world full of warmth. How I missed it.

As I grabbed the last bags and closed the trunk, I heard footsteps and turned to see who it was. John stood in the shadows of my garage. I peered out at the street, looking for neighbors, glancing at Batya's house, looking toward mine to see if Barry was gazing out a window. Where had John parked? How did he know where I lived? Oh God, how could I explain his presence? My heartbeat quickened, and my face flushed with heat.

I grabbed John's arm and pulled him into the garage, pressing the button to close the door. For the first time, I was glad it was detached from the house. No one would hear us.

"What are you doing here?"

He moved close, stroking my cheek. "You didn't respond to my emails. I had to see you again. I couldn't wait."

"You have to. I'm a married woman. My kids are here. And my husband is home this morning!"

Suddenly, I was self-conscious about all my hair tucked up inside the snood and my frumpy shirt. I hadn't put on lipstick or traced my eyes with makeup.

I pulled off the snood and shook out my hair.

"You look beautiful even with it on," he said.

"John. Seriously. You cannot be here. Imagine what would happen if someone saw you! I would be a pariah. And my kids! My husband! Do you want to ruin my life?"

"You're being dramatic," he chided. "I thought you'd be happy to see me."

"Why would you think that? Did you hear anything I just said?"

My heart thumped madly.

"Hey, it's okay. I'm sorry." He put a hand on my shoulder. His face was gray. "I'll leave. But meet me somewhere. Tonight?"

"Yes. Yes. Just go. I'll email you a time and a place."

I pushed the button, and the door swung open, bright daylight washing over us. I scurried into the house.

I was putting the last ingredients away when Barry closed the book and looked up.

We locked eyes.

"Barry," I pleaded. "Talk to me."

Please. Release me from this loneliness.

"It's funny that you want that now," he said.

"Why is that funny?"

"Because you're so fond of berating me, I didn't think you remembered how to be loving."

What the hell? This was my fault?

I struggled for words, anger rising like bile in my throat. This standoff began with him. Yes, I added to it, but he could not escape blame. Or maybe I had perpetuated it, but still. He was the man, the stronger one in the relationship, in our world divided by gender lines. Shouldn't he make the first move?

But then I remembered something Shiri taught me when I was engaged in kallah classes, the lessons for a bride before her wedding, about how to be married the Orthodox way. "While the man is the public-facing person in your relationship, the woman is the backbone," she said. "It's up to you to keep a happy home. Your husband will look to you to set the tone and pace of your marriage. That is no small thing. It always comes back to you."

Dammit. The strong, silent, behind-the-scenes role carried the day, and so it was up to me to make things right.

I cranked open a can of tuna and drained out the oil, flaking the fish into a bowl. Pulling a jar of mayo from the fridge, I plopped a spoonful onto the tuna and mixed it in with a fork. Bread sat by the toaster, the bag still open from breakfast. I reached in for two slices then twisted it closed, tying a knot in the end. I placed the slices open on a plate, heaping tuna salad onto one slice. "Tomato?"

He shook his head.

I cut the sandwich in half, grabbed a jar of pickles from the fridge and placed two spears on the plate beside the sandwich. I handed him the plate.

"Thanks," he said.

Simi padded into the kitchen. "Tati!" He flung his arms around Barry, whose arm encircled his son. He was such a good father, such a tender man. I could do this. I could close the rift, bring him back to me.

"Hey buddy," he said, leaning into his curly head.

Simi yawned, and I was grateful for the break of an impending nap. Maybe I could finally start cooking and shake off this mess of a day. People hovering, needing me, forcing their way into my path, and the only man I really wanted keeping his distance.

I scooped up my son. From the family room, the jangling refrain of *Sesame Street* tinkered. Shira sat, rapt, on the couch. Donny thumbed through the pages of another book.

By the time I got Simi settled, Barry had finished eating, cleaned his plate and put it away and left. I clicked off the TV. "Hungry?"

Shira and Donny jumped up and scurried into the kitchen. This day was like one of those revolving restaurants that keep spinning and never stop.

CHAPTER TWENTY-ONE

A fter his nap, Simi bounded into the kitchen, full of energy. The fever had broken. The beginnings of chicken soup bubbled on the stovetop, a whole onion and chunks of celery and carrot bobbing at the top. The lid burped occasionally with the force of the boil. Matzo ball dough chilled in the fridge in a big metal bowl. I set a sippy cup of apple juice on the table and a small plate with banana slices and three graham crackers. Simi's blankie occupied a chair to his right, and his teddy bear sat on the floor.

"Do you want to color once you finish your snack?"

He nodded, his mouth fumbling mid-chew with gooey graham cracker.

I wiped his face with a napkin and brushed his hair back from his forehead.

In a cabinet, I kept coloring books, boxes of crayons and thick markers. I grabbed the smallest box with the fattest crayons, perfect for toddler fingers, and a Thomas the Tank Engine coloring book.

As I measured bread flour and dumped it into the mixer bowl, I heard the mail carrier shuffle past the door and lift the metal lid, dumping letters and manila envelopes into the box.

"Mail!" Simi yelled, spitting fragments of food across the table.

I had so much to do, but I yearned to run, to be free under the open sky, the breeze on my skin, to shake off all the questions of the past week. *Meet John for a run*, a little voice mumbled. I would email him a destination far outside the community and take charge of the situation. We'd run together, making it easier to have a deeper conversation, and I would send him away so I could return to my family with renewed focus. I would come home to Barry and heal the rift between us.

Wiping my hands on a kitchen towel, I whisked into the study and clicked open my email. There was a new message from John. Boy was he eager.

Sally – close call today. I am so sorry for showing up out of the blue like that. It wasn't fair. I am letting my imagination, my memories, get the better of me. Please forgive me. If you still want to meet, let me know.

He was making it easy. Ball in my court, I had the control. Which I needed in some aspect of my life. And he was giving me an out. I could say *no thanks*, right here, right now, and end it.

But I didn't.

Thank you. Meet me tonight at 8:30 at Green Bay Trail in Wilmette. We can run and talk.

I returned to the kitchen to add wet ingredients to the mixer—eggs, oil, yeast bubbling in warm water. As I watched the mixture swirl into a sticky mass, I pictured the park where I would meet John: a hilly expanse of thick forest and gravel paths. The woods deepened the coming darkness, fireflies winking sparks in the gloaming. I liked to run on hills rather than paths. It was easier on my knees, and it provided a challenge. Up and over on uneven grass, again and again, the skirt I usually wore over running tights catching between my legs, my long-sleeved wicking shirt growing damp with sweat.

The dough was thick and tight, so I shut off the mixer and twisted the paddle free. Pulling out the bowl, I scraped dough from the blade and pressed it all into one smooth ball. Setting the dough on the counter, I coated the bottom of the bowl with oil, then dumped the mound back in and covered it with plastic wrap. It would grow bigger overnight. In the morning, I'd find a foamy puff threatening to burst beyond the plastic and create light, airy loaves for my family's Sabbath dinner.

The soup had been cooking for two hours. I pulled the matzo ball dough from the fridge and set another pot on the stove, pouring in a carton of chicken broth and three cups of water to dilute it.

"I want to help!" Simi called, jumping off his chair and pushing it over to the stove. This was his favorite part of Shabbat prep, squishing the gooey matzoh ball mixture between his pudgy fingers and watching it ooze over his skin, all the same color.

"Wash your hands," I said.

He pushed his chair to the sink and clambered up, lifting the faucet and running his sticky hands under the water. "Too hot!"

I adjusted the faucet until cool water ran over his hands and squirted soap onto each palm.

"Make bubbles," I said, smiling as he rubbed his hands together in fierce concentration, watching the soap foam between them. "Well done," I said.

He reached under the running water to rinse his hands, and when all the soap was gone, I handed him a towel, which he rubbed before flinging it aside. I caught it just before it fell to the floor.

"Hold on," I said.

He gripped the chair as I slid him to the stove. We had a routine. I filled a bowl with water for dipping hands between ball-formation. The bowl of water sat in front of Simi, beside the dough, which sat to the side of the boiling broth.

"We'd better hurry up!" I said.

His eyes danced with enthusiasm. He dipped his hands in water then scooped some dough into his palms and started rubbing it around to form a ball. I did the same. Satisfied with the roundness of his ball, he gave it to me, and I deposited it into the boiling broth. We laughed as we worked, forming matzo balls until the bowl was empty. Every so often, Simi peered into the pot, watching the balls sink then bob up and gradually expand, growing big and fluffy.

"Yum," he said. "Can I eat one?"

"Let them finish cooking," I said, both of us knowing that I would scoop a steaming matzo ball into a bowl and give Simi a child-sized spoon to consume it.

I still had broccoli kugel to make, and the roast, but both could wait for Friday. I could do the kugel now and get it ready to bake but not put it in the oven until an hour before Shabbat.

Because of all the cooking for Shabbat, Thursday night dinner was pizza carried out from the crowded shop six blocks from our house. We walked there, Simi in the stroller, just to get a change of scenery and some fresh air after being cooped up all day. I cut up cucumbers, carrots and celery and scooped hummus into three little glass bowls for the kids to dip into, gave them each a slice of pizza—cutting Simi's into bite-sized chunks—and filled plastic cups with water.

"Remember, I have that Shabbos party this week," Shira said between bites.

"Yep. Don't talk with food in your mouth, honey," I said.

She wiped a hand across her lips.

"Napkin!"

She grabbed the napkin beside her plate and fisted it in her hand but did not use it to wipe her face.

Barry was quiet at dinner. He'd pulled in just as we turned the corner with the pizzas. I gazed at him across the table, my heart pounding, wanting so desperately to cup my hands around his face and breathe him in. For all the years we'd been married, he'd prance into the house with the biggest smile and, during the weeks that we could touch, brush a warm, lingering kiss against my lips. But not for the last few weeks. I'd be happy with just a warm glance, though I desperately wanted more.

I should cancel my plans with John. But even as I knew what I should do, I reached in the other direction.

"I'm going for a run later, okay?" I said.

My husband nodded. Finishing his last bite, he carried dishes from table to sink, where I washed them and set them to dry.

"If I do baths, can you do bedtime, so I can run earlier?"

He nodded again.

I hoped I'd come home to find him asleep and the house still. I didn't trust myself to talk to my husband after meeting John.

CHAPTER TWENTY-TWO

When I got to the park, John was waiting, leaning against his car. I had whipped off my hat as soon as I left the neighborhood. A block from the park, I'd pulled over, parked the car and shimmied out of my skirt, fluffing my hair with my fingers. At the trail, I zipped my keys into the fanny pack I wore when I ran and hid my purse behind the back seat. It felt strange to only wear running tights and a shirt, my hair flowing. I felt exposed.

His appraising eyes told me a different story. One look at him, and I knew I should have canceled. It had been so long since I'd relaxed into my husband's embrace, and John was tantalizing, all lean lines and chiseled concentration.

"Hey," he said, and his voice, his clear yearning, sent tingles along my skin.

I gulped back my desire and forced my focus on the run. It would clear my nervous energy. Distract from his hungry eyes. Calm me to think clearly.

"You up for a good cleansing run?"

He nodded. "Like the old days," he said.

When we dated, John and I ran together often. It was one way we shed the stresses of college and our budding careers. It was also how we found our way back to each other after hours apart or in the wake of an argument.

I started running in high school, on the cross-country team, where I learned to lose myself in the motion and the air, to get hold of my thoughts and make sense of them. While I ran, I didn't have to think, and my worries and tensions unknotted as my feet pounded the ground and my heart pumped. By the end, I felt calm and confident, like I could handle whatever came my way.

When I became religious, it took a while to feel comfortable running in the neighborhood. I had to get used to running in skirts, and I didn't want neighbors to judge me. But then I met frum ladies who also ran, including Batya. It was one element that bonded us early in our relationship and made me feel that I could keep some parts of my former self while I blossomed into a religious woman. Barry never ran with me, but he saw how it worked out my kinks, so he wholeheartedly supported it. Even when the kids came, he took them without question so I could breeze out the door. In the early years of our marriage, I wished he would join me, but he did not enjoy stamping the pavement and getting all mottled with sweat and heat, so I let the topic go. Barry was devoted to his own workouts in our basement, and he loved riding his bike on weekends. He had his outlet, and I had mine.

The night was inky and cool. John wore shorts and a T-shirt tight across his chest, a sweatshirt tied around his waist. He had always been chiseled, with just the right contours and muscle definition. Crickets clicked in the grasses. In the dark of the trees, an owl screeched.

My feet burned as they slapped the path, my shins seizing as I pushed harder, faster. "Come on!" I called, veering onto the grass, up one hill and down the next. The soft ground held me up and pressed me on. A light wind cooled the sweat on my forehead, my temples, the skin above my lip. John followed, quiet, seething, breathing hard through his nose, his lips a tight line.

I went faster. The night fell in curtains around us, the trees in the distance deepening the darkness. Fireflies popped. On then off. Illumination then shadow.

I headed for the trees. I was hot and wet, sweat dripping down my cheeks, pooling at the back of my neck. I shoved the sleeves up past my elbows, the cool night air slapping my arms with relief. Sweat gathered behind my knees, between my toes, between my legs. I kept going, hearing John's feet thump rhythmically behind me. Taller and stronger, he could run faster than me, but he never did, allowing me to take the lead. We were in the middle of the trees now, tall oaks and maples and old pine. The forest smelled of evergreen and sweet sap and the promise of summer coming.

I slowed my pace until my breath stopped burning in my chest. Then I stopped moving altogether and bent at the waist, heaving.

"Running something out?"

I nodded. Some things never changed, like my need to run to escape the difficulties in my life and his ability to read so much from the way I ran.

My eyes were adjusting to the night. I could see the outline of his face.

"You up for sitting, talking?"

He nodded, and we plunked down against two close trees, cross-legged in the darkness.

"Interesting spot for talking," he said, but he knew why I had brought us here. I was hiding in the open, burrowing into the natural world to avoid being seen in the world in which I lived.

"Yesterday, I was going to say something totally different to you," I said. His smile faded.

"I was going to tell you not to contact me again," I said. "That I need to focus on my marriage and my family. That I can't do this, even if I am mad at my husband."

Something flickered in his eyes. An open door? A chance?

"Why are you mad at him?"

I chewed my lip, tasting the saltiness of sweat and blood as I tore into the soft tissue.

"My son was abused at school," I said. His eyes became steely. I shook my head, indicating that I needed to say it all at once. He leaned back against the tree.

"We were both horrified, of course, but we have different opinions on how to handle it."

"And..."

"And my way is the right way. His is a cop-out. His first instinct is to protect the community."

He inched closer to me, taking my hand in his. "I would never do that," he said.

"You don't know what you would do, John," I quipped, pulling my hand back. "You would never be in this situation. You haven't married or had kids. You don't know what it's like to live in an insular community."

"I haven't been married or had kids, no," he said. "But who are you kidding? I grew up Catholic. Don't tell me I don't know about abuse and communities covering it up."

Stunned, I realized that what we were going through was not, in fact, unique. Horrible, yes. But unique? Not at all.

"If he loves you, if your marriage is as solid as you say it is, he'll come around and you'll find your way back to each other," John said.

"Are you actually giving me marital advice? Encouraging me to reconnect with my husband?"

He laughed. "I guess so. And I can't believe I'm saying this. I do not want to encourage you to go back to him. I want you to choose me."

I grunted.

"So that's it? We say goodbye?" His eyes pleaded with me for a different answer.

I bit my lip. It felt good, familiar, to sit there with him, to hear the rumble of his voice, to relax into his nonjudgmental gaze. I didn't want to let John go after finding him again, but what choice did I have? We could not be friends, and I could not have more.

I pulled his hand back into mine and ran my fingertips over his knuckles. Those strong hands, each finger long and lean. How I'd loved those hands, stared at them longingly. I remembered how those hands had touched me, brought me such immense pleasure. *But your husband brings you pleasure.*

How could I never hold John's hands again? Never see his face, never hear his trilling laugh, never feel his hot breath on my neck? He'd said I was the love of his life.

But Barry, my kids, my life. John knew me in one way. The way I used to be. I would never be that person again. I was better than that person. I did not miss her or that life. But here I was, with an old lover, mucking up the life I'd built. The life I'd chosen and would choose again.

I was cold now, drenched with sweat that had cooled as we sat in the shadows of the trees. Night was full on, a brilliant moon bright in the sky. I could just make it out between the leaves.

John leaned toward me, his eyes closed, his breath almost still. His lips found mine, and I closed my eyes, wanting to taste him, to feel the pull of lips against mine, to taste the saltiness of his tongue. A single kiss couldn't hurt.

Who was I kidding? Just being there with John was bad enough. There was a reason the rabbis created fences around the law. They knew how fragile humans could be. *Lead me not into temptation…* Because once there, we had no choice but to give in to it. The animal pull was so much stronger than the intellect.

Just being in John Hogan's presence was a betrayal to my marriage. Just writing him secret emails late at night. A kiss was far worse! As much as I hated the parameters around touch in my community, I knew that one touch could unravel every tight coil of propriety that our delicate system rested upon. One kiss was never just one kiss.

I am a married woman, and I love my husband. I said it like a mantra in my mind, even as I leaned in and let him kiss me and felt my lips kissing him back, my body moving toward him, the electricity between us a live wire as the night pulsed around us.

Hidden in the cloak of the woods, no one could see us, if anyone was out this far into the park at this late hour. Technically, the park closed at sundown, or so said all the signs around its perimeter. But there were always people like us, flouting the law, skirting around it.

John untied the sweatshirt from around his waist and laid it on the ground then settled me back against it. I let him lay me down, hover over my body, pierce my eyes with a gaze that was familiar and enticing. I let him run his hands along my arms and down my legs and between my thighs. I let him pull up my shirt and take my nipple into his mouth, and I let myself arch up in response to the tingle of his sucking. I let him lead me down the path of temptation until my running tights had been peeled away and his shorts pulled down and our bodies rocked as if they were one, our hearts beating in unison, our breathing carrying the pulse of betrayal with every exhale.

We couldn't have been there more than a half hour before it was all over, and we lay side by side, staring up at the black silhouettes of leaves fanned against the sky. It was hard to pull my sweaty tights up over my legs, but I struggled into them until I was fully dressed, the dirt and loose leaves from the ground brushed from my hair and shirt.

What had I done?

I looked at John, who stared at me with a satisfied grin.

"Stop it," I said, swatting at him. I could not smile back. While it had been sweet and searing to lay with him and feel the familiar connection, the way his fingers were drawn to the pleasure points of my body as if he knew exactly what to do—which, after ten years, I could not believe he still did—I could not let go of the idea that I had just cheated on my husband. I was an adulteress. A *sotah*. Everything I had built for myself over the past decade, all the incredible love and beauty of a life I deliberately chose and leaned into with all my heart and all my soul, hung in the balance.

Barry could never find out. And I could never see John again.

Ever.

"I have to go," I said, standing up.

"Sally..." John reached for me, but I recoiled.

"This was a horrible mistake," I said. "It can never happen again. I can never see you again."

I took off at a rapid clip, knowing he would not try to catch up to me. I sprinted through the woods and made for the path, too panicked to enjoy the rumbling roll of the grassy knolls. I pounded the concrete path hard, each step searing a shock up my shins and jolting my knees, but I didn't care. I needed to get home. I needed my husband. I needed to know I hadn't ruined everything.

CHAPTER TWENTY-THREE

I crept into the house, leaving my muddy shoes by the back door. In my closet I peeled off the dank clothes, convinced I could smell sex on them, and buried them beneath other items in the hamper, far down so Barry would not sense anything. *I'll do laundry first thing in the morning*, I vowed.

The hot water of the shower needled my shoulders and my back, and I sudsed body wash into every inch of my skin, rubbing myself raw as I tried to wash John Hogan from my body. The scent of watermelon and vanilla seeped into my pores as I dumped more into my palms and frothed the soap into my skin again and again. Emerging from the shower, I shook my hair, and cold droplets rained down on the bathroom floor. I was wild with awakeness, frozen in the fear of being found out. Thank God Barry was asleep! He would know just by looking at me that I was a horrible excuse for a wife and a betrayer of the highest order. I had to calm down before morning. I stared out the window at the full, round moon, bright white in its knowing gaze. *You didn't see anything*, I bit back at it. *The trees blocked your view.*

But I felt everyone would know, could see through me, and I'd lose my place in this community, among my friends and neighbors, who would disappear like smoke trailing off as the fire was stamped out. They would forget about me after they turned their backs, and when the gossip died down, they would move on while I would be left alone once again, always destined to be alone. *You are so stupid, Sally! You had everything. You should never have responded to John's email. What a fool you are.*

I climbed under the blankets of my bed, wishing I hadn't separated it from Barry's. I gazed at his sleeping hulk in the dark, watching it rise and fall in calm evenness. I lay my head against the pillow and wept.

CHAPTER TWENTY-FOUR

Friday night was sweet and quiet, the kids eating quickly then scuttling off to bed later than a usual night but early for a Shabbat. They were exhausted from the week, as were we. We cleaned up in silence, put the food away, then sat on the living room couch in the dark, our hands interlaced, our breathing almost in sync. I had been sweet at dinner, kind and calm, begging him silently to return to me. That morning, I had pushed the beds together, so when it came time to retire, I pulled Barry to me and we made love slowly and quietly, moving in unison, finding pleasure in a way that we never had before. We didn't talk about the change of tone between us. I didn't want words to disrupt the possibility of a reunion. I knew I'd say the wrong ones and ruin everything. When we reached an ecstatic climax together, which was rare, tears trickled down my cheeks and I clung to his warm back, holding him tightly to me, not wanting to let go.

"Hey," he said, swiping at the tears on my face, which only made me feel worse. "Hey. It's okay. We're finding our way back. You'll never lose me."

I wanted so badly to believe him.

The next day, Barry went off to synagogue while I got the kids ready. I dumped mushy cereal from the kids' plastic bowls into the garbage to avoid clogging the disposal on Shabbat and rinsed the bowls with soap and cold water. On the street and at *shul*, I nodded good Shabbos to the women I knew, smiled during conversations in the playroom as Shira and Simi busied themselves with toys and books. For the first time in months,

Donny ventured off to youth minyan in the small sanctuary. Barry looked resplendent on his side of the sanctuary, puffed up with enthusiasm in his dark suit and tall hat. I envied his quick transformation.

When services ended, we gathered around the strollers in the front of the synagogue. It was a slow and quiet Saturday, the air heavy as before a storm. It would rain later that day, and I hoped we got home before the skies opened. Whenever we had a meal at Batya's house, we often stayed until dusk, too caught up in conversation and games and fun to leave.

"Let's go!" Batya called in her singsong voice. My best friend was always happy, always cheerful.

Talya was asleep in the stroller. Simi sat upright in ours, calmly watching the birds, the flowers, the people passing. He would fall asleep before we made it to Batya's, and I'd heft the stroller into the foyer to let him sleep.

"I haven't seen you all week," Batya said.

"I know. It's been a week."

"What's up?"

"Oh, you know, the usual."

We walked in silence, our steps beating a reassuring rhythm. Whenever I wore my sheitel, which I always did on Shabbat, I grew warm quickly. The extra layer of mesh cap and human hair sewn into it raised my body temperature by a couple of degrees easily. To compensate, I always chose my lightest-weight outfit. Today, I wore a silk dress with a peplum waist and a scalloped hem. It was one long periwinkle sheath with pearl buttons at the wrists. A beaded necklace hung long down the front. I slipped along the pavement in slim ballet flats that made it feel like I was walking barefoot. A raincoat slung over the stroller handle, and I gripped the fabric as I pushed.

Barry walked ahead with Tzvi, Donny at his side and Shmueli shadowing his father. The girls walked behind us—Shira, Ahuva and Bracha, with Ephraim tagging along, silent as the girls chattered.

"Your girls are sweet to include Shira."

"They're nice like that," she said.

"Good parenting," I remarked.

"Oh, I don't know." She blushed.

Barry was alight in Tzvi's presence. I'd missed weeks of the tehillim group and the last three WOL meetings, focused on Donny at first and then distracted by John. No wonder Batya was probing. I was doing a bad job of hiding. I was sure my absence threatened my position on the WOL board, where I served as secretary for a term of three years, but what could I do about it? I couldn't tote Donny everywhere, and I could not admit my transgression, even to my best friend.

By the time we got to Batya's house, sweat had pooled under my armpits. I pinned my arms to my body so no one would see. Barry appeared at my side and lifted the heavier end of the stroller to bring a sleeping Simi inside. I depressed the safety lock on the back wheel so it wouldn't move and pulled the visor down then headed for the kitchen.

"What can I do?"

We had stopped at home to grab the salad and dessert. They sat on the counter, sealed in plastic wrap alongside rows of foil-covered dishes of what were likely cold salads and baked kugels.

"You are a wonder," I remarked, peeking under the foil as Batya swatted my hand away.

"You're like a child," she said.

"I'm hungry! And you're the best cook I know."

She smiled at the compliment. While I loved to cook and was really good at it, my best friend surpassed me in every way. She really was a shining star. Happily Orthodox, shepherding a true brood of children, adoring her handsome, kind husband and creating delectable meals without seeming to stress or grow tired from the effort. Her eyes never darkened with circles from lack of sleep, though I know she got four or five hours each night at most. She never gained weight. She looked impeccable, even on a Thursday or a harried Friday morning. I did not know how she did it, but I did know that I loved our friendship, not only because of our deep conversations and shared interests, but because I admired this woman so much that it made me want to be better.

"*Kiddush*!" Tzvi called from the dining room.

A stampede of feet pounded in from the yard and the family room as the children ran to the table. I found my seat next to Batya, glancing warmly at Barry, who sat beside Tzvi.

After the prayer over the wine and the washing of hands, Tzvi held up two huge homemade braided challahs like they were manna from heaven, and I helped Batya carry in twelve bowls of vegetables and salads—hummus, baba ganouj, tabouli, roasted carrots with parsley, pickled beets, pickled turnip, tart cucumber pickles, satiny stewed tomatoes with garlic, shaved hard-boiled egg over homemade chopped liver, a lettuce salad with balsamic vinaigrette, roasted corn and pepper salad, and smooth roasted eggplant with char streaks on the soft flesh. It was like a leisurely lunch in Tel Aviv, overlooking the Mediterranean.

"You've outdone yourself as usual," I said.

"And these are just the appetizers," Batya replied.

"Oh boy—we will never leave!" I turned to Barry, who smiled. "Seriously, you'll have to roll me out of here. Or let me sleep on your couch for a few hours."

They joined me in a hearty laugh.

The kids dragged challah chunks through the spreads on their plates while forking pieces of carrot and pickle. They'd eat quickly then shuttle away from the table, leaving the adults to linger and talk. In time, they'd return for bowls of steaming cholent and bites of kugel—Batya made three kinds: carrot, broccoli and Yerushalmi—and her cholent was reassuring with its melding of flavors from hearty meat to soft, peeled potatoes to pieces of crisp onion. They'd flee again, only to return for dessert, as if radar pinged them when sweets were within reach.

Just as I had predicted, the children finished their food with such haste that I wondered if they remembered to breathe as they chewed. Before we had cleared away the salad plates, they had all disappeared, and I could hear Simi and Talya stirring in their strollers, readying to call out. I carried plates into the kitchen with Batya, placing them on the counter or in the sink, repeating the task until the table was clear.

"I know something's going on," she said in a low voice as she rinsed the plates and stacked them in a corner of the deep metal sink.

I looked at her from the other side of the kitchen island. "I can't talk about it," I said. "I need you to leave it alone until I can."

She nodded, wiping her hands on a terrycloth towel. "Okay, fair enough."

I circled the counter and pressed a hand on her arm. Her sleeves were rolled up to the elbow to avoid drenching her clothing. Her skin was soft, like satin, and pale. My good friend. My dear, caring friend who could see me more than I wanted anyone to.

CHAPTER TWENTY-FIVE

After lunch, sleepy from eating so much, we moved to the living room, while the children played in the basement. Outside, soft rain pelted the roof and streaked the windows. I wouldn't be surprised if one or two of the children were asleep on the basement carpet. I could not imagine eating another bite, but Batya was eager to fill the table with desserts, and I knew the kids would come running if they heard sweets were on offer. But before that could happen, Shira tore up the stairs from the basement and burst into the dining room.

"Is it time?"

"For what, honey?"

"Esther's Shabbos party!"

Shoot. I had completely forgotten and had nothing to bring. Most mothers armed their children with cookies or brownies or a bag of chips as thanks for being invited. They were never too young to show gratitude and manners. I looked at my daughter's eager face, her eyes round and searching. As if I weren't bad enough as a wife, now I was shirking my maternal responsibilities. How could I have forgotten?

"No problem, honey." I glanced at the clock. It was half past three, and it would take a good twenty minutes to walk to the Finsilvers' at my daughter's pace. But we could make it. I sent a beseeching glance to Batya, and it was as if she read my mind.

"Let me pack some cookies in a Ziploc for you to take, sweetheart!" Winking at me, she put a hand on Shira's shoulder and steered her into the kitchen as I mouthed the words *thank you*.

"What's going on?" Barry quipped.

"Shira has a Shabbos party at the Finsilvers'," I said. "I'll walk her."

The other kids swarmed behind and around me suddenly, hearing only that I was about to depart. "Me too!" Simi called.

"You can stay with Tati," I said as tears pooled in his eyes. "Okay, okay, I'll take you, too. Grab a cookie and head for the stroller."

"I can walk! I'm big!"

"Not this time," I said. "Stroller or stay with Tati."

Simi affected a pout, and I averted my gaze. He was so damn cute, even when he was protesting. "Those are your choices, kiddo," I said.

And then Donny was at my elbow. "Hey honey, what's up?"

"Can I go, too?" His voice was meek.

I'd thought he was bouncing back! Did something happen at youth minyan? I could hardly turn him away if he needed to be under my embrace. I raised my eyebrows at Barry, who shrugged.

"Sure," I said, and then his arms were around my waist, his head pressed against my belly. "Hey, hey, it's okay," I said, rubbing his back.

Batya and Shira returned with a bursting bag of homemade chocolate chip cookies and ginger snaps. "They'll be the best treats at the party," I said to Shira, who lit up in a smile. "Did you say thank you to Auntie Batya?"

She tilted her head up. "Thank you," she sang.

"Of course! Have fun!"

I pulled Batya aside and whispered, "No idea what's going on here, but all three want to come with me. So I'm leaving Barry with you and abandoning your Shabbat party. So sorry."

She squeezed my shoulder.

"Did everybody *bentsch*?" Batya called out. I'd forgotten the after-meal prayers. I was a true mess! I could not leave without saying them and setting an example for my kids.

My hand flew to my mouth in mock surprise. "Hurry up, everyone! The faster we do this, the sooner we can leave."

The kids flew to the table, shimmied into chairs and flipped open *bentschers*, little booklets with all the Shabbat and holiday prayers and songs that families gave out at every wedding and bar mitzvah. These were from Ahuva's bat mitzvah six months earlier. I opened a bentscher, my lips fluttering with silent words. It was custom to mouth the words as a demonstration of piety. I flipped the pages as I raced through, noticing Shira glancing at the clock even though she could not yet tell time.

When we had all finished, the four of us got up from the table and shuffled into the foyer. Simi climbed into the stroller, and I buckled him. Shira hugged the plastic bag of sweets in her arms like a baby doll. Donny hovered at my elbow as I gripped the stroller handle and wheeled my brood outside.

"Do you want me to come?" Barry bellowed.

"Nah, stay and enjoy yourself. I'll see you at home."

The rain had stopped. We settled into a brisk pace along the sidewalk. Few people were out, as Shabbos meals were still going. People lingered at table on a Saturday afternoon, with no urgency to finish, especially as the days extended longer with the welcome of summer. We would remain in Sabbath mode until three stars sparkled in the night sky, about forty-five minutes after sunset, and in the height of June, it could go as late as 9:30. Better to take our time at people's homes than count the minutes until we could resume our weekday activities.

Simi sat at attention in the stroller, taking in all the sights of the neighborhood—houses with painted shutters and metal awnings shading porches, cement driveways clogged with parked cars, open garages with children's toys scattered on the concrete, tulip hedges and close-cut shrubs beneath wide picture windows. The houses were old and sturdy. They'd been on these sleepy streets since World War II, and some even longer, changing hands as the neighborhoods turned over. The Orthodox always moved in after a neighborhood started to decline but before it fell into full disrepair. We kept our houses clean and neat, tidied the grass and the garden, but never planted anything too ambitious. The flowers came from bulb sales for school fundraisers, so many of our yards looked similar.

We got to Esther's house about ten minutes late. The front door was open with only a screen door closed to keep out the bugs. Shira went to grab the handle and pull it open, when I reached a hand to stop her.

"It's better manners to knock," I said.

She pursed her lips, not wanting to listen but knowing she had no choice. Her little fist pounded on the door. Esther's mother, Tova, shuffled to the door with an eager smile. She wore a Shabbos robe and a snood, her eyes painted in last night's makeup.

"Good Shabbos, Shira!" she called.

As my daughter smiled and bobbed her head, I said, "Good Shabbos, Tova. Thank you so much for inviting Shira to Esther's Shabbos party."

Tova pushed the door open wide. Shira shot into the house, handing the plastic bag to Tova as she whizzed past.

"Thank you! Such treats. They look scrumptious," Tova called after my disappearing daughter. "The girls are in the basement!"

I glanced back at the stroller on the grass and Donny standing close to his brother, watching me.

"When should I come back for her?"

"Six? We'll do a *shalah-shudis* and sing some songs, and then the girls can go home."

"Sounds great. Thanks again."

I closed the door behind me and collected my boys, heading down the road.

"Nice sheitel!" Tova called out after me. A hand went to my head to touch the wig that perched there.

"Thank you." I turned my head, forcing a smile. What an odd thing to say.

I pushed the stroller off the grass and onto the sidewalk as Donny walked alongside. Simi had missed his full nap, only sleeping in the stroller at Batya's house, so I imagined if I walked long enough, he would relax and fall back into rest. If I walked up and down the streets, maybe even to the park, perhaps Donny would start talking.

We rounded the corner, and I looked before crossing the boulevard. There was less traffic on a Saturday in our neighborhood, simply because everyone who lived there was religious and would not drive on the Sabbath. But of course, other Chicagoans drove through on their way to somewhere else, so it was not empty of traffic like some neighborhoods of Jerusalem. I remembered blissful silence and the absence of street traffic in Geulah, the ultra-Orthodox neighborhood of that holy city. Barry and I had walked along those streets when we were newly married. We'd stayed in a hotel in the middle of Jerusalem and joined hordes of religious Jews at the Western Wall as night fell on Shabbat, but we davened at The Great Synagogue, more part of the contemporary crush than the ultra-religious huddle. Later that afternoon, though, we walked into *haredi* neighborhoods. He had lived in Israel after high school to study in *yeshiva*, but it was my first time there, and I wanted to know it intimately, to fully inhabit the world I had chosen. I was eager to take it all in, to learn every detail of my new, fascinating path.

A sudden crack alerted us to the coming storm. When the skies opened up, I draped my raincoat over Donny's head and pulled the stroller awning tighter. Simi shrank back from the blowing rain. At home, I had a plastic cover that wrapped fully around the stroller, but I had not brought it with us. My sheitel would be a doused mutt by the time I got home, requiring an urgent call to the sheitel *macher* after Shabbat for some hasty maintenance.

"It's too far to run home, so let's just enjoy the storm," I said. The boys looked at me like I was crazy. "Sometimes you have to deal with whatever comes your way." I walked at an even pace as the rain poured down on us.

CHAPTER TWENTY-SIX

John emailed every day, sometimes twice a day. I guessed he hadn't meant it when he said he'd respect my decision! I didn't respond until the middle of the week, when the children were playing in the yard and Barry was at work.

John,

I meant what I said. We cannot meet up again. I should not have let things go as far as they did. It's been nice reconnecting, but I need to leave the past in the past. I wish you all the happiness in the world. Please respect my decision and stay away. Stop contacting me.

Sally

Barry and I had not spoken of Donny's situation, though we were no longer ships passing, no longer silent in the ominous night. *Great. Done. That chapter is closed, a mere memory. And no one has to know what I did.*

I went through my sent emails and deleted anything with John's name then flicked off the computer. It was time again to plan for Shabbat. Damn, there was so much to juggle! I was dragging that morning, though it was a beautiful day—cool but not too cool, with the promise of late afternoon warmth—but I couldn't shake a heavy blanket of exhaustion. The sun was buttery in the sky as it rose, a few clouds dancing against the blue. I pulled on comfortable clothes—a terrycloth skirt and a roomy, long-sleeved T-shirt, my hair in a snood, and no makeup—and got the kids ready. Simi had nursery on Wednesdays and Shira had school, so I'd just have Donny with me, and I needed to do a big shop for Shabbat.

Donny's Shabbat melancholy had dissipated. I hadn't gotten much out of him, just assumed his clinginess had more to do with being at shul among his old friends than anything else. I was certain no one had touched him or been inappropriate.

Most days, I chastised myself for not seeing his sadness throughout the school year, for allowing the abuse to last as long as it did and remain oblivious to his pain. He was still little, for goodness' sake! Seven was an innocent age, when all should be protected and safe, and I had failed to shield my son. I was dedicated to making up for past mistakes. How had I not noticed his need for attention? I should have picked up on subtle mood shifts.

In the grocery parking lot, Donny hopped out from the back seat. "I haven't been here with you and me alone in a long time, Mom!" he said brightly, though it had only been two weeks since we last came just the two of us.

I tousled his hair and pulled him to my side. "Well, now you are! What shall we make for Shabbat?"

I had a partial menu in my head of my family's usual favorites—chicken soup with matzo balls, cholent, deli roll, the ever-present salad as an attempt to get some veggies into my kids, and my favorite kugels, broccoli and lokshen sweet noodle. But there was always room for requests.

No one was calling with invitations to join them for a Shabbat meal, not even Shiri, and I had resigned myself to not inviting guests—except Batya's family—until the school situation resolved itself. I wanted to reach out to Shiri and ask about her distance, and her silence, but I was afraid of what she'd say. An inner voice nagged at me to come clean with Batya about, well, everything, so I was hesitant to spend too many hours alone with her. It was like she had X-ray vision and could see to my very core. I was a terrible liar and hated lying to my best friend and, even more, to my husband. I had been avoiding her, which was painful for me and I was sure hurtful for her, but I wasn't ready to put everything on the table. We had talked at length after Donny's abuse came to light but not returned to the topic since. So we had no guests coming this Shabbat, and no one had called to invite us. Which no longer surprised me.

Word had circulated around the community about our accusations against Mr. Fineman. A few mothers called to whisper in hushed tones that they, too, had had "run-ins" with him, and I wondered if that was code for abuse. I didn't know how to ask. I wished I could go back to the reporter version of me and ask probing questions of strangers, but the ways of my community were fully instilled in me, so I remained silent, nodding at the phone.

Others said they, too, had endured "uncomfortable situations," or questioned his behavior with the children, all code for something much darker, but again I couldn't probe deeper to uncover exactly what they had suffered. Too many did not call, and their silence was glaring. Women I had considered friends, women I had admired. The headmaster was trying to negotiate with Barry to keep this quiet, to sweep it away as if it had never happened. He did not want to fire Mr. Fineman, but he had removed him from the classroom to administration and replaced him with a substitute teacher. As far as I knew, Mr. Fineman was in the office, away from children. But that was nowhere near good enough. I wanted a lawsuit. I wanted the police called. I wanted to make an example of this teacher and chase him away from the community. I wanted the community to rise up and say *we won't stand for this! This goes against everything good and right that our Torah teaches us*. I wanted fallout in our community so the rumor mills and gossips could carry the story far and wide, to all Orthodox communities, so he would never again work in close proximity to children.

Barry and I had arrived at a silent understanding to not revisit the topic until he had exhausted all options with the headmaster. Thankfully, I had taken photos of Donny's initial bruises and documented what he told me so neither of us would forget. I didn't understand what was taking so long to resolve or why Barry had such infinite patience with a predator at our children's school, but I didn't want to upset the balance of our renewed closeness, so I kept quiet.

I grabbed a shopping cart, and Donny tagged along, a content smile on his face.

"So, what should I make?"

"Deli roll!"

"Already on my list. For Shabbat lunch?"

He nodded.

"Okay, and cholent of course."

Another nod.

"What about Friday night?"

"Chicken soup."

"Of course."

"With matzo balls."

"Always."

"And breaded chicken with rice pilaf!" He bubbled with the possibilities.

I plucked two bottles of kosher wine from a shelf, gathered Israeli yogurts for quick snacks or easy Shabbat morning breakfast—four chocolate, four vanilla, two plain for me. I chose a cold eggplant salad and a package of tangy Israeli pickles and several kinds of hummus for Shabbat lunch. Easy and ready to eat. At the deli counter, I ordered a pound of turkey and a pound of salami, sliced thin, for the deli roll and for sandwiches, and then added a half pound of corned beef, just to have. They had prepared chopped liver behind the glass counter, so I asked for a half pound of that. Barry liked it on matzo crackers as a snack.

"Make it a pound," I said.

"Can I have a pickle?" Donny pointed to a barrel of brine that held fat whole pickles.

"And a pickle, please," I said to the man behind the counter, who smiled in Donny's direction. With tongs, he pulled out a thick one, wrapped it in wax paper and handed it directly to Donny, whose eyes lit up as he reached for it.

"And the price tag, so I can pay for it at the checkout?" I asked, but the man shook his head.

"It's on me," he said.

"Wow, that's nice. Thank the man, sweetheart."

Donny bobbed his head and gushed, "Thanks," pickle juice spraying from his lips.

I clucked at him, chuckling, and the man laughed along with us. I wheeled the cart to the meat section, choosing flanken and chicken breasts and a whole chicken cut into eighths for the soup.

"Gefilte fish?" I asked Donny, who nodded. I grabbed a frozen loaf from the horizontal freezer at the end of the dried goods aisle. I filled the cart with boxes of rice pilaf and matzo meal and breadcrumbs, two cartons of eggs for making challah and kugels, two frozen packages of broccoli, and in the produce aisle, lettuce and cucumbers and tomatoes and carrots and one red onion and parsnips and celery for the soup along with fresh dill and parsley, plus rosemary for the cholent. At the bakery, the pickle a faint memory, Donny lit up at sight of black-and-white cookies, and I asked for a box of them, lifting one out to give to my boy to nosh as we finished shopping. I needed a box of Shabbat candles from the paper goods aisle, along with foil cups that caught the dripping wax, to keep my gleaming candlesticks clean. I grabbed a jar of silver polish for the kiddush cups and finished our tour by pulling nondairy ice cream cups from the freezer section along with puff pastry for the deli roll.

As I wheeled the cart toward the checkout, Esther's mother, Tova, passed us.

"Sally!" she called, stopping her cart next to mine, blocking anyone from getting through the aisle. She eyed me, as if she wanted to ask a question, but didn't speak. I remembered how oddly she had complimented my sheitel when I delivered Shira to her house on Shabbat. It just wasn't customary to comment on something like that. I didn't know her well but now wondered about her fascination with my hair covering and with me.

"Shira had such a lovely time at Esther's Shabbos party," I said, hoping to exchange a few pleasantries and move on.

Donny munched his cookie, oblivious.

"I'm glad," she said, smiling. "She's a sweet girl."

She pointed her eyes at Donny. "Is he home sick from school?"

I glanced at Donny then back at Tova. Surely she had heard about the situation. She had boys in the same school, one near Donny's age.

"Donny is learning at home for a while," I said. "He needed a different environment."

I patted his shoulder.

"Have a good Shabbos," I called, preparing to push my cart away.

Tova reached out, gripping my cart to stop me from moving on. She looked at me hard, all the smile gone from her eyes. Then a tart grin returned to her face and she lifted her hand. "You, too!" she said in a singsong voice and pushed past us down the freezer aisle.

What was that about? My heart pounded in my temples, but I pasted a smile on my face, hoping it would change my mood. At the checkout, I spotted Mrs. Fineman, the wife of Donny's predatory teacher, waiting in line. She looked up and saw me before I could dart away, her eyes locking on us. There were only four checkout lanes in the store, and everyone could see everyone else. It wasn't a big space, and there was nowhere else to wait. I couldn't even turn back and linger in an aisle until she had left. I took a deep breath and pushed forward, lining my cart behind hers at the register.

I grinned in her direction and nodded, pulling out my phone as an excuse to not engage in conversation. I scrolled aimlessly. Could she hear the pounding of my heart? I glanced at Donny, wondering if he knew who she was. He tapped his shoe. She lifted items from her cart, placing them on the conveyor. The cashier scanned each one, *bleep bleep bleep*. Prices scrolled on the screen. Mrs. Fineman emptied her cart and pushed it to the register, where a young man bagged her groceries. She swiped her credit card and took the receipt from the cashier. *In the clear.* But then she turned to me while the man stacked the bags in her cart.

"You ruined my husband's career," she hissed, her voice barely audible but loud enough for me to hear. Donny looked up with wide eyes. I dropped my phone into my purse and patted my son's arm, moving in front of him to block his line of vision and hopefully move him out of earshot.

"I did no such thing," I whispered. "He did it to himself."

Her eyes blazed, but at the same time I saw something else in them: doubt. She knew the truth. She knew it, and she covered it up to protect her husband. The wives of predators always knew, even if they would never admit it. To protect herself and their eight innocent children. She sacrificed other people's children—my son, and who knew how many others?—to save herself. I raged. What self-respecting adult could be such a coward? What woman could stay with a sick man, knowing the repercussions of his actions? Knowing, as she likely did, that the abuse would reach its bony fingers into her own home, down the line of her own children, if it hadn't already. And that those who are abused often become abusers.

Something snapped in me. Neither she nor anyone else in this enclave would keep me from doing what was right to defend my son—and any other child who had suffered at her husband's hands. I would report him, my husband and marriage be damned. Someone had to stick a neck out for our children. After all, if we didn't, what hope did our community have of enduring? We were supposed to be *a light unto the nations*, for God's sake! And we were doing a terrible job of it.

"Ma'am?" the cashier called to me. "You're holding up the line."

"Sorry," I said, pushing forward and throwing my items onto the conveyor. "I'm so sorry." I turned to the woman waiting behind me, a squat older lady with a thick brown wig and a boxy black dress, apologizing for the delay.

"Stay away from my family," Mrs. Fineman hissed before pushing her full cart toward the exit.

"You can bet I will," I muttered.

Chapter Twenty-Seven

On Shabbat afternoon, Batya slid open the glass door in my family room as I was clearing the lunch dishes and scraping food remnants into the garbage.

"Halloooo," she called out.

"In the kitchen!"

I stacked the dishes in the sink for cleaning later that night. Barry had gone upstairs to change. The kids were quiet in their rooms. I fully expected Simi to be dozing on the carpet, toy trains and stuffed animals scattered around him.

She deposited a paper plate of brownies on the counter. "We had leftovers," she explained, though I knew her well enough to know that she would have made extra for the sole purpose of bringing them over as a peace offering and to prompt a conversation. I wiped my hands on a towel and embraced her.

"Is it time to talk yet?"

I sighed. "I cannot avoid you, I know," I said. "And I don't want to, you must know that. But sometimes I have to get my house in order before I can talk about it outside the house."

"I get that. I understand. Really, I do."

I nodded and pointed to the living room. "Coffee?"

She shook her head. The hot water urn stood on the counter. It was my Shabbat anchor, the way I made my morning coffee, and the second cup I would sip with dessert, and a tea or a third coffee for late afternoon, when I was feeling tired but could not sleep because the children needed looking after while Barry napped.

I poured hot water from the urn into a mug, scooped two spoonfuls of instant coffee over it, stirring to blend. I carried the mug into the living room and sat opposite Batya, who had settled into the couch.

"I'll start with the easiest piece," I said and told her about Donny's school situation and the ongoing argument between Barry and me. "He wants it kept on the down-low, which is already not possible, given how fast news travels."

I rolled my eyes, and she nodded.

"I believe my son, no question. Barry says he believes him, too, but he wanted to hear the teacher's side of things. I really don't care what he might say. My son needs my unwavering support. I was pissed that Barry is concerned about how this will affect the community or reflect on the school or harm future *shidduchim* for our kids. He's been negotiating with the headmaster, which again, I am not in favor of. I want to file a lawsuit. I want to call the police.

"Anyway, you know I am homeschooling Donny, which he likes way too much." I chortled. "Barry wants him in school. He's concerned about socialization. I don't give a shit about that—and don't chide me for swearing, please. I'm more worried about permanent emotional trauma than whether he feels left out amongst the kids in the community. And honestly, he seems really happy learning at home."

Batya sighed and looked out the window. A woman in a pale—yellow dress with a matching hat passed, pushing a double stroller, two children walking on either side of her. A man walked quickly on the other side of the street, holding his hat to keep it from flying off in the wind.

"He's not wrong, you know," she said. "Of course we need to stamp out abuse. No question. But we also can't let the outside world see a fractured frum community."

"You don't honestly believe that, do you, Bat?"

She nodded vigorously. "A few bad apples can't spoil the bunch," she said.

"But they do," I countered. "If we are to be 'a light unto the nations,' then we have to admit our own frailty. We are, after all, only human. There are bad Orthodox Jews. Just like there are bad humans in every community."

"Okay, we won't come to agreement on this right now. But that's not all, Sal," she said, peering at me. "I know you too well. There's something else."

Would I tell her about John? I wanted to. But she would judge me and admonish me. Hell, I judged myself. I needed to share this burden with someone so I didn't accidentally admit it all to Barry. I could hear her already— *What are you doing to your marriage? It's a major transgression. It could ruin your whole family.*

And I would say, *Yes, I know, you're right. I love my family. I love my husband. I made a mistake. I wish I could erase it.*

What good would come from telling her?

"Sal?" She tapped her foot against the carpet.

Let's do this. "John Hogan has been emailing me," I started.

"Are you kidding? Like you need this now?"

"Stop. Please. I know it's bad. I told him I can't be in touch."

"But you saw him."

"How do you do that? How can you know things?"

"I knew there was something. Sally, think about this for a minute."

"You are far too late, Batya, and anything you say will be kinder than what I've already said to myself."

"You've only seen him, right? Nothing more?"

I listened for sounds in my house. It was too quiet upstairs. Could my words float through the ceiling to my husband's ears? I motioned to Batya to follow me outside.

On the deck, I spoke in hushed tones. "It's over now," I said. "We met up twice."

"You slept with him?"

Seriously, how did she do that?

I said nothing, but even that spoke volumes.

"Sally..." My name was a sigh in her throat, nearly blowing me over. "Oh Sal," she said. "This can ruin your marriage."

"It doesn't have to," I spat. "Barry never needs to know."

"You can live like that?" Her face was blank.

"I may have no choice, Batya," I said. "I can't lose him. I was utterly stupid. And I won't ever be again. I love my husband more than I can say. I don't want to lose him."

"I could never keep something like that from Tzvi," she said.

"You would never do this," I said. "You're too perfect."

She pursed her lips. "Thanks a lot, but this is not about me," she said.

"It never is."

"Why are you mad at me? I haven't done anything here. I love you like a sister."

"It's just sometimes not easy to be friends with the perfect woman."

I thought about my actual sisters, two of whom lived near our parents and were much like them and one who resided with her husband and daughters in Scottsdale. I rarely spoke with any of them and only heard about them when I made an obligatory call to my parents. Ours were relationships of mutually proscribed distance, in the vein of my parents' aloof stature. So Batya claiming she loved me like a sister stuck in my craw. I wanted more than a sister. I wanted a soulmate. And I had her in Batya, which meant I had to face the harsh truth she was saying right now. That was part of such a close relationship. Total, unadulterated honesty.

I looked at my friend, thinking of her lovely parents. Sheila and Eddie had completely and unquestioningly embraced Batya's religiosity from the start. They lived in Evanston, and they were over all the time, helping with the children, sharing meals, permanent friendly fixtures in my friend's home. Eddie and Tzvi were chummy, as if he were a true son, and to hear Batya tell it, her parents and her in-laws—the *machatunum*—were real friends. Whenever Batya and Tzvi had a new baby, the four grandparents gathered as a tight group, eager to be together, connected by shared life experiences. I couldn't picture Barry and my father huddled over a page of Torah like Tzvi and Eddie. At least I had my grandparents, but that was also new, since I'd become religious. Batya had depth and longevity. Everything in my life was too fresh, too easily lost.

"Mommy!" Simi peeled open the door and threw himself onto my lap. I nosed into him, catching the scent of sleep on his blond curls.

Doors were opening upstairs, Donny and Shira bouncing down the stairs. My house was waking. The hours until nightfall and the end of Shabbat would be full of energy and demands—for food, for attention, for stories and for snuggles. I was exhausted from revealing so much to Batya, and we hadn't even finished our conversation. Well, it was done for now. I shot her a pleading glance. *Don't abandon me.*

"I'd better be getting back," Batya said, rising. "And I bet someone is hungry!" She tickled Simi under his arms, eliciting a cascade of giggles.

I smiled at the sound of my son's happiness, wishing I could mirror it.

"To be continued?" I looked at Batya, who nodded. "Maybe tonight, after they're in bed?"

"Sure, just knock on my door. I'll be cleaning up as usual."

I reached for her hand and squeezed it then turned to Simi and said, "What would you like to eat?"

"Cookies!"

"How about cukies?" I stroked his cheek and ushered him into the house.

He wrinkled his nose. "What are those?"

"Cucumbers?" Simi did not find this as clever as I had.

"Not cookies?"

"Not at first," I said. "Maybe after you have a healthy snack."

Batya kissed my cheek and whispered in my ear, "I'm not going any-where. Promise."

She really could read my mind.

CHAPTER TWENTY-EIGHT

"I'm going for a run with Batya later, okay?" I said after Havdalah. I was washing the Shabbat dishes, and Barry was drying them with a towel. The kids were upstairs brushing teeth and putting on pajamas.

"Do you have to?" he said as I handed him a bowl streaked with hot water. He rubbed the towel in circles to whisk away the wet.

I winced. I had so few windows of freedom; I didn't want to lose this one.

"Why?"

"I just thought it might be nice to spend a little time alone together."

"Can I make it a quick one and then come back to you?" I dangled the towel in front of him in a mock-sensual pose, and he broke up laughing.

He nodded, swatting his towel at my hip. God, I loved this man. Why had I been such a fool? He placed the dry bowl in the cabinet. I chewed on my lip, scrubbing at a particularly hard piece of food stuck to a plate. Finally, it wrested free and flung into the drain, and I gave the dish one more good swipe before handing it, dripping, to Barry.

The window was cracked to let in the cool night air. I glanced at the clock on the microwave. It was already 9:30. The freedom of a night run would make it easier for me to talk to Batya. I dialed her number.

"Hey," I quipped. "I'll be over shortly. Can you get in a quick run with me, and we can talk while we go?"

"You read my mind," she said. "I'll let Tzvi know. Knock when you're ready."

In the all-encompassing blanket of night, I would get lost in the motion. Cease thinking and breathe in like each gulp of air was my last chance to stay alive in a roiling sea that threatened to consume me. I wiped my hands on my apron and untied it from my waist, folding it over the oven door handle, where it would dry in the night. I pecked at Barry's cheek. "An hour, tops. Thank you."

I tucked my curls into a bun and tied a *tichel* over my head, laced up my sneakers and jolted next door. Batya opened the door on the second knock and slipped outside, clicking it closed behind her.

We set off, the wind kissing our faces. The night fell in shades of gray and blue, gorgeous at every turn, falling into deeper hues as darkness lengthened. But the streetlights of Skokie never allowed full darkness, as if we always needed a light on to see the cloying truth.

"So I was thinking," Batya said as we rounded a corner. "You have to tell Barry. Otherwise, it's going to eat you up. And wreck your marriage."

I had thought the same thing. But how could I tell him? What if he left me?

"I can't imagine him divorcing you, Sal," she said.

"It's incredible," I said, chuckling, "how you read my mind."

"Yeah, whatever. It's just that I know you so well." She huffed as her feet hit the pavement. "I far prefer the softness of the street."

"Me too, but I'm afraid of running in the street in the dark. Drivers are so distracted these days."

"Yeah, we forgot the reflective vests."

We fell silent for a few minutes, our feet syncopating, our breathing heavy but fluid, like the way the wind called and breathed past houses, shaking the frames but never quite entering. On windy days, I shuddered into warm blankets safe inside. Running outside with Batya evoked the same security, even as the brisk night left us open and vulnerable.

"If I tell him... I mean, why tell him? John has gone quiet. Barry never needs to know."

"Obviously, it's your call," she said. We had circled the block and would do a few more rounds before landing in our yards and calling it a night. "You know how I feel. No matter what, I am here for you. And I know you don't believe me, but I'm not judging you. I wouldn't do it, but I don't think you normally would either. I think it was a response to this whole mess with the school. Extreme circumstances. Not excusable. Understandable."

"Maybe I should be married to you instead," I laughed.

"You wish." She elbowed me, and we turned another corner, looping through the neighborhood.

When I got home, I left my shoes by the door and tramped upstairs to shed my sweaty clothes. I took a three-minute shower to wash away the stink then pulled on sweatpants, a sweatshirt and thick socks and ran a brush through my curls, turning them fuzzy but soft.

Downstairs, Barry had neatened up the toys. The carpet was free of mess, the window cracked open. He'd dimmed the lights in the family room and was sitting on the couch. I plunked down next to him.

"I needed that," I said. "Thanks for understanding. And thanks for cleaning up!"

Every time I looked at him, shame flooded over me. I had a magnificent husband. A lovely man who loved me. How could I betray him? And how could I go on with this secret boiling up inside me?

"Of course," he said, fingering my soft hair. His hand slid underneath my mane, and he gripped my neck, pulling me to him. I inhaled his musk and a tang of cologne underneath the collar of his shirt. My heartbeat quickened. He grazed my neck, pulling back the collar of my shirt to plant feathery kisses along my neck and shoulder. He pulled the sweatshirt over my head and dropped it to the ground, pressing his lips to my chest, biting my nipples, moving lower.

We slid to the carpet. The light of the moon cascaded through the window. He peeled off my sweats, dropped his pants and shirt to the floor. I lay next to him then under him, my temples pulsing with his careful touches, his urgent need. I rose in response, closing my eyes, giving in to his fingers and the demand of his mouth. For a time, I ceased to exist, my body braiding into his, pulsing with questions and thriving in silence. We had always been this good. I opened my eyes to see my husband's dark ones, his thick curls, the angles of his face, and I ran my palms over his beard.

After, we lay on the carpet, our hands clasped.

"You are my world, Sally," Barry whispered into my hair.

I pulled him to me, my hand on the back of his head. "I am so lucky I found you, Barry," I said, meaning every word.

Chapter Twenty-Nine

That night, I dreamed horrible dreams. John Hogan came at me like a monster with no teeth, gawping a wide hole of a mouth, mocking me. His face was overlarge and gleaming in a wicked grin as he cackled with that gaping toothless mouth, spitting words like *you will never be free. I will never leave you alone. Everybody will leave you in the end.*

As that terrifying image faded away, Barry came into view, his dark curls and deep eyes haloed by a bright sun. I held out my hands to him, but he hung back, just beyond my reach. *I know what you did*, he taunted me. *I gave you everything I have, and you betrayed me. I'll take the kids and run, and you'll never find us. You were always destined to end up alone.*

I grabbed at the air to shake myself awake, but I could not open my eyes. I dropped down a well, clawing at the clay earth for a grip to hoist myself up and out of my unconscious state. I climbed and climbed but could not awaken. I called out, *Help me! Help me!*, from the bowels of the earth, having no clue who I was calling for or who might answer.

I finally woke to being shaken. Barry hovered over me, a worried look creasing his brow. "Wake up, Sally! You're having a bad dream."

I stared at his mouth, finding his neat white teeth and soft lips.

"I'm okay," I said, breathing in through my nose and smoothing the blankets.

He wrapped his arms around me and hugged his body to mine. I glanced at the clock: 2:36 a.m. I lay in my husband's arms, willing sleep to take me but afraid to descend into another deep well of fear. How long had it been since my last visit to the mikvah? We had been in this bed together for more than the usual few weeks. I searched my brain for the calendar dates, flipping through them until I counted eight. Two months with no period. Could it be?

The house was silent. Not even the normal creaks of floorboards expanding or contracting. Everything was still. I traced the rooms in my mind, surveying my home. The black leather couches in the living room, chosen because they would reject spills and be hard to tear. The antique dining room table, purchased on a Sunday driving spree early in our marriage when we wandered near the Wisconsin border in search of eclectic furniture to fill our empty home. The chairs with vanilla linen seats, a red stripe down the center of each, with carved seatbacks. The contemporary light fixture over the table, rectangles of glass dangling to reflect and magnify the sixty-watt bulbs.

The kitchen was warm and light. Moonlight shone through the windows of every room, wide gaping maws of glass, bringing the outdoors in. I could pretend I lived in the middle of a forest, searching for the baby blue sky, the scudding clouds dancing across it, traced by the winged flight of birds. By day, sunlight streamed in to wake us up, and by night, we basked in the glow of the moon. The metal kitchen sink, easy to *kasher*, beside counters made of white granite with gray veins weaving through the stone, chosen because we would not have to cover them on Passover, only pour scalding water over to transform them for the holiday.

Time advanced slowly. 3:15 a.m. Barry's even breath rolled in my ear. I would not sleep any more this night but recall the place where I lived, ponder the state of my life. By four o'clock, I peeled myself from my husband's grasp and lifted my worn body from the bed. My hands cupped my belly. A new life grew there. Barry would be excited. Maybe I could tell him about John after all and advance into a fresh start with this fourth child.

From the kitchen, I stepped out into the night. It was cool, but I welcomed it. I stepped onto the grass, the wet stalks like soft pinpricks against the soles of my feet. I closed my eyes and inhaled: damp soil, stagnant exhaust, the sweet fug of garbage in cans at the side of the house burrowed into by creatures that thrived in the night, rats and raccoons and possums, creeping in under cover of darkness while the people in the houses slept unsuspecting.

I leaned against the bark of our sole tree, pressing my nose up to its rough skin. A sentient being in my yard, clinging to the depths of the soil, its roots holding tight, its limbs reaching up and out over an expanse that grew with each passing year. This tree found a way to thrive despite its small setting. It was planted and firm, determined to persevere despite the encroachments of a playset and a sandbox and the motions of human life growing up and around it.

We would be like the tree: persevere in the face of adversity, find a way to not only grow, but thrive even in the most confining of circumstances. We would turn our faces to the sunlight, drink it in as sustaining nectar. My toes gripped the shoots of grass that forced their way up amid the gnarly tangle of tree roots.

CHAPTER THIRTY

On Sunday, the kids woke up out of sorts. Donny came downstairs lethargic and grumpy, hunched over his cereal bowl as the morning sun beamed through the window, the glare in his eyes so bright that he picked up his bowl and spoon and cup of orange juice and moved to the other side of the table, his back to the dawning day. Shira was quiet, though not surly. When Simi woke, he called out from his room for me, rather than dragging his stuffed animal and blankie down the stairs on his own.

They could sense my tension, I was sure of it. It was a thick fog, choking us all. I sat on the edge of Simi's bed.

"Mommy!" he spat, his little arms crossed in front of his body.

"Morning!" I replied, lying down beside him. He curled into me, wrapping one arm through mine in a tight hold. I closed my eyes and turned on my side toward him. The shades were still drawn, holding the room in a gray half-light. The tiredness hit me, and I started to doze.

I should have suspected something. My youngest child was usually the first one awake, energetic and ready for the day with enthusiasm. This morning, he had been the last up, and when I went to him, he simply nestled in, rather than leaping from the bed. We slept until Shira peeked her head in an hour later and called out, "Mommy? Are you sleeping?"

I shook awake. "Sorry, honey. What time is it?"

"Nine o'clock."

I shot up in bed, realizing she had missed the start of school. "I'm sorry, sweetheart. Do you want to stay home today?"

She shrugged.

"I didn't sleep very well last night. I must still be tired. I'll call it in."

Shira climbed onto my other side. I nudged a sleeping Simi closer to the wall to make room. "You okay?"

She shook her head and looked down. Simi continuing to sleep was highly unusual and probably meant he was sick. The fever from the other day must have been the start of something, which would likely run through the house. I looked at my daughter's sweet face, lined with worry. "What is it?"

"Esther's not my friend anymore," she said.

"Oh? Since when? You went to her Shabbos party last week."

"All week," she said.

"What happened?"

"Her mommy said I can't be friends with her anymore."

"Did she? That wasn't very nice. Did she give a reason?"

I thought about Tova's oddness toward me. I was the reason. Our complaints against Mr. Fineman, to be more precise. I knew there would be fallout.

"Mommy, why doesn't Donny go to school anymore?"

We hadn't said anything to the kids about what happened with Mr. Fineman, only that Donny would be learning at home for a while. I wondered if she heard chatter at school, if other parents talked too loudly in their homes, fueling their children's imaginations. I could actually see the wheels of a gossip mill churning.

"Donny's teacher wasn't very nice to him," I explained. "He was hurting him. So we decided to keep him at home until the teacher is no longer at that school."

"Okay," she said. "Am I safe at my school?"

"No one is hurting you, are they?" I asked.

She shook her head.

"Good. Tati and I will always protect all of you. We love you so much. And if anyone ever hurts you or tells you not to tell us something, you make sure to tell us, okay?"

She burrowed in, and I wrapped an arm around her narrow shoulders. She lay her head against my chest. I felt like a bird whose wings had lifted and spread to their full expanse, my baby birds under the umbrella of my protection. I could lull into sleep again, their warm bodies pressed to mine, the dim light of a new day holding the room in stillness.

But Donny was downstairs, grumbling into his cereal bowl. I could not lie there. Sundays were filled with house-cleaning, grocery list–building, and since Shira and Donny, previously, had only half days of school, I usually took all three of them to the park in the afternoon for fresh air and energy release among other neighborhood kids. Many of the mothers followed similar routines, gathering to talk while our children climbed and ran and swung and played under the trees. If I hadn't shopped in the morning while the older two were at school, we'd go on the way home, and dinner was often Shabbat leftovers or, if I wasn't feeling it, frozen pizza or fish sticks and a hasty salad.

I pressed my palm to Simi's forehead—sure enough, he was warm to the touch and clammy. I nudged Shira out of the bed and rose, trying not to disturb Simi. We padded out quietly, into her room, lifting stuffed animals and dolls and wrinkled Shabbos clothes from the floor. I placed the animals and dolls on her rumpled bed, the clothes in her wicker hamper.

"How about you get dressed?"

She stripped off her nightgown and dropped it to the floor.

"Hamper?"

She picked it up and dropped it in the basket.

"Good. It's a beautiful day. How about a jumper and T-shirt?"

She chose a pink and orange plaid sleeveless dress and a yellow T-shirt to go under it.

"Socks?"

From another drawer came fold-over white socks with lace edging.

"Underpants?"

She giggled and opened another drawer, stepping into panties.

"Great. Now brush your hair and clean your teeth."

She attempted to speak, likely to tell me both had been done, but I put up a hand to stop her, seeing the mess of curls and smelling the funk of morning on her breath.

"You know better than to lie to me," I said.

She twisted her lips as I pulled the brush through her knotted hair.

"When was the last time you brushed your hair?" I asked. "Hold still while I try to get the knots free."

Once her locks were smooth, I gathered fistfuls of hair on either side of her face and secured them with pink ribbons into low pigtails. Then I sent her off to the bathroom to brush her teeth and prayed she would actually do it. "Let me hear it," I called. The water ran, followed by the scratching of bristles against teeth.

I pulled the covers on Shira's bed to make it then peeked into Donny's room and found my son sprawled across the bed on his back, staring at the ceiling. "What's up with you?" I asked.

An arm came over his eyes to block out any vision. "Nothing," he mumbled.

"I know when something is wrong," I said. "Talk."

"I don't want to go to the park today," he said.

"That's good because we're not going," I said. "But out of curiosity, why not?"

"All the boys will make fun of me for not being at school," he said.

"Did the boys say something at synagogue?"

He nodded.

"It's going to take some time," I said. "An awful thing happened to you. You were probably not the only boy who suffered under Mr. Fineman's wicked hands, honey. Other families may not want to admit that this bad thing is happening. They may blame us for a while rather than admit the truth. And for some boys, their parents may not have pulled them out of school to stop it. They could be resentful or scared."

"Shlomi and Natan," he mumbled.

"What?"

"He was hitting them, too," he said.

I ran through the faces of the boys in Donny's class, trying to conjure who Shlomi and Natan were, what families they belonged to. Shlomi was Rachel Tobias' son, the middle child in a family of seven. I didn't know her well, only to say hi on the street, so I didn't know if he would tell her what happened or if she'd believe him. Which one was Natan?

"What is Natan's last name, honey?"

"Fabelinski."

I didn't know that family at all. I'd mention both to Barry, see if we might build alliances and shut down the gossip. Maybe now we'd have leverage to fire Fineman. Maybe they'd want to file criminal charges, too. I doubted it, but I could hope.

"Are they nice boys?"

He shrugged. "They're okay," he said. "Kind of quiet."

"Like you?"

He nodded, chewing his lip.

So the teacher sought out the quieter boys who might not raise a fuss. The picture was growing clearer.

"Anyone else?"

He thought for a moment then shook his head.

"Thank you for telling me," I said. "We are going to try hard to put this behind us and make new friends." I smoothed a hand over his dark hair. "And you like homeschooling, don't you?"

His eyes lit up as he nodded vigorously.

"Me too. I don't yet know what we'll do about the fall, but we have time, and if this keeps working, we'll keep doing it. Your brother isn't feeling well, but when he's better, we'll go to the library, get some books, spend more time together and enjoy the summer. Everything will be okay in the end, I promise." I kissed his cheek.

He sat up on the bed and threw his arms around me, holding on tight. I squeezed him, rubbing my hands in circles on his back.

"Come on. Let's get you dressed, and then we can figure out how to redeem this sorry day," I said, chuckling. I stroked his hair and smiled at my son.

I pulled up the blinds, washing the room in light. "Some fresh air?" I asked, opening a window. I pulled his blankets and sheets straight, tucking at the sides. "Let's make your bed," I said. "And pick up the Shabbos clothes from the floor." I dropped them in his hamper, which was shoved into the closet. "What do you want to wear?"

"I can do this, Mom," he said, going to the closet to look for pants and a shirt. "Can I wear playclothes?"

"Of course," I said. "Be comfortable. We are not going anywhere today."

A shower would wake me up. I peeked into Shira's room, where she sat on the floor, playing with her tea set. Simi was still asleep. I'd give him juice when he woke to make sure he stayed hydrated and take his temperature. I'd warm leftover chicken soup from Shabbat, Jewish penicillin. We'd spend the day on the couch watching TV or in the backyard playing if they grew restless.

In my room, I peeled off my clothes. Pinpricks of hot water pelted my back and arms. I dropped my chin and let the water massage my neck, dousing me from head to foot. I wanted to awaken, but the heat was soothing, lulling.

As I scrubbed my body, I noticed the rounding of my stomach. How had I not seen it? I'd take a test to confirm, but I knew. I stepped out of the shower, dripping onto the bathroom rug.

In a denim skirt and long-sleeved T-shirt, I combed out my hair and hung my towel to dry. Downstairs, I washed the breakfast dishes, made a list of meals for the week and a corresponding grocery list, set up Donny and Shira with paints, water cups, brushes and watercolor paper atop of newspaper laid flat on the table, and arranged an awake and listless Simi on the couch with a sippy cup of apple juice, his blanket, and Elmo on the TV. Barry returned from morning minyan, dropping his keys by the cookbooks and kissing Shira and Donny on the head.

"Got one for me?" I asked with a hopeful grin.

He leaned in for a peck, grazing my cheek. I motioned to the door, and he followed me outside.

"Donny named two other boys that Fineman abused," I said.

"Really? Which families?"

"Fabelinski and Tobias."

He nodded. "Where there's smoke, there's fire."

"Exactly. They can't be the only ones. Could we reach out to the families? Strength in numbers?"

He shook his head. "They won't raise a fuss. They're both scholarship kids. Those families struggle, and they'll want to keep it under wraps, see him go quietly without drawing attention to themselves or their other children."

I slapped my hands against my legs. "I don't get it."

"I don't condone what happened," he said. "Mr. Fineman was wrong. I never thought otherwise. I just don't want a scandal in the community. I don't want us, or Donny, to be the subject of scorn. I want to handle it quietly, make it go away."

"We're already being shunned, Bare," I said.

His eyes flew open. "What do you mean?"

"Have you noticed we haven't been invited anywhere for Shabbat in weeks? Women are odd to me at the grocery. And Shira said that Esther's mother told her she can't be friends anymore, as of last week."

He raked his fingers through his hair.

"It cannot be avoided, Barry," I said. "The scandal is here. So let's come out on the righteous side of it, rather than slinking off into the shadows. Fineman has to go. Children must be protected."

He pulled me to him, and I folded into his open arms. It felt good to press against his chest, hear the vibrant beating of his heart. It was strong, fast, consistent. Reliable.

"This is good," he whispered into my ear. "This is really good. We will face this together. I promise."

CHAPTER THIRTY-ONE

Barry graciously agreed to stay with the children so I could zip to the grocery, and on my way, I ran into Walgreens to buy a home pregnancy test. My breasts were tender and heavy, and I had become more exhausted with each passing day. With each of my previous pregnancies, I'd never suffered from morning sickness, only an insatiable hunger for odd foods like boxed macaroni and cheese or hot fudge sundaes, things I normally would scoff at as kids' indulgences. All the telltale signs were there, but I wanted to confirm it before I told Barry the good news. Which would pave the way for sharing some bad news a day or two later.

I returned home laden with bags, the home kit stuffed in my purse. Shira and Donny were pumping their legs on the swings, and Simi lay across Barry's lap on the couch, the tingling refrain of Uncle Moishy ringing from the stereo. I put away the groceries—eggs and juice, cans of tuna, a jar of mayonnaise, prepackaged shredded cabbage to make into coleslaw. Cucumbers, carrots, a sheath of celery. Apples and oranges and bananas. A jar of Nutella, and another of tahini. Hummus and yogurt and chicken breasts and ground beef. Boxes of rice and pasta. When it was all tucked into cupboards and refrigerator drawers, I made cheese sandwiches on individual plates with pickles and chips for the kids when they came in, starving. Then I snuck upstairs to take the test. Sure enough: a pink plus sign appeared. A thrill rippled through me. A new baby! Maybe a sister for Shira, finally, or another sweet boy. A new baby was always reason for celebration.

With each child, my capacity for love had multiplied. After Donny, gripped with fear when I learned I was pregnant with Shira, I could not imagine how I could tear myself away from my darling son to pay attention to another baby. And then she arrived, all scrunched up and squalling but with a soft fuzz of light hair and those bright eyes, and she looked up at me once, as if diamonds sparkled in her gaze, and I was more deeply in love than I had ever known I could be. And when I glanced at my firstborn, only two and still a baby himself, my heart swelled with a tidal wave of love, and I saw that, in fact, I could love them both more than I had ever loved anyone, more than I loved Barry, more than I cared about my own well-being. And when Simi came and I saw how his older siblings adored him, I was overcome by the strength of my love for these precious beings, created out of the unspeakable love I shared with my husband, and satisfaction radiated from the top of my head all the way down to my toes.

I crept downstairs. Donny and Shira squealed on the swings, the chains creaking as they pumped forward and back. Sensing my presence, Barry looked up. I bit back a smile and beckoned him toward me. He slid out from under Simi and followed me into the kitchen, where I thrust the stick into his sight. A grin spread across his face, which flushed pink, and a hand clapped to his mouth.

"Really?" he asked, his eyes wide and bright.

I nodded.

"Oh, Sally!" Barry scooped me up in a swinging hug, and as my feet left the floor, I breathed in his familiar scent. This was my home. Everything would be okay. He would forgive me.

"When?"

I shook my head. "I think it's about two months," I said. "I'll go to the doctor to confirm, though."

He braided his fingers between mine and squeezed my hand. "I am so delighted." He nuzzled my face.

"Me too," I whispered.

Barry gripped my face with both hands and planted a deep and penetrating kiss on my mouth. I sucked him in, breathing for us both, becoming one with my husband in an instant and wanting him, too. Another symptom of these early months. I chuckled.

"What?"

"Think we can sneak upstairs?"

He flushed, his face reddening. "Are you serious?" Then realization hit, and his eyes smiled. "Ah, I remember. Oh boy, here we go. The next seven months are going to be fun." He ran his hands along my back, squeezing my bottom then pulling me in for an innocent hug. "I would love to," he said into my ear, "but the kids are awake and aware, and, well, I don't think we can get away with it."

I clucked my tongue. "Too bad," I said.

"Rain check?"

I nodded. "Definitely," I said.

Chapter Thirty-Two

D inner that night was macaroni and cheese from scratch, swirling butter and milk and shredded cheese in a pot for the sauce and coating the noodles before pouring the mixture and three hefty spoonfuls of cottage cheese into a baking dish and sprinkling breadcrumbs on top. I tore lettuce for a quick salad, chopped cucumbers and tomatoes and carrots into a wooden bowl.

Tylenol had lowered Simi's fever. He'd spent the day on the couch, sipping juice. Barry called our neighbor Yossi, a pediatrician who didn't mind popping into houses on the weekend to render a medical opinion. Despite my son's illness, I felt good about my family. Barry and I were floating in the high of our news, and everything seemed right again. I'd go for a run later that night then fall into my husband's arms. And sometime this week, I'd come clean about my mistake with John, and we would work through it. We had to.

But I forgot how persistent John could be, how used to getting his way. When I checked my email, there was a long missive from him.

Dear Sally,

There was so much left unsaid years ago, and it's all my fault. I take full blame, and I can't apologize enough. I don't know what it will take for you to trust me again, but I'll do anything to get there. It's not just the thrill of the chase. I am 35 years old, and I've tried to find love since I left you, but I have never found someone who really belonged with me, like you do. You are my one and only. I was an idiot to let you go all those years ago, and I have to try to win you back. I'll always regret it if I don't.

I don't want to ruin your life, and I would never want you to lose your kids! Even if you want me, I realize you may not be able to act on it. I fucked things up back then, and this is the consequence of my stupid, immature, dramatic actions. I have to live with that. But I really want you. I. Want. You. For now, and always. Believe me, Sally. And please give me another chance.

Love, John

I deleted the email. I wished I could delete John entirely from my mind and memory, but his face loomed large, like a carnival clown taunting me. I would *delete delete delete* until the emails stopped coming. They had to stop, didn't they?

A tap-tap-tap on the front door, and Barry scurried across the foyer to open it. Yossi.

"Thank you so much for coming," Barry said. "I know it's an imposition on a Sunday."

He shrugged. "I'm happy to serve the community."

I followed Yossi and Barry into the family room, where Simi lay, clutching his blankie and sucking his thumb. His golden curls were damp and matted to his forehead. I sat beside him, stroking his soft hair, my fingers trailing down his clammy face. He lay his head on my lap.

"Hey, buddy," Yoni said, sitting on Simi's other side. "Your Tati says you're not feeling well."

Simi pouted and shook his head.

"Can I have a look?" He opened a bag and pulled out an instrument to look in Simi's ears. He shone a penlight into the darkness.

"Wow, those look angry red," he said, peering into the left ear then the right.

Simi's eyes went wide.

"Can I have a peek into your throat?"

Simi nodded and opened his mouth wide, tilting his head back onto the couch.

"Really good," Yossi said, nodding, peering into Simi's mouth and using a wooden depressor to hold his tongue flat. "That's red, too. Wow, your insides are really angry right now!"

"They are?" Simi croaked.

Yossi turned to us. "It's either an ear infection or strep throat. I can't tell without a culture, though the ears are incredibly inflamed, so it's a good bet that they're affected, even if it is strep. I'll prescribe amoxicillin because we would do that for either or both. Where do you want me to call it in?"

"The Walgreens on the corner," I said.

"I know the number by heart," he said.

"You are so kind to come on a Sunday and do us this favor," I said. "We can't thank you enough."

"He won't be going to nursery this week, okay? There's enough of this going around. Watch the other kids for signs of it."

Barry walked him to the door.

Shira and Donny went to bed without much fanfare, tired from playing outside and, I worried, perhaps coming down with whatever plagued Simi, who whimpered beside me in my bed, his body clammy and sticky. I'd changed him out of two pairs of pajamas already and cradled him in my arms, his head heavy against my chest. Barry had picked up the antibiotic, and we gave him a dose, hoping to kickstart the healing, but I heard the doctor's familiar refrain, *It takes at least 24 hours before they start feeling better.*

Barry sat against the headboard, reading in the lamplight. I had so wanted tonight to be special! To dissolve in my husband's embrace and reignite the passion that pulsed through our marriage.

Simi was heavy in my arms, eyes clenched shut. "Mommy," he moaned.

"Shhhh, honey," I said, reaching for the sippy cup of an electrolyte drink beside my bed. "Drink this, baby. It'll soothe your throat."

He pinched his lips together and shook his head.

I shot Barry a look, and he smiled. He was thinking what I was thinking, missing what I was missing. Maybe I could get Simi to fall asleep then carry him to his bed? I was officially the worst mother, caring more about having sex with my husband than cradling my sick child.

Finally, Simi fell asleep in my arms, which ached from the weight of him. I eased his head out from under the bend of my elbow, sliding his body off mine and onto the bed. His sweat had drenched through to me. My shirt and skirt clung to my skin. I nodded to Barry and tilted my head to Simi. He got the message, moving to the other side of the bed and sliding his arms under the boy to cradle him and carry him to his room.

I stripped off my clothes, thinking I might squeeze in a run, but then Barry was back in our room, silhouetted in the closet door, backlit and tantalizing. I hadn't decided what to put on, so I stood in the closet in my underwear. He blocked the door, staring me up and down.

"My wife," he whispered, stepping closer.

He stroked my hair, my cheek. I could feel his breath against my face. My hair spilled over my shoulders. He combed his fingers through it.

"Drop your panties," he said.

My heartbeat quickened. I slid them down my legs and stepped out of them.

He kissed me, pulling my body to his. He pressed toward me, breathing into me. We were one breath on a rise, then a plunge, then rising again. My pulse beat at my temples. My body responded to his nearness without any effort or thought. Every nerve ending was alight with electricity—my fingertips, the skin on my neck. My arms and legs buzzed.

I got lost in the fervent kisses, and then my husband scooped his arms under me and lifted me off the ground, kissing me all the while, as he stepped backwards and out of the closet and lay me on our marriage bed, the arc of moonlight cascading into our room. We made love slowly, taking our time, tracing the contours of each other's bodies. The hills of his muscular arms, the moss of dark hair on his chest silky under my fingertips. I traced his jaw with my fingers, tasting his skin. The first time was fervent and intense, as if we needed each other desperately. But then, a second time began as he rained kisses along my body, ending up between my legs, bringing me to incredible hills of ecstasy and I cried out in the night, unafraid of anyone hearing, free to feel and to be heard. And then, after I quieted, he brought his face back to mine and entered me quietly, urgently, moving our bodies as if they were one, riding the crest of those hills again and again until we both exploded into a million tiny pieces, raining down on the remnants of who we used to be and re-forming as entirely new people, starting over.

CHAPTER THIRTY-THREE

The next morning, Simi was less damp and clammy but still subdued, and Shira stayed longer in bed than usual, complaining of aches when I went into her room and pressed my hand to her forehead.

"I don't feel good, Mommy," she said.

"I'll bring you juice," I said.

In the kitchen, I poured an electrolyte drink into a cup for my daughter and called the school to let them know she'd be out sick. I called Simi's nursery teacher, too. Donny came into the kitchen. "Are you feeling okay, bud?" I smoothed his hair back from his forehead and kissed his cheek. "Your sister is sick now. How are you doing?"

He shrugged. "Okay," he mumbled.

"Cereal?"

He nodded.

I pulled a bowl from the dairy cupboard and poured Honey Nut Cheerios, dousing it with milk. I laid the bowl in front of my son, handing him a spoon and a napkin.

By Tuesday, Simi was on the mend, but Shira and Donny had fallen ill. I felt cooped up in the house, so when Barry returned each night, I breezed out the door for a much-needed run.

We made love every night, desperately, as if we couldn't get enough of each other. Barry was ecstatic, and it was like no time had passed and nothing had come between us. I decided against telling him about John. My mistake would fade into memory.

As my husband slept, I watched his profile in the moonlight—that sloping nose, his pale cheeks, dark eyes glimmering. His dark curly hair, and when we came together, I tugged at those curls, threading my fingers through and between them, pulling him closer to me, tasting him and breathing him in. I needed his body close, to feel his pulsing heart meld with mine, to reassure me that we were one unit, forever. To reassure myself. I concentrated on his heartbeat so keenly that eventually, I lost sight of two beating hearts and felt only one.

CHAPTER THIRTY-FOUR

While Barry and I were closer than we had ever been, we made no progress on pursuing criminal charges against the teacher. He reached out to both other families, who played dumb about the abuse. Finally, Barry was as furious as I, and while we were united in our pledge to right this atrocious wrong, we stood alone before the school and the community.

"What the hell are they thinking?" He swiped his hands through his hair, pacing in the kitchen after the children had gone to bed. "This can't be the first time Fineman's hit a kid. And now we know it will not be the last. Why is Headmaster Schwartz protecting him?"

I loved my community—its unequivocal embrace, its warm welcome and festive routine. Every week, a day to celebrate the beauty of life. And the rhythm of the calendar, through highs and lows, we lived in unison, tied to the incredible moments of the deep past that formed us as a people and spurred us on as a community. But this was the price of insularity. We had only each other, and backs turned like a mass of Viking warriors, their shields overlapping on the battlefield, a sea of beating, breathing bodies close together to prevent a break. We were causing that break—or rather, our reaction to a transgression. We stood alone in the middle of a bustling community that could not admit its weak spots. One day, it might cave in on itself, and there would be no one to blame but ourselves.

"Honestly, Sal, I had thought finding those two other kids would give us strength in numbers to at least prod Schwartz to fire Fineman," he said.

As he swept past me, I reached out, hoping to stop him with a hand on his arm and the nearness of me. "Three of us cannot stand against an entire community, and there aren't even three, honey," I said. "There never would be. This is how I felt when we first discussed it, when you insisted on going to the headmaster instead of taking legal action. Alone and misunderstood."

Dark eyes pierced through my skin, penetrating my heart. "I am so sorry I made you feel that way," Barry said, pulling me to him.

"It is always us alone against the world," I whispered. "The community is a fort, and we stand on the other side of the barricade, drawbridge up, preventing us from entering. It is a lonely place to be."

"That it is."

He caressed the back of my head, pressing me to him. "Even the threat of filing charges would prompt Schwartz to send him packing," I said. "We might be ostracized, but maybe the story would follow him, maybe it would prevent him from working with children in the future."

Barry pulled away to look at my face. "You and I both know someone will allow him to work with children," he said.

"It's a *shanda*! This man should never be allowed around children again, not even his own," I spat. "We haven't taken any action really, and we are pariahs. It doesn't seem fair."

Barry rolled his eyes. "I love my community, but this is one of its downfalls. Head in sand. Protect our own rather than cause a fuss. Don't let the *goyim* see that we have cracks in the foundation."

"You believe that?"

He nodded. "I've always known it," he said. "You grow up with it, and you see things, you hear things. I didn't want to throw out the baby with the bathwater, but..."

"That's a horrible phrase," I mumbled.

He chortled. "Yes, it really is. What does it even mean?"

We let it go there, uncertain how to continue, how to effect some lasting and impactful change. I wanted back in the embrace of my friends. I wanted Shabbat invitations. I wanted to go back in time and choose another school, protect my child from the menace of a predatory teacher and myself from becoming an outcast. I wanted that feeling of being utterly alone to live only in my deep and forgotten past. Suddenly, I was the little girl in suburban Detroit, lonely in an echoing house, with a hired nanny for a playmate, longing to live inside the books that promised happy families full of friends and parents who lavished hugs and kisses and listened long into the night.

With the kids' illnesses, I didn't check email until late on Thursday, when I discovered twelve unread messages from John. My stomach clenched. *What will it take for him to go away!* Panic rose in my throat with the acid taste of bile as the red dots signaling new messages throbbed. I was no longer angry; now I was afraid of what he might do. He wasn't thinking straight. He'd lost focus. And that could be dangerous, threatening.

I opened one after another, reading each, not responding to any. So many pleas to see me. So many poetic statements of enduring love and desire. So many candid details about how he wanted to be with me, share life with me, know me better, meet my children. *Delete. Delete. Delete.*

It was clear as a new day: his passion for me had nothing to do with me. Had it ever? John wrote those emails despite my pushing him away, in complete defiance of my total rejection. He did not need me in this fantasy. John Hogan was alone in his glass-walled apartment, alone in his wealthy, lonely life, seeking out a person he conjured in his imagination who he believed waited for him at the other end of his groping letters.

For ten years, I'd clung to the belief that John saw the real me. That with him, I could be my true self for the first time in my life, be honest and vulnerable and exposed. But no. I was a prize to win and display on a shelf.

He clearly got off on the chase, spurred to run harder, faster, toward me, never seeing me even as he propelled himself forward at full speed.

My stomach turned with nervous flutters. Would he ever go away?

CHAPTER THIRTY-FIVE

I went all out preparing for Shabbat. After all, I had nothing but time to think and plan and shop and cook. My grandparents would come for Friday night as usual, and we were heading next door once again for lunch. I made a double batch of challah, freezing the extra loaves for later weeks. I laced the dough in intricate, six-part braids, sprinkling poppyseeds and sesame seeds on top of the egg wash. They baked to a golden crust, puffing up and wrapping the house in the scent and warmth of a bakery.

I sauteed peppers and onions with tomatoes and carrots to pour over gefilte fish loaves and bake until the vegetables formed a crust. I'd serve it with tangy horseradish sauce. I made the most gorgeous salad—arugula and spinach with chopped pecans, sliced strawberries and red onion, tossed in an orange vinaigrette. I made chicken with artichokes and olives and fresh tarragon and Barry's favorite brisket, with carrots and onions and potatoes softened by a long-cooked sauce of beef broth, tomato paste, and brown sugar. I baked an olive oil rosemary cake, oatmeal raisin cookies and lavender cupcakes with lemon glaze. We would eat well and enjoy each other as a family, without the intrusion of guests except for my loving grandparents, whom I needed so desperately now. I could not wait to share the news of my pregnancy with Nana and Papa, let them experience the dawning of a new life alongside us. I would revel in my beautiful family, notice the sweet moments of our rest day.

The children ran to the door when Barry returned from work. "Tati!" they yelled, throwing their arms around him all at once. He smiled, patting their backs, pulling them close. Donny craned his neck to look up at his father, and Barry patted his head.

They hovered around him like a fog as he hung up his coat and set his bag by the stairs. I hung back, watching my family. Barry locked eyes with mine, electricity pulsing between us. His eyes glimmered, his gaze wanting.

I blushed, embarrassed by his desire in front of our children. He extricated himself from the amoeba of children, chortling as he tickled each under the arms to wrest them free. Then he was at my ear, leaning close, the smell of a long day and his musk encircling me.

"I missed you," he murmured, reaching a hand beneath the tichel I'd wrapped around my hair. He loosened the knot, unraveling the layers of shiny silk until my curls spilled over my shoulders. Then his hands were in my hair and his face was inches from mine and our bodies vibrated with anticipation. "I missed you," he repeated, pressing his lips to mine. I breathed him in. I wanted him more than I had wanted anything in a long time. I wanted to push him against the stairs and climb on top of him and press my hips against his, and not let him go. I wanted to prove that nothing could shake what we had, not even unrelenting emails from an old lover, a crazy blind idiot of a man who would not leave me alone. The secret bubbled up inside me and threatened to shatter me into a thousand pieces. I had to push John from my mind forever, forget I had ever known him, send the story like smoke up into the atmosphere.

CHAPTER THIRTY-SIX

That night, Barry made good on his promise. My exquisite Shabbat dinner helped prod along our passion. I curled into him in the angle of moonlight, stroking his curls. He rumbled with little snores like small waves close to shore. There had been more emails from John before Shabbat, all of which I deleted but which heightened my panic. Maybe I should write and tell him to stop contacting me, that I never wanted to hear from him again? But hadn't I already said that? Wasn't my silence enough of a response?

Every morning, after the kids went to school, Donny climbed into the jogger stroller—a bit large at seven years old, but he folded himself into it—and Batya plopped Talya in hers, and we ran. As my body filled out, the baby rounding my stomach, I ran harder, faster, farther. "Where's the race?" Batya laughed, keeping up with my pace.

Usually, while we ran, we could talk about anything, but with my eldest son in the stroller, I was afraid to say too much. So I kept it light and easy.

But the messages were coming with greater frequency and volume. Twelve messages one day, fifteen the next. It had been six weeks since our last meeting, and I hadn't responded, but he wasn't getting the hint and he'd taken to pleading, becoming increasingly incensed with each one.

Sally – Sal, where are you? I yearn for you – I want to be with you. Please, Sally. Please.

After John broke up with me, I kept hoping he would appear, call, email, somehow get in touch and say it was all a cruel joke. For months, I believed we would get back together, that he'd come to his senses and realize how stupid he'd been. He would not find anyone better than me. Except I didn't really believe that. His breaking up with me confirmed my worst suspicions: I was not lovable. That when a person saw the real me, he would grow bored and lose interest and eventually leave.

I knew better now. I knew what real love was. It stayed. It was quiet sometimes and passionate. Love listened, discussed, and pondered in equal measure. Love was partnership. Love was understanding. Love was slow, took time to build, and when it grew deep, like it had with Barry and me, it was the true foundation for a good life. A love like ours was a home for a family. It had no end. It was fingers braided together until you could not see the two hands as separate.

Seething, I went into my Gmail and searched for instructions to delete the account. I could no longer even look at his emails. I'd have to disconnect from him in every way online, make it hard for him to find me. I unfriended and blocked him on Facebook and set up a new email as barryandsally. I sent a quick note to my friends and family, letting them know they could reach me at this new place, and sent the old email into the Internet ether.

I found a new park to run at, afraid John might come looking for me when he could not find me online, and it became my refuge, far enough from the community to lose myself in motion. It was summer now, and hot, the sun beating into my skin, so I fastened a bucket hat tight over my head to shield my face from the glare. I doubled down on modesty—pulling a lightweight cotton skirt over my full-length running tights and choosing breathable long-sleeved shirts so I wouldn't be stifled in the unforgiving heat. Still, I baked inside the Lycra, pushing at the grass as I ran up and over and down the hills until I reached the lake. The sun glinted diamonds into the peaks of waves. Dark water lapped in ripples, crashing against the shore. The shoreline here was a curve of jagged boulders beside a tall concrete wall. I leaned over the iron railing to feel the cool spray on my face, listening to the lick of the waves.

When I ran, I tucked my phone into a pocket on my tights. A mile up the lakeshore, the phone vibrated against my leg. I stopped and pulled it out but didn't recognize the number, so I sent the call to voicemail and kept running. A minute later, it buzzed again, and I pulled it out. Same number. Could it be an emergency? Something with Barry? The kids? I answered.

"Sally." It was John. "You're not responding to me."

"Where are you calling from? I don't recognize this number."

"I'm at work."

I'd forgotten that he had my number. All that effort, and he could still reach me. Anger like a whistling kettle threatened to bubble over, frothing at my ears and in my throat.

"You have to stop contacting me," I hissed.

"I need to see you."

"Leave me alone. I'm not interested," I said.

"I don't believe you."

"I'll get a personal protection order against you."

"You wouldn't do that."

"Try me."

My heart thumped a rapid beat. I was bluffing, and he knew it. To take out a police order, I'd have to let Barry know what was going on. John could read me like a favorite book.

"I never want to hear from you again," I said, clicking off the call. I blocked the number, deleted his contact information, and slid the phone into my pocket.

The lake was wild today, whipping and frothing far out from the shore. As the waves came closer, they evened out, protected by the hug of the harbor. In the winter, this part of the lake grew angry and white, matching the frowning sky. Chicago in winter was beastly gray, and there was nothing to save you from it but a thick blanket and a warm house. Which I had.

For now.

My hand touched my belly, its round hard curve. Four months in, the baby fluttered, sending shivers throughout my limbs. I ran as fast as I could all the way home.

CHAPTER THIRTY-SEVEN

As summer deepened, Donny started showing an interest in running with me. Some evenings, he laced his sneakers, traded his kippah for a baseball cap, and we stamped along the sidewalks of our neighborhood at a slower pace, our twin smiles radiating in the twilight. I couldn't get enough food—finishing the kids' mac and cheese straight out of the pot, nibbling at the last pieces of midweek pizza, making double the number of meatballs for a Tuesday dinner just to have more for myself.

The humidity was thick and heavy. Insects pulsed in the fading light. One evening, I knocked on Batya's door. "Come for a walk with me," I said.

She nodded and stepped outside. "Tzvi! I'm going for a walk with Sally. Be back soon."

We walked in silence at first, our skirts swishing against our tights. "I miss you," I said. "I want us to get back to where we were."

She sighed. "Of course! I miss you, too."

"I have some news."

She stopped walking and turned to face me.

"I'm expecting."

Her hands flew to her face, her eyes on fire. "Really! Oh, Sally! That is wonderful news!" She pulled me into a hug, and we swayed in each other's embrace. Then she pulled back, there was a look of alarm on her face. "Is it Barry's?"

I looked from side to side, up and down the street, but didn't see anyone we knew.

"Are you crazy? Yes, of course," I hissed.

"I had to ask," she said.

"No, you didn't." I began walking, at a faster pace, and she double stepped to keep up. "That wasn't very nice."

"I'm sorry," she said.

We turned down another street. A lone tree sprouted from the concrete in the middle of the block. The houses matched ours—two-story, brick and siding, with lazy shutters and open lawns, hedged by sculpted shrubs hugging the front. Some had short concrete porches.

"Slow down." She reached a hand for my arm. "Seriously. I *am* sorry, Sally. I didn't mean to overstep."

"Like you've never made a mistake?"

"Of course I have! I make mistakes all the time! And I beg Hashem for forgiveness and make amends with my fellow humans. I am imperfect. We all are."

"What a nice little speech," I jeered.

In all the years we'd been friends, we had never been so distant. We walked at a good clip now, sweat dotting my face and dripping down my back. The hair beneath my tichel grew damp.

Then anger gave way to sadness, and I stopped abruptly, doubling over, heaving breaths, fighting tears. "You are my only friend," I spat. "The only one left. And even you are gone."

"What are you talking about?" She lay a hand on my shoulder.

"No one invites us for Shabbat. Since the thing with Mr. Fineman. And my one transgression—*one!*—is eating me alive. My stomach is a ball of knots, and I can't free myself from it. You cannot turn on me, too."

"Sal..." She rubbed my shoulder. "I would never turn on you. We are friends for life, no matter what."

I swiped at my eyes, determined not to cry on the street and give everyone more fodder. Someone was always watching.

"Then cut it out," I spat. Anger could steel away the tears. *Stay angry.*

"Stop reminding me how royally I fucked up," I said.

She opened her mouth to speak, but I thwarted the attempt. "Don't remind me about my language, not now, Bat," I said. "I am entitled this once. Let it go."

She chuckled. "I have become a mother hen, haven't I?"

I joined her in laughter. The tears had subsided, and I could breathe again. "Yes, you have."

We resumed walking, this time at a more normal pace.

"Seriously, though. People have been talking, Sally. This Fineman thing—they're blaming you."

I nodded. "I know," I said. "Easier than admitting what is really going on."

Our steps were feather-soft on the hard ground. The heat kept most people inside, wrapped in the comfort of their buzzing air-conditioning units.

"There are others, you know," I said. "Two other boys who Donny mentioned, probably more."

"Those poor children," she said. "What an evil man."

"And the adults would rather bury their heads in the sand than bring down a scandal on the community by firing a predatory teacher," I spat. I pictured Donny's sweet face, his bruised, swollen knuckles, his quiet contemplation alone in his bedroom then the immediate and total trans-formation after I pulled him from that wretched school.

I felt all the air go out of me. "I can't do this," I said.

Batya put a hand on my arm. "What?"

"I can't live for the community," I said. "I can't be constantly watched and judged. It's just too much. I can't take it anymore. I have defended this community to my family, to my old friends, and the community doesn't even have my back. It seems like a very unhealthy relationship." My voice was quiet, almost a whisper.

Batya leaned in. "You know how this goes," she said softly, stroking my back. My shirt clung to my back. "It's the way it is. You walk the line, or you can't fit in. I don't like it, but I accept it. I chose it. As did you."

"I chose the special and beautiful parts—Shabbat and the generosity of people opening their homes to me, and I chose Barry," I said. "I did not choose small-mindedness and gossip and judgment and open stares and quiet glares in synagogue. I never imagined any of those things came with the package."

"In time, they'll let you back in," she said. "If you want them to. They'll just need to forget about this Fineman thing."

"I'm not sure I can let it go," I said. "I don't think any of us should. The Torah does not condone abuse."

She put a hand on my belly. I lay my hand over hers. The veins beneath her skin were tight cords. I ran my fingers over them. "You need water," I said. "Let's go home."

"Before we do..." She stood so close I could feel her hot breath on my skin. "You are my best friend. I love you, and I don't want to see you hurt."

"I know," I said, wrapping my arms around her. I closed my eyes and inhaled her scent—vanilla lotion and lemon soap and the same sharp laundry detergent I used.

CHAPTER THIRTY-EIGHT

John didn't disappear. Somehow, he found my new email and pinged my inbox daily. He called and left messages, which I erased without listening. He texted late at night and early in the morning, begging me to talk to him, to meet up one last time, to give him another chance, to consider that he was sincere in his feelings and this time was different. I blocked his number on my phone to stop the calls and texts. I deleted his emails, sent them into my spam folder.

Some nights, I thought I saw him on the street. Hovering behind a tree, hiding inside his car, ducking behind the hedges of a neighbor's house. I wondered if I was imagining things or if he was really there. He would do something like that. I wracked my brain to remember any indications of an obsessive side to him when we were dating, to anyone or anything he had trailed after long past appropriate, but I couldn't pinpoint anything. It had been too many years.

And then, one day, he was knocking at my door when Barry was at the office. All the kids were at camp, even Donny, and I was tidying the house—sweeping the kitchen, emptying the dishwasher, slicing cucumbers and carrots for after-camp snacks.

"You can't be here," I spat through the screen door. I refused to open it. "People will see you."

"Yes, they will, so let me in."

I slammed the door and bolted it.

He went around to the back and knocked at the kitchen door. From her yard, Batya could see straight into mine. I shook my head at him. I opened the window and said, "Go away. I'll call the police."

"You want that? A scandal in the neighborhood? Everyone will talk."

"About the man who stalked me," I said. "Leave, John."

But he didn't go. He stood at the door. I ducked into the interior of the house, pacing, my arms hugging my body. Could I hide there until he left? Or would he stay, knocking and calling, until someone noticed? Maybe Batya, coming out to investigate. The last thing I needed.

I strode back to the door and unlatched it, ushering him in.

"Sit." I pointed to the table. "You have five minutes. And then I swear, you must leave and you can never return. Never. Do you hear me?"

He stared at my stomach. "Are you...?"

"Yes."

"Is it mine?" His eyes danced with light, his mouth a wide smile.

"Nope."

"How can you know?"

"Because I know. And the doctor confirmed the date of conception. Long before you arrived."

He chewed his lip, continuing to stare, breathing audibly through his nose.

"I don't believe you," he said.

"You don't have to. You just have to go," I said.

He shook his head. "Sally, this could be a fresh start. It could be our chance." He reached for me, but I retreated, bumping against the counter. I folded my arms in front of my chest.

"My husband and I are expecting a fourth child," I said. "You have no role here. You do not belong here. I do not want you here. How can I make it more clear to you?"

I strode to the door and pulled it open. "You and I never happened," I said. "Now, please leave my house. And do not contact me again."

"This isn't over," he said.

"Yes, it is."

He shook his head as he left.

I locked the door behind him and sank into a kitchen chair, shaking. I counted the days in my head. I had conceived in late April, and John and I slept together in May. There was no doubt whose baby this was. I'd done the math already. This baby was Barry's, no question.

Right?

Tears leaked down my cheeks. All the hiding and sneaking and late-night emails and secrets kept from my husband came pouring out in hot, salty tears. All the months of being strong for everyone else, of being alone on Shabbat, of being the community outcast, collapsed my shoulders. My back ached, and I rubbed slow circles at the base of my spine. I lay my head against the cool wood of the table, trails of tears streaking the light burnished oak darker.

I would have to tell Barry. Who knew what John would do! Even if he contested the baby's paternity, knowing full well it was Barry's without a shadow of a doubt, the mere question of it would rankle Barry and lurch our marriage into a precarious place. John's resolve was strong, his imagination fierce. And I was no match for him.

CHAPTER THIRTY-NINE

I needed the park as much as the kids did after camp that day, though the afternoon was long and heavy with heat. I laid a blanket under a tree and pulled from my bag plastic bags of cucumbers and carrots with packets of hummus, along with a container of cleaned, trimmed strawberries. The kids dove in with sweaty hands, stuffing their mouths.

"What's the rush?" I chided. "You don't want to choke."

Camp was full of art projects and playground time and books and story-telling and music and dancing. Donny's camp was more like school, but he had been home since April, so he was hungry for time with friends. I chose a different camp than his previous school, ensuring that the counselors would be teens and twentysomethings from the community, rather than the austere teachers of the academic year, so he agreed to go. He was eager to be among other boys his age, to run and play. As much as I needed to belong, my children needed it even more.

Donny's dark hair flopped onto his forehead, his kippah tilted to the back of his head. Of all my children, he was the one who most resembled Barry. Shira and Simi had lighter hair and golden skin, like me. But there was something similar in all their faces, something I could not put my finger on but which, in a family picture, made it clear that we were a unit, the same blood coursing through our veins. A slope of the nose, the angle of a cheekbone, the way a smile tilted in a particular way. We were connected on a deep level. Here was the proof of my bond to Barry, and

I wanted to preserve it at all costs. This baby would have the same tiny resemblances, the same tender details. The same merged DNA from my husband and me.

Done with their snacks, the kids reached out open palms as I spritzed hand sanitizer to clean away the stickiness and strawberry stains. They ran off as they rubbed their hands together, Simi calling, "The swings, Mommy! Come to the swings with me!"

I secured the lid on the now-empty container and stuffed it and the empty plastic bags into my tote. Standing, I folded the blanket and pushed it into the bag as well, ambling over to meet my son. Donny held his kippah with one hand as he hung his knees over a bar high on the rounded jungle gym, dangling his torso upside down. Shira was climbing the ladder of the slide, whisking down it with her arms outstretched then clambering back up the steps to go again. Both of them had made friends in the park, and they chattered as they played.

I lifted Simi into one of the rubber basket swings and pushed him from behind. His little hands clenched the top of the seat. The wind lifted his silky curls. He smiled broadly, teeth showing, his mouth ajar, every so often a high-pitched *wheeeee* escaping his plump lips. My phone buzzed. I gave Simi a hefty push then bent down to grab it.

I didn't recognize the number. My skin prickled. I knew who it was. I clicked the phone off and dropped it in my bag.

It was a hot day, with white sun. A Chicago summer could feel as still as a swamp and as heavy. The sun bore down, heating the ground, steaming the air. Tendrils of sweat trailed down Simi's cheeks. Even his hair was matted with damp. But I felt cold.

"Mommy, push!" Simi urged.

I patted his head. "Three more pushes," I said. "Count them for me."

His little voice called out one, two, and three as I hefted him hard and the swing lifted, bumping into the air, then swung back. He giggled and gripped harder as he went high, high and then down, down. Eventually, I stopped pushing and let the swing slow on its own, giving him a last few minutes of sweet air and open sun before lifting him out.

"Let's get your sister and brother and go home," I said.

He galloped off to his siblings as I gathered my bags.

All the voices and city sounds—car horns beeping, doors slamming, footsteps trampling grass, the whine of traffic—buzzed into white noise as I walked toward the kids. Donny had rolled his shirtsleeves up to his elbows. The armpits were stained with sweat. Shira's face was red.

"Time for good, long baths," I said.

They wilted into me, and my arms wrapped around my precious children, as much to hold myself up as to comfort them, too.

CHAPTER FORTY

When I was becoming religious, I remembered Shiri asking again and again if this was what I wanted. "There is no harm in not following this path," she'd said. "I won't be mad at you if you change your mind. We'll still be friends."

I hadn't realized at the time how generous she was being and how unusual such a statement was in this world. In the years since I had married Barry and immersed myself in the fabric of the community, I had not heard anyone say anything remotely similar. It was common to hear dismay, even fury about someone going "off the derech." As if something was wrong with the person pursuing a less-religious path, a path different from the one we followed, for there were religious Jews who lived in a variety of communities in Chicago and around the world. I had lost count of how many times women like Shiri Schwartz or even the women of my tehillim group tsk-tsked at mention of someone's grown child choosing to daven in Lincoln Park, at the "modern" Orthodox congregation there.

"They don't even have a proper *mechitzah*! Just plants down the center of the sanctuary, at waist height—everyone can see everything!"

"The women carry the Torah in their section on Shabbat. Can you imagine?"

"The girls can have bat mitzvahs where they read Torah if no men are present—it's a shanda!"

I had heard of modern Orthodox Jews but never met any, since I went from secular suburbia to fast-lane frum. I imagined it as a hybrid of the worlds I knew—observing Shabbat but attending regular universities. Maybe the girls even wore pants. What I knew for sure was that it was not an acceptable form of religious Judaism to my friends and neighbors. It was too loose, and a slippery slope inevitably led to a lack of religion, a discarding of *mitzvot*, and one day, a lawless life with no hope of return, future grandchildren and great-grandchildren who weren't even Jewish. I wondered if that community would be as harsh and judgmental as mine had been to me over these last months.

When camp ended, we all felt lazy in the summer heat. It was the nine days before *Tisha b'Av*, a mournful time on the Jewish calendar, when we did not swim, took only cold showers and did not celebrate weddings or mitzvahs or even engagements. The people of my community wouldn't travel during the three weeks before Tisha b'Av, which was a solemn 25-hour fast day in the hottest part of the summer, a day on which both Temples in Jerusalem had been destroyed thousands of years earlier. It was also the day when Hitler announced his Final Solution to rid the earth of Jews. All bad things happened to the Jews during this time, so we were extra careful. I did not do laundry during the nine days. It piled up in all the hampers and on the floor of the laundry room, waiting for this uncomfortable time to end and a resumption of regular life. I was down to my least favorite skirts and shirts, and I could not run because all my workout clothes stank from use. Plus, everything had grown tight around my middle.

Jewish life was an exercise in extremes. Absolute darkness gave way to bright, hopeful light. The lifecycle calendar swayed like a pendulum, and we rode it, holding on for dear life. During the nine days, I felt sad, depressed, forlorn, like I had fallen down a well and could not gain purchase to climb out. But then, Tisha b'Av ended and everything became clean and folded and good things were possible again. Such startling despair! Such boundless hope!

Camp had been a success for Donny, but the matter of school had yet to be resolved. Mr. Fineman remained in the employ of the yeshiva, and the headmaster had abandoned our complaint.

My son was changing every day. He was at least two inches taller than he had been at his doctor checkup the previous year. He'd asked more than once where he would go to school in the fall, pleading with me to stay home, to continue learning by my side and, then in the same breath, asking when he could play with friends. I had never pictured myself as a home-schooler. Sure, I had the hippie hair and long skirts that usually went with the image, but I believed in the education system. I had grown up at posh private schools, huddled into books and obedient to my teachers, soaking up learning like it was a lifeline. I wanted my children to be educated, to have possibilities, but even I knew that the Jewish schools lacked a certain worldliness that was essential for making a sustainable life. My position in the community was already tenuous. If I chose a secular school for my son, we would never squeeze back into the fold. I hadn't even broached the idea with Barry, who was a product of Jewish schools all his life.

One night, I made a thick vegetable lasagna and bright summer salad with slivered almonds, blueberries and hearts of palm, and set the table with candles and flowers.

"It's so pretty, Mommy!" Shira exclaimed, folding the napkins into triangles and stuffing them into the water glasses.

I smiled at her and stroked her soft hair.

The kids ate quickly and left in a rush to play outside as the evening cooled the yard.

"Clear your plates!" I called.

They doubled back, dropped plates and cutlery in the sink, then sprinted into the yard.

"Close the screen!"

"And then there were two," I said to Barry.

"It's always nice to be alone with you," he said.

I swallowed. "So we have to talk about Donny and school."

"Oh. It's a setup."

"Bare," I pleaded. "Come on. We have to decide something."

He nodded.

"I'm not pushing you to reopen the thing with the teacher, but I can't send him back there."

"I know," he said. "So I guess this means we are done with that school? Even for Simi? Or any other children..."

"Absolutely," I said.

"Where to send him, then? There are only so many options."

I sucked on my lip. "We can look outside the community," I said.

"A secular school?"

"I can keep homeschooling him," I offered.

"Not indefinitely, Sal," he said. "At some point, he'll need a higher level of instruction. I guess we could keep doing this until then, maybe consider sending him away for high school, to a yeshiva."

"No way," I insisted. "My kids stay home until high school graduation. Not negotiable."

He humphed a sigh, tilting his head back and staring at the ceiling.

"We're also going to have to consider our standing in this community, Bare," I said. "We are still persona non grata."

"That's not going to change if you homeschool," he smirked. "We'll become *that family*. That family of weirdos."

"I already am," I said in a quiet voice.

"What?"

"You don't see it, Bare, because you fit, but I don't. It's hard enough to be a BT. People are blaming me for the Fineman thing. It's easier to blame a woman, and a *ba'alat teshuvah*, than to admit to a problem in the *kehillah*."

"Who?"

"Tova said something a couple months ago, a snide remark about my sheitel. Mrs. Fineman accosted me in the grocery—with Donny watching! Batya says people are talking."

I moved from the chair into his lap, pulling his hand to my belly. "Let me ask you something," I said. "If I were less religious, would you still want me?"

"Are you planning something that I don't know about?" he asked, nuzzling into my shoulder.

"No," I said. "But if we can't ever get back into the good graces of this community, I don't want to be an island alone. It's not good for the kids. They need friends. *We* need friends.

"There is going to be another little one soon," I said. "And maybe more after that. There is you, and me, and these kids. No one else matters."

"Are you asking me to stop being religious? Because that is not an option," he said. "It's all I've known, and besides, I believe this is the best way to live. I won't drop Yiddishkeit."

"I'm not asking you to. I don't want to! But is our love strong enough to find another community where we would both fit, both feel like we belong?"

"What community? What other place?"

"I don't know yet, but if I find one, will you be open to it?"

He sighed. "I honestly don't know," he said. "This community, this place, makes sense to me."

"More than this?" I said, pointing to him and back to me.

He shook his head. "No. You are my home, Sally," he said. "*Wither you goest, I will go.*"

Chapter Forty-One

When I first became religious, I was surprised to learn there were six fast days on the Jewish calendar. I had only known about Yom Kippur, and while Jews around the world took that day seriously, abstaining from food and drink as we atoned for our sins, I had not known about the others. Four were sunup to sundown, known as minor fast days, and then there was Tisha b'Av, another 25-hour whopper of self-flagellation, where we refrained from food, drink, cleansing and intimacy. While Yom Kippur was onerous, it made sense to me—clearing the focus from mundane necessities like eating or drinking or focusing on the superficial self, to go deep, ponder behavior and attitude and interaction and purpose. Cleansing yourself of past mistakes so you wouldn't make them again in the future. A soul cleanse *and* a body cleanse.

But in the summer heat, Tisha b'Av seemed like a punishment. Rabbis insisted that both holy Temples in Jerusalem had been destroyed due to *sinat chinam*, baseless hatred between Jews, and so while on Yom Kippur we turned inward to purify our souls and contemplate our actions and motivations, on Tisha b'Av, we were chastised for transgressions so far in the past that they felt unrelatable. No one thought about their own behavior today as continuing ancient examples of intolerance of fellow Jews. I wanted to wag my finger at my brethren and point out that the way they were ostracizing my children and me now pretty much fit the definition of sinat chinam to a T.

We were taught that the soul of every Jew alive today stood at Mt. Sinai as God gave Moses the commandments, that we were all witness to the formation of our people. If the brilliance of the Torah lived in us since the moment it was given, then it wasn't such a stretch to believe the gossip and pettiness of Jews long ago could live in us, too.

Observing fast days as a mother was the ultimate cruelty, having to prepare food for my children when I could not consume any of it myself. The doctor had advised me not to fast, out of concern for my low weight and pregnancy, and when I insisted it would be safe, he pleaded with me to at least drink water throughout the day, and if I felt dizzy or nauseous, to eat. Barry would be in shul, sitting on the floor and joining in the plaintive wail of melancholy created by the mournful reading of *Eicha*, the Book of Lamentations.

He flitted back and forth between synagogue and home, thankful that we were permitted to drive on this day, unlike on Yom Kippur, and when he was home, he watched Tisha b'Av services in Jerusalem via YouTube or Torah scholars' recorded lectures. It was too hot even for the kids to play outside, so we all cooped up in the house, the TV droning on with an annoying stream of Elmo and Arthur and the plaintive wail of rabbis at the Western Wall.

So when someone knocked on the door, I was grateful for the reprieve from boredom.

Until I saw who it was.

"You can't be here," I hissed at John, who stood on our porch in dark jeans and a fitted blue T-shirt. My neighbors, if they were looking, would know immediately that this man did not belong to our tribe.

"Everyone is home—it's a fast day. What are you thinking?"

I pushed the door to close it, but he thrust his foot over the lintel. The door banged against his shoe. "If everyone is here, perhaps we can have a family confab," he said.

"No way," I said. "Please, John. I need you to leave."

"I know you do," he said. "The thing is, I don't want to leave."

He pushed inside the house. The kids clamored over to meet the guest then halted, sensing my tension. "Go play," I demanded, the firmness of my voice warning them not to protest. They fled to the family room, where the TV spilled its perpetual cheeriness but otherwise remained silent as they strained to listen.

"In here." I waved John into the dining room, farthest from the hub of the house, hopefully out of earshot of the kids. Barry was in the study, watching the bobbing prayers of so many black hats.

"Have you told him?" John asked.

I shook my head.

John's eyes were bright with disbelief, rage—passion? "Maybe I should," he said.

"Have you lost all sense of reason?" I hissed, grabbing his arm to hold him still. "Think for a minute. You're acting crazy. Do you really think chasing me, breaking up my family, will make me choose you?"

He didn't blink, holding his breath, his eyes serious.

"It's no longer about you and me," he said. "There's a baby now, and it's mine. If I can't have you, at least I can have this child."

"It's not yours."

"Yeah, well, I don't believe you."

"A paternity test will prove it, John," I said. "And then? What happens when you confirm this baby is not yours." I spoke slowly through clenched teeth, as if I were explaining a complicated concept to a young child.

His breathing ragged, he seemed at a loss for words.

"What then?" I loosened my grip on his arm. "Don't turn my children's world upside down," I pleaded.

His eyes shone. All the fight had drained out of him. I steered him toward the door. "Go," I said. "If you really love me, leave me alone."

He stepped outside. I closed the door behind him, clicking the bolt.

In the kitchen, I gulped water, no longer caring about the protocols of the day. Over my shoulder, I sensed a presence. Barry.

"Who was that?"

I swallowed. "We need to talk."

My heart thumped like a rabbit's tail pounding the ground. The air conditioning whirred outside, working overtime in the oppressive heat to blow cool air into every room. I could not believe the children had sat quietly for so much of the day; they were listening to everything.

I pointed to a chair, put a hand over his. He stared at my fingers. "Who was that, Sally?" he repeated.

"John Hogan," I said.

"The guy you dated in college?"

I nodded, curling my top lip into my bottom one.

"What was he doing here? How does he know where we live?"

I couldn't hold back the tears. They spilled onto my cheeks, sprinkling the table. "I love you, Barry," I said.

He pulled his hand out from under mine and placed it in his lap, staring at me all the while.

"I made a mistake. One mistake."

My heart thundered. "He found me on Facebook, and we started emailing. It was innocent at first. I was just excited to reconnect with people from my past. And I wasn't even going to accept his request. But then we had that fight and we were distant for weeks and I was lonely. We started reminiscing, he asked how I had become religious, and then he wanted to meet up. You and I were so distant, and I was lonely and angry. I knew that I shouldn't meet him. And I wanted to tell you, honestly I did, but then I was afraid you'd leave me if you knew. I couldn't let that happen. You are my everything. My whole world."

Tears streaked my face. My nose was running. I gasped in hiccups, trying to calm down.

Barry sighed.

"I have just one question," he said.

"Only once," I said.

His eyes went wide. "You slept with him?"

I gulped. "I'm not a cheater, Barry. I love only you. It was after the thing with Fineman, and I was so angry, and he met me for a run, and it just happened."

He threaded his hands through his hair. "Geez, Sally, it can't *just happen*. I'm not a fool."

"I regretted it immediately," I rushed. "Batya said I should tell you, but I didn't want to ruin everything, I didn't want you to leave me."

"Batya knows?"

I froze.

"I didn't plan to tell her," I said. "She pulled it out of me. You know how she is."

"Sounds like you didn't plan a lot of things. Do you believe any of this is your fault?"

"Of course it is! It's all my fault. My God, Barry, I was horribly wrong, and I wish I had never even answered his email or accepted his friend request. I've blocked him and changed my email even. He just keeps showing up."

"Keeps?"

"I even threatened him with a police order to stay away from me, and that didn't scare him off," I said.

"No, it did not," he said.

"Please don't leave me, Barry." I reached for his hands, but he recoiled. "I will do anything to show you that you are my world, my whole heart."

He looked at my belly.

"And the baby?"

"Unequivocally yours," I said.

"You're sure?"

"One hundred percent," I said. "I did the math. There is no way this baby is his."

"But he believes it is." He was quiet.

"I'm so sorry Barry," I said. "It was a complete indiscretion. I don't know what I was thinking. I am not someone who cheats."

"Well, apparently that is no longer true," he said.

I went cold.

"What's done is done. I'm not leaving you. But it is going to take a long time to forgive you. If I even can."

"You are my home, Barry," I cried, gulping between sobs. "I don't want anyone else. I can't lose you."

I wanted to reach for him, to stroke his soft skin, to erase the hurt and betrayal in his sad eyes. I wanted him to pull me to him and say he understood, that we are all human, even as I knew that he would never make such a mistake.

I stared into his penetrating eyes. They were dark and direct, strong but cold. Barry stared straight at me, as if his gaze sent a message, set some ground rules. They bore into my skin, like a burn that feels cold.

"I am yours entirely," I whispered, shivering.

"Yes, you are," he said, pushing his chair back from the table and getting up.

He strode into the family room and sat on the couch with the kids, who surrounded him with little hands and high voices and a running stream of chatter. *Tati! I love you, Tati! How is your fast going? I missed you! Hold my hand. I want you, Tati!* Simi climbed into his lap, nudging his curly head under Barry's arm to drape it around himself. Shira sidled up close, and Donny sat at his feet. Barry leaned into our children, closing his eyes. *Our children.* These three precious souls we had brought down from Heaven onto the tactile earth, to walk beside us, to carry on beyond us. They were my home. I watched them from afar, afraid to lose everything.

CHAPTER FORTY-TWO

The sun took its time sinking into the distance, cloaking the trees and the houses in gradual darkness. The night came in pinks and yellows, then grays and browns, and finally the warm darkness that is at once comforting and frightening. I switched on lights in every room of the house, following the kids' dragging footsteps up to their bedrooms. I could not bathe them until the day was complete, could not start the mountains of laundry until the middle of the next day, because as history told it, the fires that destroyed the Temple burned into another day, and so we extended our mournful time even longer.

It frustrated and also delighted me how extreme and absolute our observances were. When I first became religious, I loved how a wedding went on for hours, the guests tirelessly entertaining bride and groom, kallah and chatan, dancing before them, donning funny hats and parasols with streamers, performing the antics of a crowd set on uplifting this couple on their serious day, wary of letting them slip into fear for what lay ahead. After the wedding, Orthodox brides and grooms did not whisk off onto tropical honeymoons. For seven days, friends and family entertained them further, hosting dinners every night with at least a quorum of men to sing the mandatory blessings after a good meal. The newlyweds must know that they did not only have each other, but also the fabric of a tightly stitched community to support them in the hard years to come.

As heartily as we celebrated, we mourned equally intensely, to the same passionate depths. A funeral was quick, but the *shiva*—seven days of mourning—was long and dark and dreary. The mourners carried on beyond the seven days to at least thirty, if not a full year, halting all celebration and joy so they could properly bid farewell to their loved one, properly mourn a searing loss.

Tisha b'Av, and the days and weeks preceding it, were a time of collective mourning, when we as a people were destined to relive all the atrocities wreaked upon us or brought upon ourselves. There were many. Another realization that hit me hard when I committed to this life was just how many different nations and leaders throughout history had tried to annihilate us, how long and far we were forced to wander. It seemed endless, and we powerless to erase the ugliness from our communal past. We were a people perhaps chosen by God, but at a price—that we were destined to wander the earth alone, to be a nation among nations, a light unto others but alone with ourselves. It was at once beautiful and terrible.

It was no wonder that my mother left all this behind. Jewish identity was a heavy cloak that could suffocate you. Since I became a mother, I had been trying to imagine how she had felt toward me. Did she love me? Or was that an obligation? And as we sank into the rift that separated us from our community, I saw how my parents perched on a similar precariousness in their political world—one wrong move, one quick quip, one misstep, and they'd be cast out, never to be roped back in. My religious life paralleled their lives in ways that surprised me.

I tucked the kids into bed and kissed their soft heads. Barry and I would break the fast with a light dairy meal quietly in our kitchen. I had taken a nip of yogurt and granola in the early evening to stave off a threatening migraine. Now, a salmon and onion quiche awaited in a 300-degree oven. Outside, it had begun to rain. A steady tap beat the windows. The skies were opening up to douse the dreadful heat of the somber day. A late-summer Chicago rain was rare but welcome. We could breathe, melt in the embrace of cool air. I sliced a tomato onto a plate and set our places at the table, calmed by the rhythm of the storm.

That night, though I was tired, I lay awake, lulled by the rhythm of the rain. I stared at the ceiling, waiting for Barry to come to bed. By eleven, he hadn't come upstairs, and I wanted to find him, to reassure myself that he wasn't going to leave me, to find my way back to him. Damp from sweat, I shimmied out of my nightgown and wrapped a lightweight blanket around my body, creeping downstairs. A low lamp in the corner of the living room was the only light. Barry sat in the corner of the couch.

"What are you doing?" I perched beside him, pulling the blanket tight around me.

He reached for my leg, so pale it glowed. "Are you naked?"

I smiled, suddenly needing his touch.

I watched him in the dark, imagining the words in his head dancing across his face, a veritable chorus of ideas with bright colors and quick steps. Was he thinking about my betrayal? About the silence of our community? About how our world had literally turned upside down? Was he remembering just a few months earlier, when everything was in flow, all of our friends calling with Shabbat invitations weekly, comparing it to the silence of the summer? Or maybe those were my thoughts. His head might be quiet, empty, feeling too much to form words. Or he might be regretting marrying me in the first place, confirming that to marry a woman who had not always been religious was the best way to oust yourself from the community you loved.

"I didn't mean for all this to happen," I said. "It just...happened."

"Sleeping with another man does not just happen," he said, but there was no anger in his voice, only quiet. His hand brushed up my leg. The house was chilly from central air. The damp of the storm had seeped inside, and I shivered into the blanket.

His fingers trailed higher on my thigh, under the fringe of the blanket. He reached between my legs, gently, slowly. My breath caught in my throat.

Was this a peace offering or an act of claiming? Whatever he intended, I melted into it, leaning back into the couch. As his fingers probed deeper, he stared into my face. I closed my eyes.

"No," he said. "Look at me."

My heartbeat a rapid drum, I gazed at my husband. Every nerve ending tingled. The wave reached up, up, threatening to consume me. He sat stone-still, watching me in the shadows. And then, it was over and I was quiet, and he withdrew his hand and set it on his lap and stared not at me but into the darkness.

"Barry," I whispered, reaching for him in the night.

"Shhh." He weaved his fingers between mine. Then he pulled me upstairs, wordless in the late night. In our room, he kissed me full on the mouth, pressing his tongue between my lips, and I tasted him, familiar and good and reassuring.

I dropped the blanket on the carpet and slid next to his warm body beneath the covers, curling into his chest. His arm came around me. Before long, I descended into dreams, my husband's careful breathing a sweet lullaby.

CHAPTER FORTY-THREE

The next day, the rain had stopped, and Barry was off to work while I tended to the mountain of laundry that had piled up over the last ten days. The kids wore old clothes, T-shirts just about ready for the charity bag, all that was left in their drawers. When the clock struck noon, I bolted to the laundry room, grabbing underwear and socks and shirts and shorts from the mountain of dirty clothing to dump into the machine. The first cycle set, the machine humming, I headed for the computer.

I opened Google and typed in the words *modern Orthodox*. I had gone so hard and fast into this community that I'd never taken the time to consider all the various ways that Jews were observant. Maybe there was a place where Barry and I could start over, find our way. Would he consider it? He was surprising me at every turn these days, so why not? It was worth a try.

My tehillim women scorned the modern Orthodox, insisting they weren't frum enough, too tied to the modern world. They didn't say it in so many words, of course, just hinted when someone's grown child left for another stop on the spiritual path. But I'd never been a follower until I joined this community. It might be time to reclaim my free-thinking soul, invite her to merge with the new me.

The first hit was Wikipedia—there was a Wikipedia page about this? Well, there was a page for just about everything. Or maybe it meant that modern Orthodoxy was a big enough thing to deserve a page. "...a movement within Orthodox Judaism that attempts to synthesize Jewish values and the observance of Jewish law with the secular, modern world."

I kept searching, landing on articles from a site called MyJewishLearning, the Jewish Agency for Israel, the *Jerusalem Post*. I expanded the search to *Modern Orthodox communities in America*. Another page listed 37 synagogues. I looked for one in Chicagoland and landed on Beth Sholom in Lakeview, north of here. *Good to know.*

The next day, I left the kids with Batya and plugged Beth Sholom into my GPS. The synagogue was close to the lake. I parked the minivan and listened to the scream of waves rushing for the shore. Sprinkles of splash hovered on the air. At the synagogue, I buzzed for entry.

"Yes?" called a nasal voice through an intercom.

"My name is Sally Lieberman," I said. "I'd like to meet with the rabbi."

Inside, it was quiet. My heels echoed on the gleaming floor. I followed the hallway to the first illuminated door and found the owner of the nasal voice, an older woman with a blue cotton hat tight over her hair. She wore a short-sleeved shirt and a lightweight skirt and smiled when I peered into the room.

"Hello," she said. "The rabbi will be with you in a moment."

I sat in one of three chairs opposite her desk.

"New in the neighborhood?"

I shook my head.

"From out of town?"

I'd chosen a yellow sundress with a tight white long-sleeved shirt underneath, sneakers with low socks, and I'd covered my head with a broad-brimmed sun hat, all my hair tucked up into it. "I live in Skokie," I said.

The light in the office was glaringly fluorescent, magnified by bare walls. It was an interior room with no windows. What must it be like to be cooped up in here all day with no sun? So close to Lake Michigan, and she couldn't even see it.

A man of average height bearing a broad smile emerged from an adjacent office. He wore a knitted kippah on his thin pate of hair, which was receding at the forehead.

"Welcome," he said, clasping his hands, purposely not offering one to me. Well, at least some things were familiar. Secretary with covered hair. Rabbi who doesn't shake hands with women.

I stood and smiled, walking the way he pointed, into the room from which he had come. He left the door open and motioned to the chairs opposite his desk as he eased into his own seat on the other side. "What can I do for you?"

"Well, I live in Skokie and daven at Bais Dovid, but I've been curious about what it means to be Modern Orthodox," I started.

He nodded, leaving space for me to keep talking.

I dropped my purse on the second chair and sat back, releasing a sigh. "I didn't grow up here," I said. "Or frum. And for a long time, it's been great. Until recently."

He nodded. "What happened?"

How much to tell him? His face was friendly, kind. I could walk out of here and never see the man again. He probably wouldn't remember my name. But if I liked this place, and if Barry were open to it, it might be our new spiritual home.

"My son was abused by his teacher—beaten," I started. "And when we tried to pursue it, we were shunned."

His hands on his desk were clasped, his face even, revealing no emotion. Beyond the door, the woman clacked at a keyboard.

"My husband has always been frum, but I grew up in the Detroit suburbs, and we did not do much in the way of Judaism. My mother is Jewish, but my father is not. I chose it in my early twenties, and it felt like coming home. I love living this way. I just don't love being cast out because I want to protect my son."

"I understand," he said in a gentle, soothing voice. "I'm so sorry that your son experienced this. It's a true hillul Hashem."

If we moved here, my grandparents would have to move, too. They would love an easier way of being observant, but they'd already uprooted their life once. Would they resent me for making them do it again? And could we even find a home, or two, within walking distance of this place, which was so heavily immersed in the city? I couldn't even contemplate what it would be like to pack up a house at the end of my pregnancy and move to a new enclave. My head spun.

"Mrs. Lieberman?"

I blinked. "Sorry. I'm curious about whether this could be a good community for us," I said.

"And your husband, is he open to a change?"

I shrugged. "Maybe?"

He smiled. "Why don't you start by spending a Shabbat with us. I can arrange home hospitality, or there is an inn down the block that has suites with full kitchens."

I nodded. "Yes, that would be wise," I said. "And my grandparents—they'd likely come with us, too."

"How nice! Of course, we'll find a family close to the shul to host them," he said. "Just let me know when, and we'll set everything up." He started to stand, but I reached out a hand to stop him.

"Rabbi... I don't know anything about what makes Modern Orthodoxy different from what we do," I said. "Some of the women I know..."

He sat back down. "There's a place for everyone within Judaism," he said. "We are as Orthodox as anyone else. We just see room in *Halachah* to merge traditional values with modern advances. It's sometimes harder to straddle both worlds, easier to not have any glimpse of how other people live. My congregation are committed to their Yiddishkeit and to their lives. It isn't fair to judge how anyone observes, but people are only human. We can't help it."

I nodded. I wasn't sure what he was saying really, but it sounded nice. My head buzzed with the thought of leaving everything and everyone I knew. Shiri, my surrogate mother. Batya, my best friend and neighbor.

"Thank you for seeing me," I said.

"Anytime," he said. "Let me know when you're ready to join us for Shabbat."

Chapter Forty-Four

Over the next few weeks, people smiled at me on the street as I jogged past. They seemed friendlier, like the veil of distance had finally lifted. I was growing bigger with the new baby and knew my days of hard running were numbered. I went slowly along the sidewalk, choosing even terrain to make sure I could keep my balance. No more grassy knolls until after the birth. I bought a new pair of trainers, replacing the well-trod sneakers whose treads were practically smooth from overuse. The phone rang with Shabbat invitations. It was a relief to be invited again, and I started to believe that maybe we could weave our way back into the embrace of the community. Best of all, I heard nothing from John.

The High Holidays would be late this year, so we planned a trip to northern Michigan for early September. Growing up, that had been a favorite summer getaway for many Detroit families, and it was something I introduced to Barry early in our marriage. I packed plastic totes full of kosher food, baked challah to take with us, made and froze roast beef and chicken and lasagna to transport. Simi and Shira started school, and I resumed homeschooling Donny, ordering Waldorf-inspired books online to guide my teaching, along with Hebrew and Torah tomes. The trip would be two weeks after the start of the new school year. I didn't mind taking the little ones out of school—they wouldn't miss much from nursery and first grade, and Donny could learn wherever we were.

The day before the trip, Donny and I walked through the grocery, filling the cart with cereal, milk, yogurt, fruit, rolls and cookies, more food than we would need for a week on the northern shores of Lake Michigan in a town called Glen Arbor, not far from Sleeping Bear Dunes. The forecast promised sunshine and warmer-than-usual temperatures for the time of year, but the summer rush would have ended so the town would be quiet and welcoming. I couldn't wait to feel brisk wind on my face and soft sand under my feet, cool nights and quiet skies. Out of the watchful eye of the community, I might uncover my hair and be freer with my clothing choices if Barry was okay with it. Over the last few months, he kept surprising me. I now believed we could face anything together.

But at home in my neighborhood, I wore the uniform of the community—long skirt, long sleeves, every hair tucked into a tichel, its shiny edges like a shelter. I smiled at women I knew, waving hello, blending in as if it were that easy.

At home, I unloaded the groceries and packed everything into totes and coolers before collecting Simi and Shira from school. We would leave the city late that afternoon, driving north along the eastern edge of Lake Michigan. It would take about six hours, not counting bathroom stops. I had ordered pizza and French fries from Main Pizza Chalavi on Touhy Street to pick up on our way out of town. We'd eat in the car and hope to reach the rental house by 10, since we lost an hour crossing over into the Eastern time zone. I sifted through the mail before leaving to get the kids, tossing advertising mailers and junk mail and shoving everything else into my purse to sift through on the drive north.

By three, I had retrieved Simi and Shira and carted everyone home for quick baths. "Watch him." I settled Donny in the bathroom with Simi in the bath, splashing, blowing bubbles and *vrooming* a plastic boat over the water. Donny heaved a sigh and leaned onto his palms. "Thank you." I winked.

Shira sat on the carpet of her room, surveying her open suitcase. Sparkly scarves and necklaces lay atop dresses, shirts and shorts.

"It'll be colder up there," I said. "You may not want the shorts."

She nodded. "I love this dress." She pointed to a pink and blue paisley with a poofy tulle skirt.

"A bit dressy for Up North, don't you think?"

She nodded again.

"You want comfy clothes, honey, that you don't mind getting dirty. We'll be outside a lot."

I folded the clothes she chose, tucking them into her suitcase. "Pajamas?"

She pulled open a drawer, drawing out two pairs of flannels.

Finally, her suitcase was full, and I leaned on it to zip it closed. "Take it downstairs, please, and put it by the door."

By the time I returned to the bathroom, the floor was drenched. I laid out towels to mop it up. "You're relieved from your duty," I said, saluting Donny. "Grab your blankie or your teddy bear—whatever you want in the car and to sleep with up there."

Earlier that week, I'd felt the baby flutter, like butterflies flapping their delicate wings inside my skin. I loved that feeling of new awakening, like the baby and I were talking in a way that no one else in the world could access. I felt protective, in love. It fluttered now, and I stood in my kids' bathroom, palms cupping my belly, closing my eyes to commune with this gift-child.

"Mommy, I'm ready," Simi called.

My eyes flew open. He stood in the bath, arms outreached, his body slick with water.

I grabbed a towel and reached a hand to help him step from the tub, bending to free the drain plug. The water swirled down and away. Simi peered at the spiraling water disappearing down the drain. "It's cool, isn't it," I said.

He nodded, shaking off drops of water as he did so.

"Let's snuggle you in," I said, wrapping a towel around him, and then my arms, in a tight embrace. He leaned closer. "Mmmmm," I said. "Do you want to wear pajamas for the drive?"

He nodded, wrested free of the towel and of me, and ran naked to his room, screeching. They would sleep well on the drive up.

Barry was home a half hour later, with pizzas and fries, and we stacked the suitcases and totes in the car until the trunk was full and we had to wedge items under seats for the kids to rest their feet on. Every inch of the car was filled with clothing and cutlery, paper goods, pots and pans, prepared foods, frozen dishes, and ingredients for breakfasts and snacks and quick lunches. Traveling while kosher was never easy, especially if we wanted to go somewhere off the Orthodox path.

We backed out of the driveway and headed for the highway. I tuned the radio to a soft classical station and relaxed. The car vibrated, and I found the motion soothing. I closed my eyes. Barry reached a hand over and brushed my arm.

It was dark when we arrived in Glen Arbor, the streets quiet, the night sky glistening with uninterrupted stars. The waves of Lake Michigan rolled in and retreated, like gentle thunder.

"Can we look at it for a minute before going in?" I whispered to Barry, who turned the car onto a tree-lined road that ended in a beach at the Glen Haven Historic Village. A half dozen single-story clapboard buildings led to a thin lip of beach and the roaring freshwater lake. The moon was bright, and in the distance, I could just make out the hulk of the sleeping Manitou Islands. Barry pulled into a spot in the empty parking lot, rolled down the windows, and killed the motor.

"We can leave the car doors open," I said, nodding to our sleeping children.

Barry opened his door and stepped out. I joined him, leaning against the car, hip to hip with my husband. His hair fluttered in the night air. I reached up and pulled on his curls. He leaned his head to mine. I nestled against his cheek. He turned to me, grazing my face with his nose, reaching a hand to my belly and palming over it.

"Has the baby moved much?"

I nodded. "Little butterfly kisses," I said, moving my nose side to side against his skin. His breath quickened.

"Temptress," he said.

I nodded. "I'm glad we took this week away," I said. "I needed it. We all did."

"Are you still thinking about a different community?" he asked in a sober voice. I'd told him about Beth Sholom. I would have no more secrets between us.

I shrugged. "I don't know. It feels like we're returning to the fold. Maybe we don't need to?"

"Let's see how the *chagim* go," he said. "I'm not opposed, but not fully onboard either. It's an awful ordeal to move, Sal."

I nodded. "And there's my grandparents to think of."

"And my parents—geez, they will not be happy if we leave," he said.

"Whatever we do, Bare, I'm glad you chose me," I said.

He patted my belly.

"You haven't heard anything from him?"

I shook my head. "Nothing." I laughed feebly. "It's kind of concerning actually." I snorted as if to shrug it off, but I was a little worried by John's absolute and total silence.

Barry tilted his head in a question.

"He was just so ardent," I said. "I mean, to the point of stalking. Showing up at our house? Like he lived in a state of unreality. I can't believe he would just drop it and disappear. It was like something took hold of him and wouldn't let go. But I hope that's all we'll hear from him."

The lake swelled and fell. Small waves licked at the sandy shore. There were hiking trails bordering this slip of land made up of shifting sands.

They were hard to climb and blazing hot in a bright sun but cooled by the night. Across the open expanse of lake and dune, a powerful wind sifted through the trees, whispering as it swept across the landscape.

Barry squeezed my hand. "No more John Hogan," he said. "Let's be here." He kissed my cheek, snaked an arm around my shoulders and pulled me close. In the moonlight, shadows danced along his jaw.

The rental house sat at the end of a cul-de-sac, with a gravel driveway and an attached garage that could fit two cars easily plus kayaks, rafts, paddles and other outdoor equipment. It was swept clean and free of dust. I wished my own house could be so flawless.

I punched the code into the keypad on the front door like the owner had instructed and walked into a spacious great room, with plush couches and thick carpet. Cooking and dining areas melded into one big space, and high windows silhouetted a full bright moon. Barry carried a sleeping Simi into the house, laying him on a bed in the room the boys would share. I tapped Shira and Donny, rousing them enough to stumble into the house and crawl into bed. I left the car doors open. In this small northern town, we needn't worry about theft or assault. It was quiet and welcoming, a perfect retreat.

After the kids were tucked into their beds, with nightlights on in case they woke and became startled by their new surroundings, Barry and I emptied the car. I brought in suitcases, depositing them in various rooms. He hefted totes, coolers and grocery bags into the kitchen, setting everything on the counters under pendant lights. I unpacked the food, putting perishables in the fridge or freezer, stacking dishes and cookware on the counters, tucking packaged snacks into cupboards.

It was after midnight by the time we finished, but I didn't feel tired. I wandered into the master bedroom, unraveling the scarf from my head and folding it into a square on the dresser. "How would you feel if I uncovered my hair this week?"

Barry sat on the bed, unlacing his shoes.

"Really? Like, entirely? Out of the house?"

His eyes questioned then pleaded.

"We don't know anyone here," I said. "It can't affect our standing in the community. I just want to see what it's like."

"Oh Sal," he said, riffling his fingers through his curls. "It's not about who will see. It's about doing what God asks."

"Well, you and I both know that it's not an absolute commandment—only an interpretation from the passage about the Sotah. An interpretation by men, I might remind you." I tilted my head and raised my eyebrows. "But I don't have to," I sighed. "I would like to see how it feels, though. We can talk about it in the morning. Come sit with me on the patio." I reached a hand to my husband.

We padded across the house to French doors that led to the backyard. The moon was full and bright overhead, backlighting tall trees. In the night, crickets seethed, and the leaves of near bushes rustled. Squirrels? Possum? Raccoons? Bear wouldn't come this close. We settled into Adirondack chairs, and I tilted my head to count the stars.

"There are so many," I said.

"What?"

"Stars. We can never see them at home."

"The lights of the city drown them out," he said.

The night smelled of banked campfire and moist dirt. "We could live in a place like this," I said.

"No, we couldn't," he said.

I chuckled. "Yeah, you're right."

Barry's breathing was soft and rhythmic, like a light wind caressing the darkness. Reliable. Life-affirming. We sat there for a good half hour before he dozed off, and I tapped his hand to pull him back inside. The kids would be up at their usual time. We should find a way to sleep.

I brushed my teeth and washed my face and dropped my skirt and sweatshirt beside the bed before stepping into flannel pajama pants and one of Barry's old T-shirts that ballooned around my belly. I pulled the down comforter up to my chin. "Open a window, will you?"

Barry lifted the sash on a far window and cracked it two inches. A cool breeze sifted in through the screen.

"Perfect night. How tired are you?"

"Seriously?"

"I forgot how I feel in the second trimester," I laughed.

"And the first. And the last," he chuckled.

I traced his grin in the dark.

"Well, it is a Jewish man's obligation to satisfy his wife," he whispered, turning onto his side and grazing a hand over my thigh.

"Yes, it is," I said, leaning in.

He kissed me, long and hard, darting his tongue between my lips. I moved closer, wanting to meld into him, become one. His hands trailed over my back. He ran a hand under my shirt, dancing his fingers over my nipples. I arched into him, loving every touch. We kissed and tasted and teased and breathed the same air into each other as if we were each other's life support. Then he pushed me onto my back and nuzzled his head down my torso, depositing sweet kisses and nips along my skin as he made his way over the hump of my belly and down between my thighs. I laid back into the pillow and closed my eyes. This was what I had always wanted. A deep and abiding love that endured through the years and the questions and the difficult moments. I let go of thought and let touch overtake me until I was riding on the swells of Lake Michigan, up and over the endless icy waters, roiling in the waves, tossed about until finally, I landed on the soft shore, spent, gratified, content and safe.

CHAPTER FORTY-FIVE

The next morning, the kids clambered into our room like a noisy circus, leaping onto the bed and nestling between us. "Mommy! Tati! Wake up! We're Up North!"

I rubbed my eyes and stretched. "What time is it?"

"Eight o'clock—it's late!" Donny chortled.

"And you're all hungry and want to go swimming in Lake Michigan," I said, pulling upright.

Barry hid under a pillow, burrowing deeper into the blankets.

"Let Tati sleep. I'll make breakfast. Go. Let me wash up."

I shooed them out, pulling a sweatshirt over my pajamas. The cold of the night had seeped into our room, minty and calm. It was brilliant to wake up in. I grabbed a pair of fuzzy socks from my suitcase and slipped them over my icy feet.

In the kitchen, I pulled boxes of cereal from the cupboards and lined them up on the counter, along with paper bowls and plastic spoons. "Make your choice," I said to the kids, pointing at the boxes. They clamored for Frosted Flakes, a rare treat. "Careful. Let me pour it," I said, shaking a reasonable amount into each bowl then dousing each with milk. They sat on stools at the counter, slurping their cereal, spilling drops onto the Formica.

"There are lawn games in the garage," I said. "After you finish, clear your places, and you can go play in the backyard. But wear shoes. The grass will be dewy. You'll get wet."

"In our pjs?" Simi chirped.

I nodded. "It's vacation," I said.

I scooped coffee into a paper filter in the coffeemaker, which Barry had approved for our use because it only ever held coffee, which was always kosher. I poured in water, flipped the switch and listened to the gurgling as the machine came to life. I rinsed out our travel mugs and set them on the counter as the smoky headiness filled the room.

I poured an inch of milk into my hot coffee and secured the lid, grabbed a blanket from the couch and wandered onto the patio. I wrapped the blanket around myself. The trees were brilliant with the morning light, no longer silhouettes as they had been hours earlier, but full and bold and strong. Wide green leaves and long sturdy limbs stood sentry over the yard. Bean bags for cornhole thwacked as they hit the wood or plopped onto the grass when a throw was off. Simi scampered from base to base, watching Donny and Shira toss back and forth.

"Lemme! Lemme!" he clamored.

"Give him a turn," I called.

Shira scrunched her nose and ignored me. Dewy damp darkened the bottom of her cotton nightgown. Donny had rolled the bottom of his pajama pants and removed his socks before sliding into sneakers that he didn't bother to tie. Simi was shoeless, clomping on the wet grass in footie pajamas. He didn't seem to care about any of it, only wanting in on the game. I sipped coffee, its warmth coating my throat and coursing through my limbs. I settled my cup on the table, dropped the blanket on the chair and trailed into the garage to find a game for Simi, returning with a ring toss, which I set up on the grass. His curls shone in the morning light, haloing around his face as he skittered across the lawn.

It was close to ten before Barry appeared, by which time the kids had grown weary of the games and were picking through the bushes around the border of the yard.

"Don't eat anything," I yelled.

Simi waddled back and forth, collecting sticks and depositing them by the fire pit. Donny and Shira peered at plants, huddled between bushes, the secret conversations of siblings in a world of their own making.

"Morning," I said as Barry settled next to me, coffee in hand. He nuzzled my ear.

"Morning," he whispered. "I can still taste you."

I swatted at his shoulder. "Don't let the kids hear you," I said.

"They wouldn't know what I meant if they did," he said.

The morning was still, with little wind. We were two miles from the lake, but the trees blocked any sound of crashing waves. The day's forecast promised warmth and sun.

"Swimming?" I said.

Barry nodded.

"Will you go in with them? Or will you mind if I do?"

I usually wore a long-sleeved swim shirt and leggings with a cotton skirt at the pool or lake to preserve modesty, but I wanted to wear a bathing suit like other people while we were so far from home. I'd brought a maternity one, with a gingham skirt, which looked more old lady than modest mother, but in our community, it would be scandalous. There were "modest" bathing suits on websites propagated by Mormons, Lycra and spandex swim dresses, which suited my community just fine. At least for those who went in the water. Many women wouldn't in mixed company.

If I hadn't grown up secular, I wouldn't know any different. I looked at my husband, easy bliss on his face. To know one world all your life and accept it—what a gift. It was too hard to straddle worlds. I understood what the rabbi at Beth Sholom had meant.

"I brought a bathing suit," I said. "If you're comfortable with me wearing it."

"And your hair?"

"You want me to cover my hair, but it's okay to wear a bathing suit?"

He chuckled. "Yeah, I see the hypocrisy," he said.

I stroked his arm. "I'm sorry I am pushing you," I said. "I just want to try things and see how they feel. I never really questioned anything, just followed Shiri's lead, and it's been great. But now I'm curious."

The kids tromped over, drenched from the wet grass and tired from their morning romp.

"How about a little rest in front of the TV then swimming in the lake after lunch?"

Their voices sang a chorus of cheery yesses, and they trampled into the house.

"Change into dry clothes, please!"

"Pizza!" Shira called.

I followed them in, pulling leftover slices from the fridge.

"Glad I ordered two larges," I said.

Barry snorted.

"I hope we brought enough food for this crew." I surveyed the boxes and cans, the full refrigerator shelves.

"There's always the grocery in town, Anderson's," he said. "It's expensive, but we're on vacation."

The kids dressed, dumping damp pajamas on the floor. I followed after them, picking up everything and laying it over dressers and shower rods to dry. They pulled on bathing suits, with shirts and pants over top. I stuffed towels into a wide canvas beach bag then changed into my swimsuit, with a long-sleeved swim shirt and denim skirt over top. It had been a decade since I'd shown so much skin in public. I grabbed a baseball cap, hesitating to fasten it over my head. *Baby steps.* I put it on, planning to test the waters of my husband's patience when we got to the lake, hoping to feel the wind sifting through my hair, the sun warming my scalp. Barry pulled on swim trunks. I added sunscreen and sunglasses to the bag. Would I feel uncomfortable with my skin bare to the open air and the gaze of the prying public? Or would it be like riding a bike—you never forget how?

The house was only a half mile from a small beach, but Simi would never make the walk back, so we piled everyone and everything into the car, along with a canvas tote full of granola bars, apples, juice boxes and cheesy crackers. The beach was fairly empty. Past Labor Day, all the local children were in school and the vacationers from down-state were finished with their travels. It was the perfect time to hide in the glorious landscape of quiet, rugged nature, to claim the long expanse of beach as our own. Two older couples sat in folding chairs that sank in the sand. Another couple meandered down the beach holding hands. We lugged our gear to a small sweeping dune, where I lay a blanket on the sand, keeping it from flying away with tote bags and stacks of towels at the corners. The kids pulled off their layers and dropped them in the sand. After lathering everyone with sunscreen, I shimmied out of my skirt and followed them to the water, keeping the swim shirt on. Barry trailed behind me. The cold air pimpled my skin; I was all too aware of my bare legs for all to see, grateful that no one was looking.

The water was cold and clear. The smooth rocks of the lake bed shimmered through the water, and on the shore, tiny pebbles mixed in with fine, smooth sand. In the distance, lilting swells turned from turquoise to midnight blue where the lake deepened. Carved by glaciers, Lake Michigan dropped to 922 feet at its deepest. The sun turned the water into glistening pricks of light, jewels dancing on the waves.

"Not too far!" I called to the kids.

The wind was stronger here, and loud, screaming and whipping around my head. I had left the baseball cap on the beach. My hair grazed my face, wind sifting through the strands. How long had it been since I had felt sun and wind on my hair? Before I married Barry, I had never paid attention to how the sun warmed my scalp. I had not noticed the sparkling heat prickling my skin. I had not noticed the cool gust whipping my hair into a frenzy.

Simi stayed near the shore, Barry close behind him. Donny and Shira edged deeper, cautious, glancing at me then turning to the open expanse. The water was shallow for a long way. Though the waves were fierce farther out, here they lolled rhythmically, one after another, lapping and pushing the kids closer to the beach. Unlike the ocean, the tide didn't pull the kids out, and I breathed relief into the crisp air.

That night, I warmed a lasagna and made a salad. After, we built a fire in the pit out back, huddling around it, staring at the licking flames and soothed by the crack and pop of burning wood. We all slept well and long, full of fresh air and bright sunshine and the freedom of an unencumbered schedule in a place where no one was watching. I was asleep by nine, huddled into blankets, the cool night air a whisper through the room.

The next day, we packed a backpack with water bottles and snacks and trekked up the first hill of Sleeping Bear Dunes. Simi scampered halfway then froze under the bright sun. He stared up then back down to the foot of the dune and exploded in tears and screams.

"Too high! Too high!"

He clawed at my skirt, pressing his face into the fabric. I patted his back and pulled him up into my arms.

"It's okay, honey. We can go down." I led him by the hand slowly down the dune until we stood at its base, staring up at the dramatic sweep of sand. It did look huge and scary from where we stood. Barry, Shira and Donny were specks at the top, calling and waving. We waited for them under a tree, Simi squatting to stare at a trail of ants pouring up and out of their hill like a tiny volcano spewing black.

The next day, we returned to the beach, and the day after that, we hiked up the slim dune trail bordering the lakeshore. There, the dunes were not as severe as Sleeping Bear, though Simi hovered close, sticking to my legs, while Shira and Donny sailed down the sloping ridge close to the water's edge, running with their faces to the sky and their arms wide like the wings of a bird. All the stress and tension of our home life, all the heaviness I hadn't realized had settled upon us, seeped away, draining out into the fragrant earth, absorbed by the listing hills. Even Barry relaxed into the fresh air, staying close to me, reaching out to touch more frequently than he did at home. We were free and easy, happy, content.

It's not easy to observe Shabbat far from a Jewish community, but I was prepared for a quiet one in the far north. We'd brought candles, wine and grape juice. I had made a double batch of challah and frozen the loaves. For the meals, I brought salmon to bake Friday night in a mustard-brown sugar sauce, with a salad and berries for dessert. For Saturday, I'd frozen an orange cream cake, brought puff pastry and deli meats to make a deli roll in the koshered oven, and picked up packaged salads—hummus, baba ganouj, pickles, olives, artichokes. I would cut cucumbers and seep them in vinegar and sugar to soften. I'd mix frozen corn with diced red pepper and onion and toss it in olive oil, salt and pepper. It would be simple but filling, more than enough to satisfy us. We could even have cholent here—it was easy to transport the crock pot and all the ingredients, and by midday Friday, I had the familiar stew bubbling on the counter. When we awoke on Saturday, the house would smell just as it did at home on Shabbat, hearty and warming. And for the third meal, I'd whip hard-boiled eggs with celery, onion and mayonnaise, open a few cans of tuna and finish whatever salads were left from lunch. Sunday we'd head home.

On our last morning in Glen Arbor, I rose early and scribbled a note to Barry that I was taking one last run along the lakeshore. I laced my sneakers and pulled a thin purple hoodie over my tank top. The road was empty that early. I turned onto the main road, tromping on the gravel shoulder downhill until I reached West Harbor Highway. I headed west, huffing and panting as I pushed harder. My hair was free to the air, but there was no wind in the early stillness, and my curls lifted only from the effort of my body heaving into the day, going slowly but consistently along the quiet road.

I listened for birds but could not hear them above the pounding of my heart and the whipping intake of breath. I pushed on, past the D.H. Day campground, where the first tent-campers were stirring, mixing coffee over open fires. I followed the road to its fork at Glen Haven Road and turned right. Ahead of me, evergreens were still against an open sky. To the left, swells of trees lifted over hills we had hiked earlier in the week. A mile or two up to my left lay the Dunes, but I turned right, toward the Glen Haven Historic Village, a veritable ghost town, just before the lakeshore, the place we had come the first night, staring at the vast starry sky. I sprinted down the road until it, too, ended and pushed through the empty parking lot until I reached the sand, and even then, I kept going, stumbling and slowing but pushing forward, trying for every last searing breath before I'd have to turn around and go back.

A half mile down the beach, I sank onto the sand and lay back, staring up at the sky. The baby fluttered inside me, as if begging me to slow down. I seized with a cramp after pushing so hard. I'd go slow on the way back. Walk, if I had to. No wisp of cloud marred the clear blue. The sun was slowly blinking awake behind the trees. I turned to the lake and listened for its voice. The whir and shout of a constant wind seemed to say *let everything go, Sally*. I stared at the waves. Little brushstrokes. Fingers massaging the blue. They came in and in and in, and I swore I couldn't see them retreat from the land. The lake was a boiling mass of motion that never stopped, going in one direction then changing its mind. The natural world did what it needed to do, what it knew to do, without judgment, without rumination. We humans complicated so much. I wondered which boats had sunk near here, settling on the smooth, sandy lake bottom. How many fierce nights had roiled with anger near these shores, tossing freighters and sailboats atop the waves, only to sear them in half and sink them to the depths. How must it feel for sailors to know their end was imminent and there was nothing they could do to save themselves? To the west, I saw the sleepy profiles of the Manitou Islands. No industry, just quiet nature.

The drenching sweat that had saturated my shirt was cold now, and I shivered. I'd been gone for an hour. The sun climbed higher, shifting the colors of my view from deep jewel tones to light pastels—gold to butter, ink to robin's egg, black-green firs became radiant emeralds. And the sand, once white and blinding, was now a soft cream with sparkling specks of pink and orange and purple.

I walked back down the beach to the parking lot and then took off at an easy trot, through the ghost town, back the way I had come. I jogged at a slow pace, past the campground, which was coming to life, the scent of bacon and campfires lifting on the light breeze. And then I was passing the little cafes and art galleries of Glen Arbor, until I was at the main corner, with the grocery and Boondocks, which wouldn't open until eleven. I turned right at the intersection and walked the remaining half mile to my family.

At the house, the kids lay across couches, watching cartoons. Barry was pushing eggs around a skillet and toasting bread in the oven on a cookie sheet.

"Coffee?" he asked.

I shook my head, brushing my lips across his cheek.

"Shower," I said.

He scrunched his nose and nodded. "Good idea."

When it was time to go, a sadness fell over us. Shira trailed her favorite doll along the ground, her thumb in her mouth. She rarely sucked her thumb anymore! Simi kept up a relentless whimper, clinging to my side as I lugged totes and bags and suitcases to the car. Donny sat on the couch, staring out the window. Barry stroked his hair as he passed by.

"Where are your keys, Sal?" Barry called.

"In my purse," I said.

A few minutes later, he came out, an envelope in hand.

"What is this?"

I looked at it. "I don't know. Where'd you find it?"

"In your purse."

"Oh—I stashed the mail in there last week before we left. I forgot it was there."

"It's from a law firm. A pretty precious one, downtown."

I swallowed. My stomach jumped. Of course John would not disappear that easily.

He tore at the corner of the envelope and slit it open with his finger, pulling out the paper inside and unfolding it. As his eyes scanned the letter, color drained from his face. Our perfect week of sun and clear air dissolved. Rage reddened his cheeks.

I grabbed the letter, scanning the words. *Paternity. Father's rights. Court-ordered DNA test.*

My throat vibrated. I looked at Barry, searching his eyes for that strong, assuring connection.

"You swore it couldn't be his."

"It's not," I said. "No chance. This baby is yours."

He threw the envelope to the ground. "Dammit, Sally!"

I reached for him, but he shrank back. "This will be the end of us in the kehillah. It doesn't matter that it isn't true. The hint of scandal will consume us. We will never be able to show our faces again."

"I am so sorry. You know I am, Barry." I reached for him, but he kept retreating, pulling back from me. "We've been through this. It was a mistake."

"Oh yes it was," he hissed.

I glanced toward the house. Were the kids hearing this? Even staring at the TV, they could be taking it in. They picked up on everything.

Where were they? From clinging to me and trailing under our feet as we packed up, they were conspicuously absent now. *Please God, don't let them hear this.*

"I made one mistake—one! I came clean, and I apologized. I love you—and only you, Barry! You are my everything."

"You came clean because I caught him in our house." He practically spat the words. "I wonder if I would ever have found out if he hadn't been."

"Barry." I grabbed at his arm. "I can't lose you. I don't want to lose us."

He ran a hand over his head.

"I'll do anything to make it right," I said. "Please don't leave me."

He stared up at the sky. "I told you once that I wouldn't leave, and I meant it. This is my baby," he said in the calmest voice I had ever heard from him. "And you are my wife. I made a promise to you eight years ago, and I intend to keep that promise. Even though you broke yours to me."

Calm. Quiet. Seething. My heart pounded in my ears. Outside, a squirrel scratched against the trunk of a tree.

"But we do things my way from now on," he said.

I nodded, not knowing what he meant but knowing I had no other choice if I wanted to keep my family together.

"I have been incredibly forgiving," he said. "And I will try to find a way to forgive you for this." He shook the letter at me. "But it will not be today."

He called to the kids to grab their carry-ons and get in the car. I was cemented to the floor, my body humming with fear. The baby fluttered. My hand hovered over my belly. *It'll be okay, sweetheart.* I rubbed circles to reassure my unborn child. *We will be a family.*

The drive home was long and quiet, the silence palpating inside the minivan. The children slept on and off, waking and whining in turns, worn out from an energetic week in the fresh air and likely sensing the tension between us. I didn't know how many times I glanced at Barry, wondering what he was thinking, wondering when he would speak to me. And when my eyes wandered away from him and grew bored with the road, I agonized over what might happen next.

It was still light as we pulled into our driveway. We were quiet as we carted totes and boxes and suitcase in and out, in and out, until the car was empty and the house a cluttered mess. At least we'd finished most of the food I'd packed for the vacation, so there was less to take home and nothing perishable.

We'd been home a half hour when Shira asked, "What's for dinner, Mommy?"

"It begins," I said, glancing at Barry. He didn't look up. He didn't even seem to hear me. I reached a hand toward him, offering a pleading smile.

"I'll order pizza," he said, dialing the number we both knew by heart.

"Goody!" Shira exclaimed. "French fries, too, Tati?"

Barry nodded. At least he wasn't taking out his anger on the kids.

"Take your things up to your rooms," I said, placing their suitcases by the stairs for them to drag up. "Put your clothes in your drawers. Let me know if you need help." I'd washed everything when we were still Up North, leaving very little laundry to cart home.

I grabbed the soft duffel that held my clothes and hefted it upstairs. The baby kicked in response to my clenching muscles. I patted my belly. *Sorry, I'll go lightly.* I cracked the two windows of our bedroom to dissipate the stale air and swung my bag onto the bed, pulling out shirts and skirts and several pairs of running tights, which I deposited in drawers and the closet until everything was put away.

"This is going to be a nightmare, no matter what the outcome is," Barry said, walking into the room with his suitcase.

"What are you talking about?"

"You know what I'm talking about, Sally." He was curt and unapologetic. "Even though it's not his baby—and I hope to God it's not!— he'll claim paternity, visitation. It'll be an awful mess. If it is mine, there is still the embarrassment of the lawsuit, and you know this community will hear about it. Nothing stays hidden. I mean, think of all the Jewish attorneys who will see this on a court docket. Because I don't imagine he'll do this quietly."

"It *is* your baby, Barry," I pleaded.

He rolled his eyes. "We'll see, won't we?"

"I can't believe the community buries their head in the sand about abuse at the day school, but this they want to focus on," I said.

"The final hammer edging us out," he said, pacing.

"I can ask John to keep it quiet," I said. "To do this in a dignified manner."

"You'll do no such thing," he snapped. "I want no more contact between you and him, do you hear me? And don't be a fool. He doesn't care what you or I want. He never did, Sally."

"Settle down," I said. "I understand that you're mad and hurt, but that doesn't give you the right to order me around."

"Oh yes it does!" His eyes blazed. "I've been incredibly understanding for a really long time. I have the right to explode now, don't I? You are my wife, and in this community and in the eyes of the law, that means I have a say in how our family operates. And I am putting my foot down. Do you really want to challenge me?"

I didn't. I wanted all of this to go away and to return to the blissful state my marriage had inhabited for most of the past eight years. I wanted to pretend all of this had been a bad dream that I could erase with the quick opening of my eyes. I glanced at the open window. Our houses were so close to our neighbors; had anyone heard his outburst?

He raked his hands through his hair. "I'm sorry, Sally. I am angry. And I am hurt." He sank onto the bed. "I am not normally the type of husband who makes demands, so this once, I believe I am fair to ask that you never see or speak to John Hogan again. Ever."

I went to him, a hand hovering over his shoulder. "Okay," I said. "Barry, I am eternally sorry. I love you. I have always loved you. Please, never doubt that."

He grasped my hand and looked up. "I know," he said.

"You're a good man," I said, pushing the suitcase back to sit beside him. I pressed close, kissing the side of his face. "I really love you," I said. "I wish I could make this all go away. I wish I hadn't been so stupid."

"So do I," he said, closing his eyes.

"*Mommy!* Is it time for pizza yet?" Shira called from her room.

I stood up.

Barry reached for me, pulling me back down. "To get through this, we have to be in sync," he said. "Promise me."

"I promise." I grasped his face with both hands and kissed him, full and hard, his hand gripping the back of my head, pressing me to him.

"I'll get the pizza," he said. "Get the kids unpacked and washed up."

That night, after the kids were in bed and the suitcases put away in the basement, I found Barry on the deck with a glass of whiskey.

"Wish I could join you," I said, sitting beside him and pulling a pashmina around my shoulders. It was starting to feel like fall, a cool wind lifting the leaves on the backyard tree.

"I called Martin," Barry said. "He'll help us with this. He'll reach out to John's lawyer tomorrow and see what we need to do."

The baby fluttered, and I patted my belly. This part of pregnancy was exciting—I wish it didn't have to be dampened by drama brought on by my mistakes.

"I know I said we'll do this my way," he said. "I don't know what that means yet. But I think it will mean that we'll need to find another place to live."

"Really?"

"I didn't say modern Orthodox," he said. "I said another place. It might be another *yeshivish* place—if we can find one where this mess won't follow us."

The religious world was small, and word traveled fast. Someone would tell someone who would taint us before we even got somewhere new. I would leave him to his research and hope that in the end, we'd find a place where we could both be happy, where I could stretch my wings and retain all the good I'd found in this beautiful observant community but leave behind the nastiness that had comprised much of this year.

"Okay," I said.

He sipped from his glass. I imagined the heat of the whiskey sliding down his throat, warming his arms and legs, reaching all the way to his toes. I loved the reassurance I felt from a sip of hot blazing fire.

"Can I?" I said, reaching for his glass.

"Do you think that's wise?" he said, handing it over.

"Probably not." I took the smallest sip, letting it pierce my tongue and warm my heart.

Chapter Forty-Six

After dropping Shira and Simi at school the next morning, Donny and I headed for the supermarket. The house was sparklingly empty of food, and I had only a few days to plan for Shabbat plus restock our pantry for everyday meals. After the groceries were put away, I settled Donny at the kitchen table with a math text and a notebook.

"I'm going to say hello to Batya, honey," I said. "I'll be right back."

The back door was open, and I called through the screen. "Batya! We're back!"

Footsteps swept across the floor. "Shhhh," she said, appearing around a corner, a finger to her lips. "Talya is asleep on the couch." Her baby would be two on Sukkot. I noticed Batya's shirt billowing out in front of her. I cocked my head to ask, pointing at her midsection.

She nodded, smiling. "I couldn't wait to tell you," she said. "Four months along."

"Mazel tov!" I swept her into a hug.

We settled into deck chairs. "I can hear her from here," she said. "How was your trip?"

I glanced over at my house, straining to see Donny's bowed head at the kitchen table. "Good," I said. "Great, really. Until the last day."

"What happened then?"

Birdsong pierced the silence.

I told her about John's sudden appearance on Tisha b'Av, coming clean with Barry, and the letter.

"Oh Sally." Batya hung her head. "I don't know what to say."

"There is really nothing to say," I said. "I was wrong. I regretted it the minute it happened, and I was afraid to tell Barry. I didn't want to lose him."

She reached a hand over and closed it around mine.

"You're sure it's Barry's baby."

I nodded. "One hundred percent. I did the math when I realized I was pregnant. More than a month before John and I... Anyway. Barry's attorney is calling John's."

Birds skittered in conversation—barn swallows, blue jays, mourning doves, robins, starlings. How simple their life! Collect food for winter. Find a mate and build a nest. Warm the eggs until they peck through to the raw air. Push them out when it's their time to fly. Perch on a branch and survey the landscape before you. Collect sticks and leaves and human detritus for a nest that will keep your family safe.

I had always been taught that humans were superior to all other creatures because of our ability to think. I had begun to consider this not actually a strength, but rather a threat—all this time to ponder our self-importance, satisfaction, desires and yearnings, could only lead to unhappiness.

"Any chance you can keep this quiet?" Batya asked.

"What do you think? I don't plan to discuss this with anyone other than you, and maybe my grandparents, but think of all the attorneys we know. Someone is bound to spot my name on the court docket."

"But attorney-client privilege, and we're not supposed to speak *lashon hora*," she said.

"Not supposed to," I wheezed. "We were just inching our way back into the fold. Before the trip, we'd had a few Shabbat invitations, finally. People smiled at me on the street and in the grocery. I was hoping the outrage over our complaint against Mr. Fineman was finally fading."

"It was," she said. "Especially since he packed up and left town."

"What? Wow, a lot happens in a week."

"Yes, Shmueli came home from school and said Mr. Fineman was no longer there, so I put my ear to the ground and learned that they shipped off for Des Moines. He has a job there in a yeshiva."

I sucked my lips. "He should never work with children," I said.

"I know, Sal," she said. "At least he's gone from here. Don't pursue this. It'll only waste your energy and push you further away from people."

"I can't care what anyone thinks, Bat," I said. "It's abuse of children! It should follow him wherever he goes. We should have filed criminal charges."

"It's behind you," she said. "Leave it there. Are you coming tomorrow to tehillim?"

"I'd love to, but I can't bring Donny. I'm on my own for the foreseeable future."

Batya's black rayon skirt swept the bottom of the deck chair, pooling around her like a queen holding court. She wore simple clothing but in a way that I envied. On my friend, a simple ribbed cotton long-sleeve in the prettiest shade of pink, the color of a baby's tender lips, became an act of elegance. She hid her hair in a floral and linen hat. She wore no makeup but radiated honest beauty, full of peace and energy. I envied her quiet happiness. For eight years, I'd been much like her: happy in my marriage, content as a mother, a firm part of a vibrant community. And then it all came crashing down. Or, rather, I stared at the waving trees—damn Facebook!—remembering, wondering, opening the door to people from a past I had never really wanted to revisit. Without even realizing I was doing it, I cracked open my tight little world, and once it stood ajar, I couldn't stop the swell of curiosity. Truth was, I had never missed John Hogan. As soon as I found Yiddishkeit, I was done with that period of my life, done with him, happy to bid it all farewell. Maybe there was something after all to the admonition against mixing the contemporary world with the traditional. I needed to get back to a place of simplicity, of ease, and soon.

CHAPTER FORTY-SEVEN

I was full into maternity clothes pulled from the back of my closet, shifting the more fitted items to the shadows. I pulled the stretchy panel of a khaki skirt up over my belly, pairing it with a flowy embroidered blouse. I pulled my hair into a tight bun and lifted my sheitel off the stand on my dresser, fastening it over my head and securing it with clips on each side. The hair was human, golden brown and thick, dusting my shoulders. I brushed light-pink shadow over my eyes and lifted my lashes with mascara to look fully the part of a doting Orthodox wife.

After a volley of phone calls early in the week, Barry set a meeting for Thursday, late afternoon, in the attorney's office. Martin was part of a prestigious firm in the heart of Chicago, on the twenty-third floor of a gleaming high-rise. At night, I wandered through the house while my family slept, clicking on email then shutting it down, just to see if John had messaged. I would keep my promise to Barry not to communicate with him, but I wanted to monitor his efforts. If a message came in, I'd immediately tell Barry, who would send it to the lawyer.

But John stayed silent. He had completely severed contact. I remembered how callously he'd ended our relationship. I could see the real John now and not confuse memories with dreams of a caring person. I put to rest the what-ifs of the past. Abrupt, cold and final, once before he'd cut all ties and walked away without a glance. It was no surprise that he'd do it again.

"We will contest a DNA test, on religious grounds," Barry said. "Done in utero, it can disrupt the placenta and endanger the fetus. Halachah forbids an invasive procedure that is not necessary to protect the life of the mother or baby."

I agreed, though putting off a paternity test until after the birth would only prolong the fight and keep John on the periphery of our lives for at least three months. Barry hoped it might dissuade him from going further, but I knew it would spur him on.

"*My way,*" Barry kept insisting.

Batya offered to take the kids and keep them for dinner so we wouldn't have to rush home. We might need a respite, a slow and easy dinner just the two of us to unwind and process the meeting. I had yet to hear mention of our current troubles from anyone in the neighborhood, but that didn't mean it remained a secret. John was clever—and vindictive—and if he could figure out how to penetrate our community and hurt me in the process, I was certain he would.

"He has a frum lawyer," Martin said. "At least one on his team. I'm sure that was deliberate."

Indeed, John's posh law firm had a number of religious attorneys on its rolls, including Sruli Schwartz, Shiri's husband. I knew him well, from my early days in the community, and while I doubted he was John's main attorney, he was consulting on the case. Shiri had to know. Sruli was committed to honoring attorney-client confidentiality, but this hit so close to home... I didn't see how he couldn't let something slip. But if she knew, I expected her to call. And kick me off the WOL.

We followed Lakeshore Drive downtown, Lake Michigan sparkling under the bright sun. It seemed different from the vision we'd enjoyed so serenely a week earlier—same lake, different surroundings. The lilting waves calmed me as Barry drove, turning into a parking structure, where we left all daylight and pulled into a below-ground spot.

"Ready?" he said, grabbing my hand and squeezing.

I steeled myself, following my husband into the elevator and sticking close to his side. Floor-to-ceiling windows encircled the perimeter of the twenty-third floor, which the law firm occupied in its entirety. Frosted glass walls separated interior offices and conference rooms to protect privacy. You could see shadows of people scuttling about, but all sound was muffled and faces were blurred.

John sat in the middle of a long table in a corner conference room. His hands folded one on top of the other, his mouth set in a line. What had been so alluring that night in the park? What had I ever found attractive about him? He looked grim, menacing. Funny how the same person could attract and repel in equal measure.

On his left sat a man I didn't know, and Sruli Schwartz sat to his right. *Our world is about to break wide open.*

Martin held the door as Barry stepped through, and I followed. A law clerk trailed after us. We settled into soft leather chairs, opposite John and his team. It felt like a face-off, and I stifled a laugh, remembering the seriousness of the Detroit Red Wings on center ice when I attended games as a child, waiting for the puck to drop. Did I need a helmet and thick padding for this, too?

"I'm Steven Cassidy," said John's main attorney, reaching for Barry's hand.

Barry pumped it, his face stony. Steven reached a hand in my direction, but I waved him away.

"Our religious observance prevents men and women from touching outside of marriage," Barry explained.

John snorted. Steven raised his hands in apology and sat down. I wanted to glare at John but contained myself, biting my tongue to stifle any facial expressions and kneading my hands in my lap.

I avoided looking at Sruli for fear I'd see judgment in his eyes. Even a lawyer couldn't hide his true feelings. Well, maybe a good lawyer could, and Sruli was the best. A frum attorney wouldn't have a job in a high-brow firm unless he was fierce, dedicated and super-smart, and Shiri would never marry a hack. The frosted glass cut the glare of the bright sun. I searched for the sparkling blue of the lake, but everything beyond the walls was a blur.

"We would like to resolve this matter as easily and quickly as possible," Steven said. "All we need to do is determine paternity. A simple blood test will ascertain whether we need to proceed further."

"Yes, but such a test done in utero would pose a threat to the fetus," Martin said.

"My client is willing to wait until the baby is born," Steven said.

I shifted in my seat. Three more months of limbo, John Hogan hovering over us, threatening our marriage? *No, thank you.* This lawsuit would dampen the arrival of our baby. I didn't want that any more than I wanted a long needle poking through my belly. But I stayed silent.

"Before either option is pursued, we must first determine the validity of the claim," Martin said. "My client insists that there was no intercourse with your client, and thus there could be no paternity contest."

I pressed my lips together. So we were lying our way out of this? I wanted to nibble at my fingernails or huff a huge sigh, but I did neither, sitting upright against the tall chair under the bright conference room lights, trying for a poker face. *I am a doting Orthodox wife*, I repeated as a mantra. It might have been the first time in my life that I was glad to leave the matter in the hands of the men around me.

"That an affair took place must be proven before we will agree to any testing," Martin said.

Barry reached for my hand under the table, stroking the soft skin of my fingers. When he reached my ring finger, he cradled the gold band between two of his, rolling it as a meditation. I focused on breathing evenly, staring at the point where two walls met, a right angle.

"We can prove that," Steven said a little too calmly.

My heartbeat kicked up its pace. How? I replayed the time we had lain together in the forest that night, recounting every step leading up to and away from that coupling. No one had seen us. There had been no blanket beneath us offering long-dried evidence—and even if there had been, how could John have known this would all go sideways? Or was there a blanket? A shirt? A jacket? The scene played before my eyes, until I could no longer see it clearly. I didn't trust my memory. We had only done it once, it hadn't been premeditated, at least on my part—it had happened suddenly, in a fit of passion. What was I missing?

Martin nodded. "And what evidence can you submit to that fact?"

Steven passed a paper to Martin, who scanned its contents. How did attorneys stay so calm in the face of contentious cases? They were friends recounting a golf game over lunch. Where were the drinks? Let's break out a toast! Bring me some whiskey, a fine glass of wine, and let's offer a *l'chaim* to everyone's health and good fortune.

Martin passed the paper to Barry, who showed it to me. The words swam on the page. What was I looking at. A lab report? Of what?

Steven said, "This attests that there was DNA from the defendant and the plaintiff on the sweatshirt, with the lab dating it from May 15th."

"That is not proof of intercourse," Martin said. "It merely proves that both parties were present on that day, in the same place. It does not prove simultaneity. One person's DNA could have come later and been added to the sweatshirt."

There was a sweatshirt?

"The lab speculates that the DNA deposits were within a thirty-minute window of each other," Steven said.

"Not unequivocal evidence," Martin said, handing the paper back with a scoff. "This is insufficient to assert paternity. Come back to us when you have something real."

"We'll see what a judge says," Steven said.

Out of my peripheral vision, I glanced at Barry but couldn't make out his expression. I was ready to boil over. I bit my tongue to stifle my rage, tasted the metallic tang of blood. If we went before a judge, this case would be public knowledge. We would be entangled in another grapevine, and all the goodwill and easy reconnection that we had started to enjoy in recent weeks would disappear. No more Shabbat invitations. And oh, the kids! Other mothers would tell their children to avoid mine, which had already happened to sweet, innocent Shira, and our little ones would have no idea why their friends were no longer available for playdates. How could a community I loved and been so devoted to turn on me so fast?

If John could assert paternity—which I was clear enough to know that he could not unless he fabricated evidence—he would be forever entwined in our lives. I could live without the Skokie community, but I could not live without Barry and my children.

"That is your prerogative," Martin said.

"A simple DNA test would put this to rest, of course," Steven said. "And if there is no legitimate claim, then this disappears quickly and quietly."

"It's already been disruptive for the Liebermans and their community," Martin said. "Further pursuit would not endanger their position any more than this suit already has." He closed the folder and pushed back his chair. "Please notify our offices when you've secured a date on the judge's docket."

He waved us out of the room. Barry helped me up. I swayed a little, the blood rushing to my head, wanting to speak, to yell, to stomp and throw things at John, but I firmed my stance, gripped my husband's arm and walked out. I shot a glance in John's direction, but he wasn't looking at me. He was staring at Barry's hand in mine as if his gaze could burn a hole between us, forcing us apart. I clenched my husband's hand. *Take that, you prick.* Barry turned to me, at first alarmed then elated, and planted a slow and tender kiss at my ear. When he finished, he turned his head in John's direction, his eyes gleaming, his smile triumphant. I leaned into him.

Martin ushered us into his office and shut the door.

"Let it out," he said.

"This is easy," I said. "My doctor can date the pregnancy. I know when I last went to the mikvah—there is a record of all the appointments. It proves when I finished my last cycle, when I immersed, and when I returned to my husband's embrace. We can prove this baby's conception almost to the day."

Barry's face lit up. "Yes!" He thrust a fist into the air. "Take one for the Orthodox!"

I laughed, more from relief than anything.

"Six weeks before I ever met up with John," I said, enunciating each word.

Martin blew out a woosh of air. "Hallelujah," he said. "Saved by religion."

"What do we do next?" Barry leaned toward the desk, his foot tapping the floor.

"We wait," Martin said. "This is ammunition. Get me all the documentation you can. If they take action, we counter with concrete evidence and hopefully avoid court. Of course, they could be bluffing. They can't prove anything with a sweatshirt, and his attorneys know it. They wanted to see if we'd flinch."

"He won't bluff," I said. "He'll take this until it dies, and if an attorney tells him no, he'll find one who will tell him yes. John Hogan doesn't like to lose. He won't have anyone tell him he's wrong."

"I can't wait to be the first," Barry said.

Once we were shut in the car with the doors closed, I screamed.

Barry jumped. "What was that for?"

"There was so much I wanted to say in there! How dare he? It's so demeaning, so vindictive. What did I ever do to him?" And then I started to cry, weeping into my hands.

Barry gripped the steering wheel. He had yet to start the car. It was four o'clock on a Thursday, the concrete structure echoing with the silence of the parked cars around us and the absence of people coming or going.

My sobs slowed, and I looked at my husband, but I couldn't read his face. Anger? Despair? Fear? "Can you ever forgive me for this?"

"Of course I will," he said. "I already have." His tender gaze spurred a whole new round of tears.

"I wish I could rewind time," I said.

"But you can't."

"You know, Sruli might not say anything," I said. "It's lashon hora. He and Shiri try very hard to be faithful to Halachah."

"I know she was kind to you when you came to the community, Sally, but that was a long time ago," he said. "You're right, he may not mention an open case to his wife. There is the propriety of the law, and he is a damn good lawyer. He would not challenge attorney-client confidentiality just to give his wife a juicy tidbit. He is a straight-up guy, serious about not only civil law, but Jewish law, too."

"You think?"

He stroked his curls with his fingers. "But he knows, and it's the way he'll look at me. To know is one thing, to take action another."

"What does that mean?"

"It means we might be able to slip this into the pocket of history, once it's over. Unless..."

"Unless?"

"Unless John Hogan fucks it up for us."

Barry never swore. "How would he do that?"

"If he's as malicious as it seems, he could easily find a way to release this information to our community and tarnish our reputation forever."

"I wouldn't put it past him."

Barry looked at me, his eyes a question. "What did you ever see in that guy, Sally?"

The air pulsed between us, my heartbeat a metronome. "I honestly can't remember at this point, Barry, but if John hadn't broken my heart, I would not be frum today. If only I hadn't let him in when he sent that friend request. If only I'd told you from the start."

I stroked the hard line of his fingers, grazing his knuckles with the pad of my thumb. I looked into his dark, warm eyes, and my breath quickened, seeing the honesty, the acceptance, the deep love, the putting aside of pride to stand by me even in this most difficult moment.

"I would not have found you or fallen in love with you or made this family with you," I whispered. "I can't rewrite history, Barry, but if I could, I don't think I would, because without him in my past, I would never have come to you."

He closed his hand over mine. "I know that," he said. "Let's go away for Shabbat. We can daven at Lakeview."

"We just came home from a trip! And you hate the idea of Modern Orthodox," I said. "I'm not sure I love it, anyway."

"It's not about finding a new community, Sal," he said. "It's about getting away from this for a day. There's a hotel in walking distance, and we can bring a hot plate, cold cuts, rent a suite, tell the kids it's a Shabbos vacation."

"You're amazing," I said. "I don't deserve you."

He stroked my cheek. "Yes, Sally, you do."

CHAPTER FORTY-EIGHT

That night, I showed Barry how sorry I was, making love to him slowly, running my hands along his soft skin, kissing the tender spot at the base of his neck, his furry chest, the hollow under his arm, the cleft where his leg met his torso. I needed to believe that we could be strong in the face of adversity, intact and together, no matter what John lobbed our way. He took what I offered, submitting to me, eyes closed, hands open on the sheet.

"What it is between us," he whispered after, my head on his chest, his hand threading through my curls. "I can't find words. It is the greatest power, and the greatest surrender, I have ever known."

I spent the next morning cooking, so we'd eat well at the Inn at Lincoln Park during Shabbat in Lakeview. Barry booked a double queen suite with a full kitchen, plenty of room for our little family. I didn't really want to go away for Shabbat, after just returning from our vacation Up North, but it brought Barry some comfort, so I went along with it. I was curious about Modern Orthodoxy and a little afraid. The stress of the week had knotted my shoulders. My limbs hung heavy with exhaustion. A hotel stay with three young children over what would effectively be two nights—we had to reserve the room until Shabbat ended, which meant paying for a second night, though we would not sleep there once the dark night sky signaled the end of our holy day and released us to go home—sounded worse than a lonely, silent stay in our house, where we had room to move and outside spaces to play in privacy.

Once they cooled, I wrapped the challahs and deli roll in foil. I padded the bottom of a cooler with ice packs and layered in packaged meats, potato salad, coleslaw and pasta salad with olives, red peppers and artichokes. I filled another cooler with individual yogurts and cut fruit for breakfast. Into a paper bag went plastic cutlery, plates and bowls, a bag of granola, a bottle of grape juice, wine and a corkscrew, and Barry's kiddush cup. I grabbed the challah plate and cloth cover from the dining room to bring in a separate bag along with my travel candlesticks and two white candles.

Were we running away? Even the worst scandals eventually blow over. In the religious world, though, a tarnished reputation could follow a family around the world and for generations, rearing its ugly head when you believed memories had receded to the deep corners of individual minds. Like when our children were old enough for marriage, we could meet with a *shadchan*, a matchmaker, who would dredge up unseemly details from our pasts and use them as a bargaining chip to charge more and make us settle for less-than-perfect matches. I wanted my children to have friends and opportunities, not the long dirty trail of rumors following them wherever they went. Families with a child who had developmental disabilities, or depression, or a physical handicap that could be genetic often found that there were fewer matches for their other children seeking to marry. Our calamity was still just an unproven rumor. If it remained such, it could disappear. But if John found a way to prove that my baby was illegitimate, a *mamzer*, then the only way my children and Barry could remain untarnished would be if they were to leave me behind.

I already had it harder than my frum-from-birth peers. *Ba'alei* teshuvah were praised for returning to the faith but remained on high alert, having to double down on observance, cover hair more zealously, wear skirts five inches below the knee instead of the minimum requirement of four. I knew the flavor of freedom, and I could taint the whole community if I strayed. I came from a place where you could eat anything, do anything, wear anything and still be awash in the golden light of God's approval. Which, where I came from, no one sought anyway.

Shira bounced into the kitchen as I finished packing the food. "I've never slept in a hotel!"

"It's an adventure." I smiled as she threw her arms around my legs, since my waist was too thick for her to reach around. "That's a hug." I squeezed her. The simple act of holding my daughter calmed my nerves. To be a child unaware of the pressures and stresses of the adult world!

"Where are your brothers?"

"Simi's stacking blocks in the family room. He keeps pushing the button on the CD player to hear the same Uncle Moishy song. I hate that song."

"Which one?"

"'Hashem is Here.'"

"Yeah, it's annoying." I laughed, patting her shoulder. "Where's Donny?"

"On the swings."

"By himself?"

She nodded and scampered out of the room. I pushed open the door to the yard. Donny dangled his legs, listing in the breeze. One foot traced circles in the grass.

I wedged into the second swing, which was becoming too narrow for my expanding hips. The chains squeezed my thighs. "Hey," I said. "Whatcha doin?"

He shrugged.

"Something wrong?"

"I miss my friends is all," he said. "I'm the only one learning at home."

I ran a hand along his back, gave his neck a squeeze.

"It's temporary, you know," I said. "Until I can figure out something else. I can't send you back to that yeshiva, honey."

"I don't want to go there anyway," he said. "They'll all look at me funny and call me a troublemaker. Like that lady in the grocery."

So he *had* heard Mrs. Fineman. Kids always picked up on tension between adults, even if they didn't understand it. They couldn't give it voice or explain what ate at them, but it refused to leave, souring the way they understood the world.

Were we all wounded husks of humans, pawing through life the best we could? Early disappointment and trauma tainting any chance of focusing on beauty and wonder? I had become religious because I believed in the possibility of redemption and goodness. I hadn't expected all this chaos and confusion to accompany it, though. Perhaps I was idealistic. No people are perfect, even if they try to live according to sound rules.

"Ma, I like learning at home with you," he said. "I'd keep doing it forever! But it gets lonely sometimes with no one else my age."

"We could change that," I said. "Plenty of families homeschool. They aren't frum, though, or even Jewish."

"I don't care. I just want friends."

Well, that changed things. We could tie into a homeschooling group, find a community of families who paved their own path. He'd have friends, and I would have support. And maybe I'd inspire other frum parents whose children had endured beatings at school to join us. Lawsuit and tarnished reputation be damned—we'd blaze a new path, show a new way to be religious *and* thoughtful.

"Honey, what Mr. Fineman did to you was wrong," I said. "I am certain it wasn't just you or just this year. Bad men are bad to the core. They are bad to lots of people until they're punished for it."

"Is he being punished?" Donny looked up with hopeful eyes, planting his feet in the grass to steady the swing.

"He's left town." I tried for a smile.

"But he's not in trouble for hurting me?"

My chest ached with the truth of it. The baby beat inside me, sensing my unease, nudging me to be truthful.

"Well, he lost his job at the yeshiva," I said. "But Tati and I are trying to make sure that he is punished for beating you and other boys."

Donny's lips arched in a meager smile. "Thank you, Mommy," he said, leaning his swing in my direction to snake his arms around me.

"We'll have a quiet Shabbat in a different neighborhood and take a moment to breathe," I said.

"Why are we going away for Shabbat? We just came back from Up North."

"It's a lot of travel in a short time, isn't it?"

He nodded. "I'm tired."

"We all are."

"So why go?"

"Tati thought it might be fun to check out another synagogue."

The afternoon light was fading, shrouding the yard in shadows from the tree. Soon, the leaves would fall. Soon, we would leave for Lakeview, to wend through weekend traffic and settle in before sunset rendered travel off-limits.

I stood and held a hand to my son. "Help me pack up the car."

CHAPTER FORTY-NINE

I n our shul, the men sat near the *bimah* and the Ark that held the Torah scrolls. Women were out of reach and out of sight to ensure no distractions to the men's holy focus. We sat far from the action, the music of men chanting drifting across an open expanse, through a curtain, reaching us in muted tones, and we shifted and shuffled with our prayer books, piously praying without making any sound. When the men sang, we mouthed the words and swayed to their harmony, careful to not participate, lest a female voice divert the men's attention from their mission.

At Beth Sholom, potted plants lined the center of the sanctuary. Three rows of folding seats were available for congregants, men filling the thick center row, while women and small children veered toward the two outer ones. It was open and calm, still adhering to the mandated gender separation but giving everyone a full view of religious worship. Voices swelled, male and female, as the congregation became one unified body of respectful observance. I could not distinguish between a man's voice or a woman's, and the idea of a true congregation, where all voices melded into one flowing harmony, began to take root. This could be our legacy, to come together with fellow Jews and focus on the words, prayers written centuries earlier, not concern ourselves with the minutiae of whether a woman's very presence taunted men away from the pious path.

Donny followed Barry to the men's section, while Simi and Shira trailed after me into the women's seats. I could see my husband and son in full view throughout the service, which made me smile. It felt like we were all there together. I laid a tote bag with books at my feet and lifted a prayer book from the back of the seat in front of me.

A woman in the next row, who wore a drop-waist maxi dress and silver-threaded multicolored scarf around her head, turned and whispered, "Good Shabbos."

I smiled and nodded.

When I sat, Simi climbed onto what was left of my lap. My round belly made it hard to make room for him, but I managed to set him on an angle and still see the words on the page, peering over his shoulder. When he nestled back into me, I gave up, closing the book and slipping it into the sleeve on the chair in front of me. *This is why women are not obligated to pray as men are.* I was content to listen to Friday night *davening*, led by a man in a dark-blue suit at a podium in the center of the bimah, chanting Kabbalat Shabbat. I hummed to the tunes. No one glared. Some women were not only humming, but singing in full voice. Though the synagogue was far from full, the voices lifted into a beautiful chorus.

After the service, I shepherded the kids out of the row to make our way to Barry, when a woman stopped me. "Shabbat Shalom," she said. Young and pregnant, she wore a smock dress with a long-sleeved silk T-shirt beneath it. Her hair was tucked into a gray hat with a wide brim, sparkly Michal Negrin earrings dangling from her lobes.

"Shabbat Shalom," I said.

"And who's this?" She turned to Simi, leaning to his level.

He melted into my legs.

"Simi, say Shabbat Shalom," I said.

He hid behind my legs, peering at the woman. Shira gripped my hand.

"They're tired," I said.

"Are you new to the neighborhood?"

"We're just here for Shabbat," I said. "We live in Skokie."

"Oh! What brings you downtown?"

"We wanted to try something different." I was the only woman in a sheitel, but everyone had a covering of some kind on their head. All the women wore dresses or skirts. It wasn't so different from what I knew.

Barry was talking to three men, in no apparent rush to leave. Donny had struck up a conversation with another boy who looked to be a similar age and who I assumed was one of the men's sons.

"Do you have a place for lunch tomorrow?"

"We brought food to the hotel," I said.

"It'll keep. Or bring it with you! Come to us. I'm Tzipi." She extended a hand, which I clasped and shook.

"That's very kind! Let me talk to my husband," I said, nodding to Barry.

"Sure, sure. He's talking to my Asher," she said. "I bet he's already invited him." She chuckled.

Indeed, Barry and Donny were making their way to us, snaking through the rows until they reached us. "Sal, this is Asher, Michael and Aaron," he said, pointing to each man in turn. "Asher has invited us for lunch."

"See!" Tzipi laughed. She sidled up to her husband, who beamed at her. "So you'll come?"

"We'll come," I said. "Can we bring something? I've brought so much food to the hotel."

"Sure! Bring whatever you want," she said. "We'll have plenty. We'll leave from shul together."

Simi yawned.

"It's getting late, Barry," I said.

"Right. Good Shabbos. We'll see you tomorrow."

In the cool night, Lake Michigan crashed against the breakwater and danced up the walls of Lakeshore Drive. The hotel was a block from the water, but anywhere we walked in the neighborhood, we could hear the constant soothing music of the lake. In the suite, the kids kicked off their shoes and scampered to the table I had set before we left for services. Soup, chicken and couscous warmed on a hot plate. I had made a salad and sliced gefilte fish. On the counter sat a cinnamon babka and chocolate chip cookies. We stood around the table as Barry sang "Aishet Chayil." His eyes sparkled under the low lights of the hotel room. The curtains were drawn to keep out the night. We huddled in our cocoon, content and contained within the sustaining warmth of family. I could not look away from his gaze, as if we were magnetically connected, a powerful thriving energy pulsing between us. For a moment, I forgot the kids were there, so entranced was I by my husband's gaze.

He poured wine into the kiddush cup and chanted the prayer over wine. *Yom hashishi*... Then we trooped to the sink, doused our hands with the double-handled cup I'd brought among other Shabbat ritual items, and shuffled to the table silently until Barry recited the prayer over bread and tore chunks of challah. The kids gnashed at fistfuls of bread. I tasted the sweet softness, at home in this ritual even in completely foreign surroundings. That was the grounding thing about this life: no matter where I went, I knew who I was and what I was supposed to do. My religion was my routine, my reassurance. My home.

It was a quiet, easy dinner. I served salad with the gefilte fish, then soup, and then cleared away the smaller dishes to bring out the main course. Simi was asleep on the couch before dessert.

In bed that night, I huddled into Barry so our chatter wouldn't wake the children. Donny and Simi shared the other queen, and we'd opened the sofa bed for Shira.

"It was a nice night," I said, stroking his face, my fingers trailing along his soft skin. My hand dropped to his neck, kneading the tight muscles of his shoulders.

"That feels good," he muttered, closing his eyes.

I nosed close to his face. "It doesn't matter where we go," I murmured, "as long as we have this."

Lunch with Tzipi and Asher was easy and delicious, and we lingered at their house until late in the afternoon. Since Tzipi and Asher had no children yet except the one they were expecting, and were in fact newlyweds as I had guessed, my children grew restless without their usual trove of toys and books, so we didn't stay as long as I would have liked, opting to walk along the lakeshore before returning to the hotel. The waves were mesmerizing. We stopped to stare at the froth and crack as water washed the jagged rocks protecting the road from the lake. I didn't want to stay in the hotel another night, so after Shabbat ended, we packed up the minivan and headed home.

"Up to bed." I pushed the kids into the house. "Brush your teeth!"

Simi groaned.

"That's not going to happen," Barry chuckled, hefting a tote into the kitchen.

I riffled through the mail, pulling out a note in Batya's handwriting. *Come over when you get home. Doesn't matter how late. B*

I showed it to Barry.

"Go," he said. "I'll put everything away."

"Thanks."

Her back door was unlocked, so I tapped then slipped inside. "Bat?"

"Kitchen!" The water trickled into the sink as she washed Shabbos dishes.

"What's up?"

She shut the faucet and wiped her hands on her skirt.

"There's talk," she said.

My breath caught in my chest. "It's starting," I said.

"They're couching it in concern for Barry," she said, "to avoid admitting that it's full-on lashon hora. No one has any business discussing it. Especially since it's a legal situation, but..."

"What?"

"I heard some women saying things about you that weren't pretty," she said.

"Do I want to know?"

She lifted her shoulders and shot me a questioning glance. "Do you?"

I sank into a kitchen chair. "I honestly don't know. Does it even matter? There's nothing I can do about it anyway."

She nodded. "You're probably not going to be able to stay on the WOL board," she said.

I shrugged. "That's okay," I said. "I don't want to be in a club that doesn't want me as a member. Didn't Groucho Marx say that?"

She grabbed my hand. "You'll never lose me," she said. "Or Tzvi."

I patted her hand. "I know," I said. "And I am grateful."

"It has nothing to do with gratitude," she said. "This isn't a pity party! I actually love you."

"Even if my friendship costs you in the community?"

"I am impenetrable," she said, thumping her chest with her fist. "My piety is beyond question."

"Lucky duck." I snorted. "Bat, whatever happens, it's okay. I am fine with it. And Barry is, too. We are solid. This has actually been a turning point, leading us in a good direction."

"I'm glad." She squeezed my hand. "So what's going on with the case?"

I shrugged. "We met with the lawyers. John's threatening to go to court to contest paternity. We refused a test on religious grounds of potential harm to the fetus. Our lawyer says they first have to prove we actually had sex. Which they can't. But John hired Sruli Schwartz. That's where the gossip's coming from."

"You think? I don't know. I can't see it. He and Shiri are so pious, and they love you."

"Who else?"

She shrugged. "How was Lakeview?"

"Fine," I said. "But this is home. I don't need to be Modern Orthodox."

"Really?" The night reflected through her kitchen window, dark and silent.

"I am happy as I am, Bat," I said. "Finding my way."

Chapter Fifty

Weeks went by with no word from John's lawyer and no date to appear before a judge. I almost began to hope that it would fade away. Women looked away when I passed them in the supermarket and on the street. I focused on teaching Donny during the day and found that I loved it—lingering over a Torah passage, debating its meaning, poring over a piece of prose for his English lesson, carefully following the formulas in his math text. His intelligence delighted me, and when we studied Jewish texts, my own understanding of this way of life deepened. I loved how his eyes danced as he pursued a subject, his voice rising in a swell of passion as he made a point. I ordered more books and called the Chicago Waldorf School for support. I looked online for homeschooling groups and started a list of places to call and people I wanted to meet. But I was in no rush. I loved how the Waldorf curriculum wove math and art together, connected movement and play and outdoor exploration as part of his learning. A whole new side of me was opening as my son started to awaken. He was happy. And so was I.

I contemplated pulling Simi and Shira from their schools and home-schooling as a family. By two months after the initial lawyer meeting, the communal whispering had dissipated, and we walked into shul without shuffles of avoidance or acrimonious glares. Friends resurfaced, calling with Shabbat invitations. We had returned to Beth Sholom three times, and while Barry surprised me by embracing that community, I found I was more comfortable in our insular enclave. I had dropped the tehillim group without regret and resigned from my WOL post with apologies to Shiri, who said nothing about the legal battle. She was curiously quiet—my first friend in this community, all but a wisp of memory. But again, I was surprised by how effortlessly it all rolled off me. I didn't ruminate, didn't lose sleep worrying about where I belonged.

Aseret b'Tevet, the tenth of the Jewish month of Tevet, is a minor fast day just after Chanukah. Because I was pregnant, I was not obligated to fast, but Barry was, and he was cranky by the time he got home from work.

"Mac and cheese in the oven," I said. "And a salmon quiche. I'm making a salad."

He glanced at the clock. "The fast is over, and I'm starving!"

I laughed as I set plates on the table. "You can go twenty-five hours on Yom Kippur or Tisha b'Av, but you're complaining now, on the shortest fast day of the year?"

"I know," he chuckled. "Feed me!" He stood behind me, gripping my hips and kissing my neck.

"Call the kids," I laughed.

"Kids!" he yelled, sifting through the mail. "What's this?" He held out the law firm letter.

I shrugged. "I left it for you to open."

"Damn," he said. "I'd hoped this was all over."

I watched his face as he read the letter. His eyes were blank, his mouth set in neither a grin nor a frown. The kids thundered down the stairs and climbed into chairs at the table.

"He's dropping it," Barry said.

"What? Why?"

"I don't know," he said. "But he has one condition: he wants to meet with you. Alone."

I pulled the steaming Pyrex from the oven and set it on a trivet on the table. "It's hot," I warned the kids. "I'll serve."

I pulled out the quiche and grabbed a serving spoon and spatula. I poured vinaigrette over the salad, tossing the lettuce and cucumbers and tomato chunks until it was well mixed.

Barry dropped the letter on the counter and took his seat.

"Me first!" he said reaching to Shira and Donny at the same time and tickling them.

They giggled. "Tati!"

I scooped salad onto Barry's plate and slid a steaming piece of quiche next to it then served each kid before taking my seat. My belly was big and round, the baby pushing against every organ, visibly kicking and fisting at my skin. I had trouble getting comfortable at night, and Barry massaged my lower back and legs until I could find my way into sleep. Soon, this baby would arrive, and we would continue on the path we had carved, moving forward in the brisk air of a harsh city and a forgiving community.

Why did John want to meet with me, and alone? I stared at Barry across the table. He dug into his food with gusto.

"I'll clean up," Barry said. "You put the kids to bed." He carried the dish and pie plate to the counter, kissing my forehead as he passed.

"C'mere," he said, putting down the dishes. His hands cupped my face. "I love you, Sally." He kissed me deeply and hard. "The one good thing to come out of this nightmare is this, us. I never knew I could love this deeply."

I leaned into him and laid my head against his chest. The steady, pulsing beat of his heart was reassuring. I inhaled my husband—musky, from a long day in a closed office, the subtle tint of sweat. My hair was uncovered—since our trip north, I'd taken to uncovering it in the house, no matter who came over, grounded in an interpretation of Jewish law, if not custom, which was enough for me. For now. Maybe it would change in the future. Maybe I'd return to more religious ways. Maybe I'd fold back into the hug of the community, the star student, stepping into her long skirts and long sleeves with eager ambition, to reaffirm the place of the always-been-religious ladies who needed validation from an outsider that this way was, in fact, right.

The truth was, there was no right way. Only choice. And my choice was to be observant, to cover and to quiet and to live a subtly beautiful life in the embrace of a doting husband and the routine of prayer that freed me from needing the acceptance of others. It had taken all of my 35 years to find my home.

His hands combed through my curls, pulling at the knotted ends. He burrowed into my hair. I heard the deep inhale rather than felt it and leaned as close as my belly would allow.

"I'm getting so big," I said.

His hand crept down my back and settled on my bottom. "You're so hot when you're pregnant," he said. "Evidence of the power between us."

"Evidence that I am yours," I laughed.

"Hmmm mmmm," he murmured, rubbing slow circles on my low back. Then he pulled away. "Go to the kids," he said. "I've got this."

CHAPTER FIFTY-ONE

I arranged to meet with John in the lobby of the Westin downtown on a Tuesday morning in December. Donny was with Batya, who was all too eager to play the role of teacher for the morning. Her belly had grown, too. She was three months behind me, in that blissful state of showing and enjoying the baby's swift movements but not yet cumbersome. I was counting the days until my baby's arrival.

I'd hefted our Waldorf books into her kitchen and dumped them on the table. "Good luck!" I said. "Have fun." I kissed Donny's head. "And you'll get Simi and Shira from school?"

Batya nodded.

"Mother of the year!" I called as I left.

Barry would meet me after, and we'd go to lunch. He was taking the afternoon off. Once tax season hit and the baby came, it would be a rare opportunity to squire away time just us. The baby was active that day, shifting and kicking, assuring me that I was not alone. My hands hummed with nerves. John sat on a couch in a far corner. There were few people in the lobby, in that gray time between hotel check-out and the arrival of new guests. My shoes against the shiny floor echoed louder than I wanted. I was conscious of every step, fearful that people could see my mistakes, know my awful truths as I approached this man from my past, a man I wanted out of my life once and for all.

John looked smaller than I remembered, shrinking into the couch. His face was pale, his eyes deep in his face. He looked sad, diminished. Through the ugliness of these past months, any attraction had disappeared, and now I could not recall what had drawn me to him in the first place.

He stood when he saw me, a weak smile playing at his lips. "Sally," he said, reaching for me.

I shook my head. "Let's not," I said, settling onto an opposite couch, sitting stiff and upright.

He cleared his throat. "Thank you for meeting me," he said.

"Did I have a choice?"

He looked down, twisting his hands. "You're mad."

"Yes."

"Why?"

"Really, John? You've ruined my life with this game," I said, wincing at the words because I knew they weren't true. I was lucky that people had short memories. This scandal would not taunt me or my family as I had feared, and surprisingly, it had strengthened my marriage. But I wasn't going to let him know that.

"It wasn't a game," he said. "I just wanted you back."

"Well, you made sure that wouldn't happen," I said. "Anyway, why are we here? Why did you want to meet? And why did you drop the paternity claim?"

"Because I couldn't possibly be the father," he said.

"Why not?"

"Because I'm sterile," he said. "I always wondered why I never got anyone pregnant in all my years of dating and relationships. When this came up, I was so excited at the thought of finally becoming a father, so I had my doctor draw blood in preparation for a DNA test. That's when I found out. It is not biologically possible."

His eyes glistened. And in that moment, I pitied him. This man I had once loved so entirely, as if the sun and the stars revolved around him.

This man I wanted to be the center of my universe and whose absence I mourned for far too long. This man whom I thought understood me, saw me, knew me in a deep and lasting way that no one else possibly could but who actually never saw me at all. I had everything he wanted and nothing he could have.

"I am sorry," I said.

"Thanks. Once I knew that, I didn't think it was fair to put you through anything more. It would only be out of spite."

"Well, thank you for that," I said.

"Has Barry forgiven you?"

I nodded.

"I'm happy for you, Sally."

"I hope you find love, John," I said. I stood, looking at the angle of his nose, the curve of his chin, memorizing the details so I could let them go to sail away into the theater of memory, lifting on the wind.

Barry was waiting for me outside the hotel. The wind was sharp and tingling as it hit my face. I leaned into my husband. "Everything good?" His arms came around me, and I huddled into the cocoon of his warmth.

"Yes. Let's go."

Chapter Fifty-Two

L abor began in the gray shadows of night, while my house was quiet with sleep. Even the floorboards didn't stretch their bones and creak as usual. It was utter silence when I felt the first thunderous wince of muscles contracting and releasing, the baby shifting in its warm cave, readying to burst into the cold air of this world. I tapped Barry on the shoulder.

"It's starting," I whispered.

While Donny's birth had been slow in coming, Shira whipped out into the world in a frenzy. Simi had taken his sweet time, prolonging my agony much longer than I had been prepared for. I had no idea what to expect with this one. She could be quick and easy or stubborn and long. I was convinced the baby was another girl, a companion for Shira, a tender heart to add sweetness to our family. And she was announcing her arrival.

I paced the carpet in our room, breathing slow and long. Barry sat up in bed, watching me.

"I promise I'll tell you when I need you," I said.

He'd cracked a window to bring in a cusp of minty winter air, and I felt invigorated by its rawness. Plus, I was hot. I had twisted my curls into a loose bun atop my head and fanned my face with a folded paper. I was barefoot, a sheer nightgown swishing against my legs. A fierce contraction seized, and I leaned against the wall, swaying. Barry shot to my side, his body shadowing mine, swaying in rhythm with me, holding me up. Then it subsided and I could breathe evenly again.

"They're coming faster," he said. "The shower?"

I nodded. "Call the midwife first," I said. "Let her know."

He dialed the number, and she told us to head for the birthing center when the contractions were two to three minutes apart. I dialed my grandparents.

"Nana? I'm sorry to wake you, but the baby's coming."

"We'll be over soon," she said and hung up.

The spray of the shower pelted my belly, soothing the twist and release of contractions. Barry stood in the open door, watching me. I pressed the tile wall for support, angling my belly into the spray. A fierce one gripped me, and I winced.

"Breathe, Sal," he said. "Breathe."

"It's coming faster," I said. "We should go."

He shut off the water and helped me out, wrapping my immense body in a thick bath sheet. My teeth chattered. I always shivered before a birth, my body turning into itself.

"You're too close," he said, watching as I slipped into a cocoon of my own, oblivious to anything outside my body. "I hope we make it."

He helped me into a sweatshirt and maternity skirt, slipping socks then sandals onto my feet for ease and time. Downstairs, I heard the rustle of my grandparents, who had let themselves in with the key I'd given them. I murmured prayers under my breath, in a trance.

"Get me there," I whispered to Barry, who guided me down the stairs by the elbow.

My grandmother's eyes were wide as she took in the sight of me, and I knew that I had little time before this baby would arrive. Barry led me to the car and eased me in, pulling the seat belt over my belly, then raced to the driver's side, starting the engine and peeling out of the driveway. The hospital was only two miles from our house, but the drive felt long and agonizing, every rumble of the tires sending jolts through my body, searing, burning pain, and I cried out, gripping the armrests and door handle, crushing back the urge to bear down.

He wheeled into the circle drive of the emergency room, and a white-clad orderly pulled open my door.

"Baby coming, now!" Barry barked.

The man pulled me into a wheelchair and pushed me through the yawning doors into the harsh glare of the hospital and down the hallway to a waiting elevator, which we rode to the birthing ward. I doubled over in pain, the contractions like waves of a furious lake, piling one on top of the next, never stopping, never retreating, pounding the shore.

"It. Won't. Stop," I seethed.

The doors flung open, and he wheeled me into a room, where two nurses waited, each grabbing an arm and hefting me onto the bed.

And then it was all a blur. There was light and there was no light. A sea of faces and a series of screams. Were they coming from me? Arms reaching, a blur of limbs and eyes, cold air on my skin, *where were my clothes?* And then Barry was there I leaned on my arms and knees and the screams were mine, and he threw a blanket over my back, a tent shielding my heavy presence from sight, and then I was pushing with every muscle, clenching, gripping, tearing. There were sounds and they were coming from me, and I was under the cold water, pawing at it to move it away and let me rise to the surface, to gulp air, to taste the sharp ice of winter, to know that I was alive.

When it was over, my daughter's sharp cry pierced the precious silence of a still room that I had no memory of entering. I sat back on a plush bed, blankets gathered around me, my curls cascading over my shoulders, draping curtains around my face, tickling the soft skin of her scrunched face. She opened her eyes at me, and they were dark pools just like her father's, and in them I saw all the hopes and dreams of a future yet to be written, the innocence and trust that she was placing in me with the expectation that I would guide her forward and protect her from harm. Tears spilled from my eyes, dampening my cheeks. My nose ran. I tasted salt at the corners of my lips, and I wept, for the opportunities that each day brought and for the recognition that we always have a chance to start again.

"We'll call her Shachar, for a new dawn," I said.

Barry peered over my shoulder at her sleeping face. He kept his distance from me as was customary after the start of bleeding, after a birth. But I no longer feared the distance. We were connected at a soul level. Nothing could come between us.

"It's a perfect name," he said.

Chapter Fifty-Three

Although Barry named her in our shul the next day at minyan, three weeks later, we returned to Beth Sholom, staying with Tzipi and Asher, who had welcomed a son a month earlier. I brought kugels and deli roll and picked up salads from a kosher carryout in our neighborhood so she wouldn't have too much burden feeding our brood. On Shabbat morning, the rabbi called Barry up to the bimah for *birkat hagomel*, the prayer of gratitude, recited after a person recovers from a serious illness or completes a dangerous journey. I was so used to sitting far from the action in services and watching everything from a distance that I was startled when Barry called me up to join him. The synagogue had created the sanctuary so women could reasonably and legally, under Jewish law, stand just near the bimah when their presence was important to the proceedings. All eyes turned toward me and the baby in my arms as my husband waved me over.

"What are they doing, Mommy?" Shira whispered, reaching for my hand.

I made my way to the end of the aisle, past the women seated near me, all of whom were smiling. No harsh glances, no glares, just compassionate and encouraging eyes. My heart thumped as I walked down the aisle to the bimah. Barry reached for me, and I threaded my fingers through his, shifting the bundle in my arms.

"*Baruch ata Adonai, Eloheinu melech ha'olam, ha'gomel l'chayavim tovot she-g'malani kol* tov," Barry recited. *Blessed are you, Lord our God, ruler of the world, who rewards the undeserving with goodness, and who has rewarded me with goodness.*

The congregation recited in unison, men and women in full voice from all sides of the room: "*Mi she-g'malcha* kol *tuv, hu yi-g'malcha* kol tov selah.*" *May he who rewarded you with all goodness reward you with all goodness for ever.*

What a year it had been! I looked around at the faces of the congregation. The seats of the sanctuary were hugged by walls of tall, frosted windows, through which the bright light of a winter day illuminated the room. All the faces turned to us seemed to shimmer with angelic light, the smiles genuine, the eyes accepting. We were happy, healthy and whole. I squeezed Barry's hand. The voices of the congregation rained down on us, shouting "Mazel tov!" And in that moment, I found a contentment that I had been looking for all my life.

BOOKS BY LYNNE GOLODNER

Poetry
Driving Off the Horizon (Lynne Cohn)
Living Inside: The Poetry of Prayer (Lynne Schreiber)

Nonfiction
Hide & Seek: Jewish Women and Hair Covering (Lynne Schreiber)
In the Shadow of the Tree: A Therapeutic Writing Guide for Children
with Cancer (Lynne Schreiber)
Residential Architecture: Living Places (ghost-written for Dominick
Tringali)
A Patient's Guide to Understanding Cutaneous Lymphoma
Stand Out from the Crowd: The Your People Guide to Beside-the-Box,
Funky, From-the-Heart DIY Marketing, PR & Social Media
The Flavors of Faith: Holy Breads

ACKNOWLEDGMENTS

I started writing Woman of Valor in 2011, when it was a very different book. I picked it back up in 2020, wanting to tell a story about compelling Jewish characters who fill their lives with passion and purpose – and who are strong in their identity even if, at times, they question the behavior of their fellow Jews. There are so many stories out there of people who left religious Judaism because of dissatisfaction or not being able to be their full self within the confines of the community. I wanted to write a different story. Too many novels are stories of angst and disappointment; I wanted to write a novel about someone who is happy with her choices, who chooses to stay even when things get tough.

At the heart of this story is the enduring power of love, which I am fortunate to have with my *beshert*, my soulmate, Dan Golodner. I am so glad we found each other. Dan's belief in me and my writing gave me the confidence to pivot my entire career to focus on putting my words into the world. Back when we first met, and I was working mostly in marketing, Dan insisted that he thought of me first and foremost as a writer. That enduring belief has influenced and inspired me and allows me to live my passion every day. Dan, I love you and am so grateful for your continued support and encouragement!

Thank you to my children – Asher, Eliana, Grace and Shaya – for giving me the time and space to write this book. I poured my love of motherhood into Sally's zest for parenting. And it's not entirely coincidental if some of the sweetest traits of her children were inspired by my amazing kids.

I am fortunate to have grown up in a family that believed in my writing and encouraged me to put my words in the world, even when they were brutally honest. Thanks Mom, and to my late Dad, for believing in my talent. Thank you also to Auntie Suz for seeing the real me, and Jody and Amanda for being interested in my writing.

I am grateful for the enduring support of friends and colleagues, including Katie Scott (affectionately known as Rabbi Katie), who has been writing with me for decades and gave a careful and thorough read to this book. I am part of quite a few great writers groups, who support and encourage my writing. My appreciation to my Tuesday writers group – Elizabeth Gowing, Cathy Aicardi, Rachel Weikel and Janet Bailey. Kris Spisak did a great developmental edit on this book, and Jenny Rarden did a fantastic proofread. I am grateful to work with Patrick McEntaggart and Susan Jones on the cover design. Thank you to Adina Pergament for guiding my research into Orthodox Jewish women and running. Thank you to Rochelle Weinstein, for talking through the early process of publishing this book and eagerly reading some chapters. A shout-out to Barbara Jones, for being a great mentor and friend since 1998, Alisa Peskin-Shepherd, who is a soul sister, and Merle Saferstein and Nancy Sharp, for being kindred spirits on this writing path. Thank you to Elizabeth Gowing (again) for her guidance in publishing, and to Crosby Noricks and Amanda Ring for guiding me through this brave new world.

I have been a part of many vibrant Jewish communities over the years. Rabbi Joel and Rebbetzin Aviva Tessler showed me what it means to be modern Orthodox, and I loved being a member of the community led by Rabbi Steven and Rebbetzin Yael Weil, who remained my friends even after I left religious life. Both couples showed me that Orthodoxy can merge with modern life and you can be true to yourself while also being religious. Thank you to Rabbi Marla Hornsten for helping me transition to a more liberal Jewish lifestyle, and to Rabbi Steven Rubenstein for welcoming my family into Congregation Beth Ahm. I was lucky to be raised at Temple Israel, which instilled in me the belief that every Jew matters, and every approach to living a Jewish life is valid.

My memberships in the Women's Fiction Writers Association, the American Society of Journalists and Authors, and Peaker Writers have been hugely motivational and encouraging for my writing and publishing.

I've been writing since I was old enough to hold a pen, and it is through writing that I make sense of the world. I hope you find in this story inspiration and motivation to ask tough questions, to patiently pursue answers, and to believe in the possibility of goodness and redemption.

ABOUT THE AUTHOR

Lynne Golodner is the author of eight books and hundreds of articles and creative nonfiction essays as well as a marketing entrepreneur, writing coach and host of the Make Meaning Podcast. After working as a journalist in New York and Washington, D.C., Lynne returned to her native Detroit to pursue a freelance writing career and teach writing. In 2007, she created Your People LLC, a marketing and public relations company with a focus on storytelling that guides authors in building their brands and marketing their work.

Lynne's creative nonfiction and reportage has appeared in *the Great Lakes Review, 45th Parallel, Saveur,* the *Chicago Tribune, Better Homes and Gardens, Midwest Living,* the *Detroit Free Press, Porridge Magazine,* the *Jewish Literary Journal, The Good Life Review, Hadassah Magazine, The Forward, Valiant Scribe, Story Unlikely, The Dillydoun Review, bioStories, QuibbleLit* and *YourTango,* among many more publications. One of Lynne's creative nonfiction essays was a 2021 finalist in the Annie Dillard Creative Nonfiction contest at *Bellingham Review.*

Lynne teaches writing around the world, leads writers retreats and facilitates The Writers Community. She fuses her marketing expertise with her writing background in webinars and masterminds focused on arming writers with the tools to market their work and build consistent author brands. A former Fulbright Specialist, Lynne graduated from University of Michigan (BA, Communications/English) and Goddard College (MFA, Writing), and she earned a Certificate in Entrepreneurship from the Goldman Sachs 10,000 Small Businesses program through Wayne State University. She is the mother of four young adults and lives in Huntington Woods, Michigan with her husband Dan.

Learn more at https://lynnegolodner.com.